PER WAHLÖÖ

The Assignment

Born in 1926, Per Wahlöö was a Swedish writer and journalist who, alongside his own novels, collaborated with his partner, Maj Sjöwall, on the bestselling Martin Beck crime series, credited as inspiration for writers as varied as Agatha Christie, Henning Mankell, and Jonathan Franzen. In 1971 the fourth novel in the series, *The Laughing Policeman*, won an Edgar Award from the Mystery Writers of America. Per Wahlöö died in 1975.

JOAN TATE

Joan Tate was born in 1922 of English and Irish extraction. She traveled widely and worked as a teacher, a rehabilitation worker at a center for injured miners, a broadcaster, a reviewer, and a columnist. She was a prolific writer and translator, well known for translating many leading Swedish-language writers, including Astrid Lindgren, Ingmar Bergman, Kerstin Ekman, P. C. Jersild, Sven Lindqvist, and Agneta Pleijel. She died in 2000.

The Assignment

PER WAHLÖÖ

The Assignment

A NOVEL

Translated from the Swedish by Joan Tate

VINTAGE CRIME/BLACK LIZARD
Vintage Books
A Division of Random House, Inc.
New York

FIRST VINTAGE CRIME/BLACK LIZARD EDITION, JUNE 2013

Translation copyright © 1965 by Michael Joseph Ltd.

Vintage is a registered trademark and Vintage Crime/Black Lizard and colophon are trademarks of Random House, Inc.

Library of Congress Cataloging-in-Publication Data for this edition has been applied for.

Vintage ISBN: 978-0-307-74476-0

www.vintagebooks.com

Printed in the United States of America
10 9 8 7 6 5 4 3 2 1

To Maj

whose cooperation made

this book possible

The Assignment

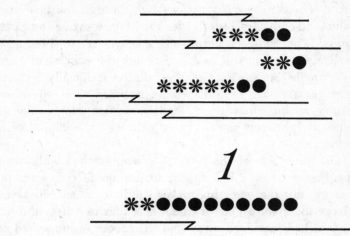

1

The car was a 1937 eight-cylinder Packard. It was black, like the soldiers' uniforms and the American motorcycles in the escort. The time was three minutes past eight in the morning, and it was already very hot. The two people in the back of the car were talking.

"Father, are you never afraid?"

"What is there to be afraid of, my dear?"

"All these people . . ."

"Barking dogs don't bite. You must remember one thing: always rely on the army—it is the only stable force here—as long as it has the right leaders. You ought to have had time to learn that by now."

"Why don't you forbid the servants to read the leaflets they drop?"

"What difference would that make?"

A silence fell in the car. The General turned his head and looked at the white villas rushing by without really seeing them. The convoy cut its way down through the long steep bends and onto a level road covered with gray-white stone chippings. The engineer corps had constructed it three years earlier and it was still usable although the edges had begun to crumble. At the foot of the hill the artificially irrigated area came to an end, the escort sounded their sirens and swung out into the wide, cobblestoned main street which ran dead straight from north to south through the capital of the province.

On either side of the road were whitewashed walls which the Fascist regime had begun to put up fifteen years previously, but the work had never been completed. In several places there were gaps in the walls, and in others the poor cement had crumbled away and the blocks of stone had collapsed. Ordinary fencing had been put up then, but now the barbed wire was already rusty and here and there the natives had cut through it with pliers and wound it into oval openings. Through these open gaps one could see the buildings behind the walls, a confused jumble of sacking, boards, and crooked shacks.

A white jeep which had been parked at the side of the road closed in behind the convoy. Four men were sitting in it. Their helmets and uniforms were white and their brown peasant faces were stiff and expressionless. They belonged to the Federal Police.

"I have seen so many kinds of policemen, under so many regimes," said the man in the car—distractedly and indifferently, as if he had not been referring to anything in particular nor addressing himself to any specific person.

The escort drew a screaming black line through the suburbs. It was not traveling very fast, but the sirens gave an impression of efficiency and urgency. Chickens, naked children, and thin black pigs leaped away from the road.

Just before the entrance into the center of the town there was a man-high inscription scrawled in red on the rough white wall: *Death to Larrinaga!* Someone had painted it there during the night. In a few hours' time the men from the administration would come with their buckets and whitewash over it. The next morning it would be there again, or somewhere else. The General smiled and shrugged his shoulders.

The escort thundered between the short, dusty palm trees along the main street. Here the buildings were tall and modern, square white boxes of glass and concrete, but there was little sign of life on the sidewalks as yet. The few pedestrians stopped and stared as the convoy went by. Many of them wore uniforms and nearly all of them were armed.

The escort officer swung diagonally across the beautifully laid stone plaza, drove up to the entrance of the Governor's Palace and raised his right hand to signal a halt. The square was large and white and empty. Only two people were outside the entrance: an infantryman in black uniform and a policeman in white. The policeman had a Luger in a holster on his belt and the soldier a submachine gun on a strap around his neck. The submachine gun was American with a straight magazine and a folding iron frame.

We still have far too few of that sort, thought the General. "Despite everything, they're more important than all the agricultural reforms," he mumbled to himself.

The Packard had stopped, but the couple in the back remained inside. The escort officer jerked his motorcycle up onto its stand, pulled off his gloves, and personally opened the car door. Then the General moved for the first time. He leaned over to one side, kissed his daughter on the cheek, and got stiffly out onto the sidewalk. He returned the guards' salutes and walked through the swinging door. The escort officer followed three yards behind him.

General Orestes de Larrinaga went into the white marble hall. Straight ahead of him lay the wide staircase and the elevators, to his left a long smooth counter, and behind that a messenger in a uniform cap and a black sateen jacket. The General gave him a friendly look and the man smiled.

"General," he said, and then nothing more.

He bent down and took something from a shelf beneath the counter. The General paused and nodded amiably. The messenger was a very young man with an open face and dark-brown eyes.

He looks frightened, thought the General. People are frightened, even here.

Ten seconds later General Orestes de Larrinaga was dead. He lay on his back on the marble floor with his eyes open and his chest shattered. Red patches were already spreading over the material of his uniform, as if on white blotting paper.

He had had time to see the automatic pistol very clearly, and his last thought was that it was of Czech manufacture with a wooden butt and a circular magazine.

The escort officer had seen it too, but he reacted much too late.

Outside in the square the soldiers and the girl in the car heard the short hammering salvo and soon after that the more distinct cracks of someone firing an 11-millimeter Luger.

The southernmost province of the Federal Republic is the poorest and the least prosperous. Three hundred and forty thousand people live there, and the landowners number less than two thousand. Eighty per cent of the population is made up of the natives, most of them agricultural or mine workers. Nearly all of them are illiterate. The other fifth are descendants of European settlers; it is this group that owns the land and controls the means of production. The province has been deemed too poor and thinly populated to become self-governing. It is under federal administration and its chief official is an officer, the Military Governor. His seat is in the capital of the province, which has about seventeen thousand inhabitants and is situated on the high plateau between the mountains in the northern area of the district. The white population lives in the middle of the town and in the villa district on an artificially irrigated hillside to the northeast. The forty thousand odd natives subsist in the jumble of shacks which are spread out at a comforting distance from the modern buildings in the center. Most of these natives work in the coal and manganese mines up in the mountains. Straight through the town runs the wide cobblestoned highway that enters from the north, but only a mile or two south of the town boundary it narrows into a stony winding mountain road, barely adequate for ordinary traffic. At the southern entrance there is also a row of large white stone barracks. The Third Mechanized Infantry Regiment is stationed there.

The disturbances in the area began in March 1960, when terrorist groups, in patrols of about ten men, began to infiltrate the mountain tracts in the south. Trained in a neighboring Socialist state, they were well armed, and they soon gained experience and efficiency.

In the summer of that year, mopping-up operations on a large scale began, but the typography and the attitude of the inhabitants toward the army favored the guerrillas, and after six months or so the results were disappointing. In fact, far from being eliminated, the disturbances had spread to all parts of the province. The previously disbanded Communist Party appeared again in the guise of an underground Socialist organization, the Liberation Front, which sought to obtain recognition through lightning strikes and sabotage. At the same time the white population formed a Citizens' Guard, which replied to the sabotage with terrorist tactics. In September 1961 the situation had become untenable. No work or transportation of goods was possible except under military guard. Most of the properties in the southern area of the province had been abandoned by their owners, the number of terrorist murders increased, and more and more people were executed after summary trials by military courts.

At this stage the federal government fell, and in the new presidential elections, the Liberal candidate, Miroslavan Radamek, a self-taught lawyer and son of a peasant from one of the agricultural states in the north, was victorious. The elections were held in an atmosphere of powerful international pressure, and Radamek's name was put forward as a compromise designed to placate all parties.

The government made energetic efforts to put an end to the crisis in the beleaguered province. Military operations were halted, and the army received orders to hold themselves in readiness. The responsibility for public order was put into the hands of the Federal Police, which government propaganda had christened *La Policia de la Paz*, or Peace Force. When the President promised to look into the question of provincial self-government and announced agricultural reforms and numerous social improvements, it seemed that the situation would soon be brought under control.

Seven months after Radamek's accession to power, however, the disturbances flared up again. Only a few of the promises of social reform had been fulfilled, the employers harassed their employees more than ever, and the committee that was working on the self-government proposals had made no progress. Open fighting broke out between the Liberation Front and the Citizens' Guard, and the state of emergency which had been lifted six months earlier had to be proclaimed again. The President now had only one choice: to take up direct negotiations with the opposing parties before a neutral arbitration commission. A Provincial Resident was placed at the head of this commission. The choice fell upon a retired army officer, General Orestes de Larrinaga. He was sixty-two years old, had never mixed in politics, and was generally respected because of his military achievements.

General Larrinaga's arrival at the Governor's Palace brought a temporary relaxation of the tension, but a few weeks later the situation again became critical. Assaults on civilians and attacks on private property resumed. More often than not the surveyors sent out by the reform commission were chased off by the landowners before they had had time to do any work; some of them were murdered and others disappeared altogether. The Liberation Front replied with raids in the countryside, and in the town armed groups of the Citizens' Guard openly patrolled the streets.

On May 20 the Liberation Front dropped a leaflet accusing the Provincial Resident of having been bought by the right-wing element and of representing the interests of the land-owners and the capitalists. Several days later his life was threatened. Although a representative of the Liberation Front denied responsibility for the threat, it was repeated twice during the week, the last time on the evening of June 5. The threat gave rise to more violence against the natives.

The only person who seemed unconcerned was the Resident himself. Every morning at eight o'clock he drove with a military escort from his home in the residential sector to the Governor's Palace. He was often accompanied by his twenty-six-year-old daughter, who taught at the Catholic school.

Orestes de Larrinaga played his part as a national hero with imposing consistency and great calm. Although little was known about his activities within the walls of his office, he had somehow become a symbol of security for tens of thousands of people.

This, then, was the situation in the capital of the province on the morning of June 6.

2

●●***

The new Resident was selected less than twenty-four hours after the murder of General Larrinaga. His name was Manuel Ortega, and very few people had ever heard of him. The appointment reached him by telegram early in the morning on June 17, and he was given exactly four hours to decide whether to accept or decline.

Manuel Ortega was Assistant Trade Attaché at the Republic's embassy in Stockholm. He had already held the post for two years and had had time to become used to Sweden. He lived in a furnished flat in Karlavägen in the Ostermalm part of the city, and about six months earlier he had sent for his family.

Outwardly he was fairly commonplace, a Latin in some ways but no one would have been surprised if he had turned out to be a Greek or a Pole or a Finn. He had brown hair and brown eyes, was five foot ten, and weighed a hundred and fifty pounds. A badly cared-for soccer injury from his university days had left him with a slight limp in his right leg, but it was noticeable only when he was in a hurry.

He was called to the embassy just before eight o'clock, and the Ambassador himself handed him the cable signed by the President of the Federal Republic. Manuel Ortega read it slowly and carefully with that lack of surprise one usually experiences in the face of something totally unexpected.

What on earth is this lousy job? he thought coldly.

And soon afterward: Might as well say no right away.

The Ambassador was wearing a smoking jacket and had not yet had time to shave. He was standing up because he was altogether too nonplused to contemplate sitting down and he completely misunderstood the other man's attitude.

"Naturally you're asking yourself why you of all people should have been chosen. I can perhaps help to shed a little light on this point. You're a lawyer and an economist, used to dealing in a businesslike way. What is needed down there is someone rational with a sense for practical solutions. You are nonpolitical too, and always have been. We others have all got our—well, our burdens."

The Ambassador had held various ministerial posts in three consecutive half-Fascist governments, and since then had only with considerable difficulty survived a series of sensitive changes of regime.

He went on: "This is of course an interesting offer worth looking into. If you make any definite progress down there, you can consider yourself made. If you fail, on the other hand . . ."

He cleared his throat and at last sat down behind his desk.

"Sit down by all means, my dear fellow," he said.

Manuel Ortega sat down in the visitor's armchair and put the cable down on the desk. Then he leaned back and crossed his legs carefully so as not to spoil the crease in his trousers.

"On the other hand," said the Ambassador, "the assignment should naturally not be overrated, nor the seriousness of the situation either, for that matter. Our country is large and prosperous and orderly. This border district . . . Have you ever been there, by the way?"

"No."

"Well, I've flown over it once or twice. As I've said, this border district is, as you know, thinly populated and totally infertile. Thanks to a handful of farsighted pioneers and their sacrifices it has to a certain extent been made productive. These people and their descendants obviously have certain rights, which speak for themselves. The rest of the population is a backward minority which, of course, must be emancipated gradually but which is still, for all practical purposes, in-educable. There are minorities like this in all countries, even here, you know . . ."

He snapped his fingers.

"Of course, the Lapps."

"Exactly, but here it has been possible to make them into a tourist attraction thanks to the favorable geographical cir-cumstances. The country down there lacks all that and is merely scorched and inaccessible. Despite the country's efforts, and with the exception of a very small number of mines, it is still practically worthless. But you know all this as well as I do."

Manuel made a vague but polite gesture.

"In any case the present situation would never have arisen if the atmosphere hadn't been poisoned by foreign provoca-tion and lying propaganda. Before this the army was always quite capable of keeping the territory under control. If it had been allowed to continue its operation six months ago, then . . . well, then we would not be sitting here discussing the matter."

He drummed his fingers on the desk for a moment, look-ing across at the window. Then he said: "I knew Orestes de Larrinaga for a long time. He was a first-class officer and a great man. It is idiotic that an assignment like this should be the cause of his death. He was much too well qualified for the post and I don't understand why he let himself be talked into accepting it."

Manuel Ortega leaned forward and brushed a small flake of ash off his trousers. Suddenly he said: "Perhaps he wanted to do some good."

"I doubt that this was the right way. But the tragedy is, of course, that he did do some good. It opened people's eyes. Even so-called world opinion should, after this, see things in their right perspective. And as soon as foreign propaganda is silenced then the problem will cease to exist."

He paused and sighed: "In any case, I certainly don't want

to influence your decision, but I think you should be allowed to see a communication which arrived here last night."

He took a folded slip from his briefcase and pushed it across the desk. The man in the armchair picked it up with a certain hesitation, as if he did not know whether to put it in his pocket or to begin reading it at once.

"Of course, my dear fellow, go ahead and read it."

Manuel Ortega took his glasses out of his top pocket and unfolded the piece of pink paper. As he read he heard the continuous drumming of the Ambassador's fingers on the edge of the desk.

"ministry of foreign affairs to all embassies: three hours after murder of provincial resident the following communique was sent out from leaders of citizens guard: one of the most famous men in our country, general orestes de larrinaga, has today fallen victim of a murderous communist assault. this terrible crime has three aims: (1) to remove a brilliant personality and an objective and just representative of the law and the government. (2) in this way to make way for a politician and an administration which has less power to resist foreign provocation. (3) to create anarchy. his death has deeply disturbed all right-minded inhabitants of the province. the most disturbing issue is the knowledge that general larrinaga died holding a meaningless post and that his and many other honorable mens lives could have been saved if the army had been allowed to fulfil its duty. we responsible citizens in this town and this province demand the immediate intervention of the army. we hereby place ourselves under the protection of the armed forces and we promise to give the troops every imaginable support in the fight against the reds who threaten to flood our country. we demand also that the provincial resident—if a successor to general larrinaga is to be appointed at all—shall have military forces at his disposal. as resident we can only accept an officer with technical knowledge of this area. if the government should give way to undue outside pressure and appoint another official we demand that he should in the interests of the country refuse the assignment. if he does not we should be forced to use violence. a civilian provincial resident or anyone who wishes to accept this post without the full support of the army can assume that he is sentenced to death at the moment he accepts the assignment. two weeks at the latest after his arrival this sentence will be carried out. (this communique has been distributed by air, posted in public places, and broadcast in news bulletins.)"

Manuel Ortega folded up the piece of paper and placed it on the desk. He thought once again: What a lousy job. Aloud he said: "This hasn't been mentioned in the newspapers."

"My dear fellow, seen in a wider context, our problems are very minor and scarcely worthy of notice. I am not entirely convinced that even our own newspapers will take up the matter. The whole thing is futile. If General de Larrinaga had not been such a famous man, his death would certainly not have aroused any attention, at least outside the country. It all concerns just a handful of people who are far away, in their own country as well as from us."

Manuel Ortega pointed at the slip and said: "Do you think, Excellency, that this stand they have taken can be defended?"

"Not officially, of course. But I imagine their position is very difficult, very difficult indeed. The death of Larrinaga has scared them considerably. He was the symbol of their security. Now they're fighting desperately, not only for their rights but also for their lives. And the army is their only hope."

"Do you think President Radamek will give the army a free rein?"

"I am not convinced that this decision rests with the President."

"What is meant by the expression 'an officer with technical knowledge of this area'?"

"Presumably the commanding officer of the command there, General Gami, or his Chief of Staff, Colonel Orbal." The

Ambassador again looked toward the window. "Excellent men, both of them," he said.

There was silence for a moment or two. Then Manuel Ortega said: "And the Communists murdered General Larrinaga?"

"Yes, just as they will kill anyone else who works against their interests."

"The new Resident is condemned to death by both sides then."

"It looks like it. If the army doesn't take over." The Ambassador looked at the clock. "You've not much more than three hours," he said apologetically. "Or have you already come to a decision?"

Manuel Ortega rose hesitantly.

"Weren't you just going on vacation?" said the ambassador.

"Yes. Today."

"Where were you thinking of going?"

"Tylösand."

"Ah, Tylösand, wonderful. Then the choice should not be all that difficult."

"No," said Manuel Ortega.

"Then at midday at the latest you'll let me know, will you? If you accept you must figure on going this afternoon."

"Yes."

Manuel Ortega walked down into the dim hall, put on his rubbers and raincoat, and began unsheathing his umbrella. But when he went out onto the steps to Valhallavägen, the rain had stopped, so he hung his umbrella over his arm and walked slowly along the wet shiny pavement. He bought a newspaper at the stand in Karlaplan and, a bit farther on, sat down on a bench and tried to think. It was not easy; he felt irritatingly indecisive, as if the conversation had simply confused the issue for him. He glanced over the front page of the newspaper and then flipped to the foreign news. He found it there: a short item with the headline *Political murder*. The

General's name was spelled incorrectly. The Ambassador was right: their country apparently played no role on the world scene.

Manuel Ortega rose and walked on. Large drops of rain fell from the trees onto his head and shoulders. At Sibyllegatan he crossed against a red light and was almost run down by a taxi. Three minutes later he opened the door to his apartment. He did not want anything and did not know what he should do.

A little while later he was sitting down drinking coffee. He had taken off his shoes but not his jacket and he was leaning back in his armchair watching his wife as she went out of the living room. With a faint feeling of distaste he noticed her buttocks moving beneath the slightly too tight dress and he saw that she had a fold of fat at the nape of her neck beneath the heavy black knot of hair. Nevertheless, she was in no way unattractive.

He sighed, put his coffeecup down, and went across to the large french window. The rain had started again and was streaming through the trees along Karlavägen.

With a cigarette in the corner of his mouth and his hands in his pockets, he stood and watched the rain making small pools and streams in the sandy path of the avenue. He heard his wife come into the room.

"What do you think I ought to do?"

"It's not my affair."

"You've already said that."

"But if you think there's a chance you really would benefit from it . . ."

"But perhaps I might be able to *do* some good for once."

"To whom?"

"To all these people."

"They themselves have said that only the army can do them any good."

"But all the others? Three hundred thousand other people live there too."

"That mob? Who can neither read nor write? Who live like animals? What can you do for them? If you'd been a doctor or a priest, but . . ."

It was as simple as that then.

"In some ways you're absolutely right."

"But if this is a real opportunity, then you should take it. I don't want to advise you. It'd be absurd if I started advising you on your work."

"It entails a certain risk too."

"You're thinking of General Larrinaga? You're no general, Manuel. And you've got Miguel as well, if it proves necessary."

Miguel Uribarri was her brother. He had for several years been head of the criminal police in the federal capital.

After a while she said: "But if you can see quite clearly that this is not an opportunity, then you should refuse it."

Manuel Ortega clenched his fist and beat on the door frame.

"Don't you see that I too want to do something? Something real?"

"Presumably your work here is considerably more important to the country."

Dryly and factually. She was not unintelligent and was almost certainly right—from her point of view and from many others too.

"I don't want to be cowardly either."

"That's a point of view for which I have much more sympathy. If it's my sympathy you want."

She left the room. After a minute or so he went back to the chair and sat down. He looked at the clock. Quarter past eleven already.

She came back.

"Have you decided?"

"Yes. I'll accept."

"How long will it be for?"

"At the most six months. Probably not that long. Do you think it'll be difficult? With the children?"

"I've managed before. . . . Don't worry on that score," she added with a sudden spurt of tenderness.

He remained sitting in the chair, feeling empty and listless, almost apathetic. The children came into the room.

"Children, Daddy's not coming with us to the beach."

"Why not?"

"He's got some important work to do."

"Oh."

"Come on then—off to your room now."

They went.

Manuel Ortega was no longer thinking about the assignment. He was thinking about himself. He thought about himself and his marriage and his family. Everything was perfect. His wife was perfect, apart from that little bit of corpulence. From the very beginning their marriage had been successful and had never really ceased to be. Sexually, it was technically perfect even now. The children were so perfect it almost scared him. Sometimes he wondered whether the years in this perfectionist little country, with its bad climate, had not transformed them into an ideal family, into museum pieces. He could see them standing in a glass case, with labels. Father of family, 42, born in Aztacan, Latin type. Boy, 7, born in London, utterly satisfactory model. Girl, 5, born in Paris. Woman, 35, mother of two children, well preserved. Perfect relationship between equal partners. Please note their tenderness and absolute openness toward each other.

She said in a friendly tone: "Aren't you going to call His Excellency?"

He roused himself, arose, and went over to the telephone. He dialed the number direct but did not get through. Instead he got through to the secretary and told her his decision.

"Check-in time at Arlanda is three-fifteen. You must be at the airport by then. The car will pick you up at exactly half past two. Tickets and money are arranged for."

Everything was so businesslike.

Just as he put down the receiver, the telephone rang. It was the Ambassador.

"After our conversation this morning I have been thinking the matter over further. I have reconsidered my ideas. It would be wrong for you to refuse the assignment, to reject the faith that has been shown in you."

"Good. I have already said that I accept."

"What? Excellent. I am pleased that my little experiment worked so well."

"Experiment?"

"Yes. Now I can admit that what I said earlier was not meant very seriously. A stupid attempt to test your ability to deal with matters and make independent decisions. At least partly. But, you must understand, all the facts were correct. But forgive me all the same."

"Of course."

He felt his mouth go dry.

"One more thing. In Copenhagen you will be meeting one of your co-workers. A lady who will act as your secretary. She is from down there and has outstanding qualities. Called— one moment—oh, these Slavic names—of course, I've nothing against the President, ha ha, yes—here it is . . . Danica Rodríguez. She's already received her instructions. Understood?"

"Yes."

"Good luck then. You'll have a difficult but interesting job."

"Thank you."

"And, Manuel—be careful. They mean it."

"Yes."

Manuel Ortega put the receiver down slowly. The Ambassador had never used his first name before, nor had he ever used that tone of voice with him before. The conversation had been confusing, almost unreal.

Be careful, Manuel. They mean it.

Much later he said to his wife: "Where is my revolver?"

"I've already thought about that. I've heard it can be dangerous down there. It's in the bottom drawer of the desk, on the right. Will you get it yourself?"

"Yes."

The revolver lay there (as she had said), wrapped in a soft cloth and neatly tucked in the shoulder holster. He unwound the straps and the cloth and weighed the weapon in his hand. It felt heavy and firm and was well oiled. He took three boxes of cartridges too, and put them all in the top of his suitcase. Then his wife shut the lid and locked it.

A little before half past two, Manuel Ortega kissed his wife and children and got into the front seat next to the driver. His wife said: "Don't forget the seat belt."

The car drove away. His family stood on the sidewalk and waved. He waved back.

At twenty-five to four he climbed the steps into the plane. Just as he bent over and stepped inside, smiling at the girl who was standing at the door, fear snatched at his heart.

It came like a shock, without warning.

Orestes de Larrinaga had been given three weeks to live. He would not even get that much.

Two weeks at the latest after his arrival the sentence will be carried out.

Be careful. They mean it.

He was sweating, and as he pushed forward between the people in the aisle, he fumbled for something that would give him security. He thought of the revolver and how it had lain in his hand, heavy and cold and comforting.

The revolver was a 9-millimeter Astra-Orbea with a walnut butt, made in 1923 in Eibar. His father had given it to him for his twenty-first birthday. He had never been without it since then. He had never had cause to point it at any living creature, not even as a joke, but sometimes he used it for target practice on empty bottles and tin cans.

3

✳●✳●✳✳

Over southern Scandinavia the clouds seemed about to break up, and when Manuel Ortega leaned against the window he could see the contours of the land quite clearly, as if on a map. Their course was almost directly west, and to the south one could faintly discern a large town, which must be Malmö. Evening began to arrive and the sunlight that lay over the countryside was already slanting and golden red.

The plane sank lower over the water, flattened out over a level square island, and swept its broad-winged shadow across a peaceful little harbor with red customs sheds, fishing boats, and a ferry. Only a few moments later the rubber tires bit into the runway and the plane taxied up toward the airport buildings at Kastrup.

Manuel Ortega let out his breath and unhooked his seat belt. He had never been able to get used to landings, however routine they seemed, and even this time the procedure had claimed all of his attention. For a few minutes everything else had been pushed to one side.

The waiting room was the same as those in all the other airports he had seen from Dublin to Santa Cruz, and he thought that flying not only robbed the journey of its pleasure but also obliterated the individuality of the countries as well as the traveler's identity.

He drank a glass of beer in the bar and went to the men's room to wash his hands. Then he remembered the woman who was to meet him and went to the waiting room to look for her.

He saw no one who resembled the picture he had already

created in his mind, and he soon gave up. Common sense told him that the woman could look like almost anyone. Moreover, there was no guarantee that she would be waiting there.

When he returned to the bar for another glass of beer, he was detained by a middle-aged man wearing a tweed hat and a wind-breaker. The man turned back his jacket and gave him a glimpse of a press card which was fastened to the breast pocket of his blazer with a paper clip.

"You're Manuel Ortega, aren't you? The new Provincial Resident?"

"Yes."

"The man with the suicidal assignment?"

"Well, there's no reason to overdramatize it."

"It didn't go all that well last time. Are you used to assignments of this kind?"

"No. And besides, the situation is a very special one. But is the general public here really interested in our little problems?"

"Not very. But in you personally. Anyway, it might become more interesting. Would you mind answering a few questions?"

"As well as I can."

Most of the questions were foolish and irrelevant. Such as: "What did your wife say when you left?" and "How many children do you have?"

He answered in monosyllables or by shrugging his shoulders.

"Are you yourself from this province?"

"No. I was brought up in the capital, in the north of the country."

"Is your father alive?"

"No."

"What was his profession?"

"Executive in an export business."

"What kind of an education did you have?"

"A commercial education. I studied economics and law at the university as well. I worked for a while with the Ministry of Finance."

"What are your political views?"

"None."

A photographer appeared and took a few shots.

Manuel Ortega smiled with an effort and said: "May I ask you a question? Aren't you afraid of losing your press card?"

The man looked dumfounded. Then he turned back his wind-breaker and said:

"No, not at all. Look at this. I've got a safety pin which goes through the case and is fastened on the inside of the pocket. My wife fixed it for me."

He returned his notebook to his pocket and added: "One more question—a little more fundamental than the others. Are you afraid?"

"No," said Manuel Ortega.

He turned toward the bar and tapped on the glass counter with a coin to show that the conversation was at an end. Out of the corner of his eye he watched the two men walk across the floor of the hall, and he saw that the photographer said something to which the other shrugged his shoulders.

He had been unpleasantly disturbed and felt ill at ease. When he tried to analyze the sheer physical sensation he found that it could be best described as pressure on his chest.

His flight was called after half an hour's delay. It was raining, although the sky had been quite cloudless during the flight in. The concrete apron shone with pools of water, and as he had left his raincoat on board, he put his head down and half ran to the plane. He was very conscious of his limp and thought that he must look rather foolish.

Manuel Ortega sat by the window with his black briefcase lying on his knees. Everyone seemed to be in place, but the seat beside him was still empty. He peered out into the rain and busied himself with the seat belt and did not notice her until she was standing about a yard away from him. She took off her dark-green leather coat, folded it up, and put it up on the luggage rack. Then she sat down, fastened her belt, and placed a worn canvas bag on her knee. She took a pack of cigarettes and a lighter out of the bag and put them into her jacket pocket. Then she turned her head and looked at him.

"Miss Rodríguez?"

"Yes. Danica Rodríguez."

"Manuel Ortega."

She thrust her hand into her bag again and passed him an identity card in a plastic case.

While the plane was rolling toward the takeoff runway and the engines were being revved up, he studied the identity card. It was the same type as his own, issued by the department but signed by the Foreign Minister of the previous government. Everything was there, from thumbprint and details of height, age, marital status, and color of hair, to her service codes. Surname: Rodríguez Fric. First name: Danica Antonia. Born: 1931. Place of Birth: Bematanango. Marital status: Married. Height: 5 ft. 8 in. Hair: Black. Eyes: Gray.

The first part of the code he solved with ease: stenographer, correspondent, interpreter, but after that there followed a series of numbers which he did not recognize and which for a moment at least he could not figure out.

The plane had air beneath its wings when he returned the card. She took it without looking at him and it vanished into her bag. As soon as the warning lights went off, she took a cigarette out of her jacket pocket and lit it.

"Where is Bematanango?" said Manuel Ortega.

"Down there, where we're going. Right down in the south. It hardly exists. Twenty-five or thirty mud huts at the bottom of a valley, one street, a little Catholic chapel. There was a little hospital there once, but it's fallen down now."

He nodded.

She let the subject drop.

"I have a few things with me for you to deal with. Do you want to look at them now?"

"It can wait. We've plenty of time."

Manuel Ortega lets the back of his seat down and closes his eyes. A formula has once again begun to grind away in his brain: The sentence will be carried out within two weeks at the most. Then he shrugs his shoulders and thinks, without knowing it, in exactly the same words as his predecessor: Barking dogs don't bite. Then he remembers the news item about Orestes de Larrinaga, his name misspelled. He thinks about the journalist with the neat safety pin and the abrupt question: Are you afraid? It is easier to spell Ortega, he thinks. A few seconds later he is asleep.

An hour later they are over another part of Europe. The plane is a Convair Coronado 990 jet of Swissair. It is flying at twenty-six thousand feet and the air in the cabin is dry and smells of cloth and leather. The man by the window has awakened. His mouth tastes of lead and he is sitting forward with his black briefcase on his knees and he has put his right arm across it so that no one can see the chain between his wrist and the handle.

He turns his head to the right and looks at the woman in the seat beside him for the first time. Her hair is short and black and she is wearing a red dress with blue revers. She is sitting slightly crouched with her right elbow on the foam-rubber armrest and her head resting against her hand. On her knees there is an open notebook and a page of stenciled tables. She is smoking as she reads. When she picks a flake of tobacco from her lip with her little finger, he sees that her nails are cut short and the cuticle is bitten down. She is wearing no makeup and has a thin downy shadow on her upper lip, and he thinks that most young women would have this removed. There is nothing conspicuous about her. She would vanish into anonymity on any European or American street, and if she had been sitting a few yards farther away he would quite likely never have noticed her. Presumably she had been in the waiting room at Kastrup all the time while he had been looking for her.

He thinks: Be careful, Manuel. They mean it.

Then she turns her head and looks at him with her strange dark-gray eyes. She says nothing, but smiles slightly and calmly.

He looks at the clock and turns away, leaning his forehead against the windowpane and staring into the darkness.

He notices that she rises and goes to the washroom and when she comes back down the aisle he follows her with his eyes. She walks like an animal, softly and rhythmically, with gliding steps.

It was ten past nine when they touched down in Zürich. During the long wait there Manuel Ortega drank coffee and brandy in the waiting room. She sat opposite him and read an American paperback.

At one point he said: "You have an unusual name."

"My mother was a Croat."

"Not your father?"

"No."

Another time he asked: "Have you a clear picture of the job we've got ahead of us?"

"Only in principle."

"I must admit I've not really had time to look into the matter. I didn't get my instructions until eight o'clock this morning."

"Mine came even later."

"As soon as possible we must get the negotiations going again from where they . . . were broken off."

"I don't think there was time for much negotiating before Larrinaga was shot."

When she said this she looked straight into his eyes.
"Your knowledge of the province will be extremely useful."
"I wasn't there for very long."
At that point the conversation ceased.

As the plane bounced in the air pockets over the Alps, Manuel Ortega sat with his legs crossed and wrote. He had put his notebook with its black oilcloth cover on top of his briefcase and he was trying to write down his thoughts. This was a habit he had acquired long ago; he had often found it useful.

The woman had fallen asleep, and when he looked at her he realized how tense and nervous her face had been when she was awake. Now it was open and relaxed, and he noticed that her features were finely-drawn and pure like those of a little girl. She was breathing through her nose and her breath played in the soft hair on her upper lip.

He wrote: Am I afraid? Yes, but not rationally. I have never concerned myself with politics in their active and more extreme forms, but on the other hand I have come across many other and similar situations, for example in the commercial world, and have handled difficult negotiations between obviously incompatible parties. In these cases it has always been possible to come to some agreement in a rational way. A small group of people working on the same problem sooner or later always come around to what is possible and what is absolutely out of the question. Politics prove this: in situations in which it is a question of saving everyone's skin, compromise solutions always appear to be quite honorable. One assumption is that the parties are represented by people who are neither mentally ill nor entirely without talent. The work that lies ahead in this unhappy province should then, on my part, be accomplished with reasonable expectations of progress. The first step must be to create a state of peace and guarantees of public safety. Then it should be possible to find practical solutions which would to some extent satisfy and benefit the backward masses without the occupying (and, one supposes, the more able) class suffering any real damage. There should, of course, be found within this "upper" class technically and administratively trained people who must not be pushed out, but who must be won over to a sensible project of cooperation. I cannot believe that either side would gain anything by doing violence to me personally. They must realize this themselves. The murder of Larrinaga was surely a tragic mistake, committed by some lone fanatic. (What has, for that matter, become of the assassin? No one has said anything about that. Presumably he was caught. In which case his trial should prove productive.) Moreover, it was a provocation to give the post of Resident to an army man, even if he was retired and a national hero. A stupidity on the part of a Liberal government. What I am now embarked on is a matter of the well-being of three hundred thousand people. It is a great task. No, I am not afraid. But I shall naturally take all reasonable precautions. The best thing would be to rely entirely on the Federal Police. Without physical security one cannot work efficiently.

Manuel had filled several pages of his notebook. He closed it and put it into the outside pocket of his briefcase. Then he leaned back and was lulled to sleep in the air pockets.

At midnight they touched down at Lisbon. They still had the cold, raw chill of northern Europe in their bones, and they were taken by surprise by the night air which billowed up to meet them, heavy, hot, and suffocating.

Like a small taste of the day to come.

4

✳⬤✳⬤✳✳✳

The plane went down from twenty-six thousand feet to six hundred and drew a shining aluminum spiral over the capital of the Federal Republic. Manuel Ortega sat on the inside of the curve and through the window saw the city gradually become larger and nearer. It was white and beautiful with parks and wide tree-lined avenues, the sunlight winking on the cathedral's copper roof and reflections glittering in hundreds of thousands of windowpanes. At this time of the day most of the shutters were not yet closed. The pilot flattened the plane out just above the rooftops; the circular bullring and an oval soccer stadium slipped by beneath the wing, then blocks of apartments and a suburb of dirty small houses and sooty black factories, but even they seemed neat and tidy. It was obvious that this was a great city in an orderly country, a country to be proud of. Then came a chicken farm with thousands of shapeless white blobs fleeing in all directions below the great shadow, then grass and the windsleeve and the first bounce on the concrete runway.

As the plane was still rolling and long before the warning notices were switched off, a uniformed official, presumably the radio officer, came aft down the aisle and said quietly: "Would you and the lady kindly mind waiting in your seats until the other passengers have disembarked?"

So they stayed seated and waited. When the plane was finally empty, a police officer in a white uniform stepped in through the doorway. He saluted and said: "Welcome home, sir."

His tone of voice was gruff and his face serious, as if he were on a difficult and important mission.

At the foot of the steps stood a white American police car with a radio aerial and spotlights on the roof. The white paint was marred by the word *Policía* painted in (black) block letters across the doors. Ten yards away stood a white jeep. The engine was running, a policeman sat behind the wheel and another was standing upright in the back. Otherwise there was not a soul in sight. The plane had stopped unusually far away from the airport buildings.

The officer opened the car door for them, made a commanding gesture to the guards on the steps, and then got into the back of the car himself. He was fat and it was quite a squeeze. The jeep drove past with its siren wailing and took the lead. Then the little convoy drove three hundred yards over to an annex of the airport buildings which was seldom used for anything but ceremonial welcomes for prominent visitors. Manuel Ortega threw a confused glance at the woman at his side. Her face was completely expressionless.

The car had stopped, and although the distance to the entrance was no more than three yards, the arrangement with the guards was repeated before the Resident and his secretary were allowed to enter the foyer. This room was ostentatiously equipped with luxurious furniture and colorful wall decorations. A policeman opened a door in the far wall and at the same time made a sign to the woman to stay where she was.

Manuel Ortega went into a small room containing low tables and leather armchairs. Two men were already in there, one whom he had only heard of and seen in pictures and one whom he knew of old. The former was Jacinto Zaforteza, Minister of the Interior in the federal government, the other Miguel Uribarri, Chief Inspector of the C.I.D.

Manuel shook hands with Zaforteza and embraced his brother-in-law.

The Minister of the Interior was a large, coarse man with a bull neck and short gray hair. Several heads of government had considered him invaluable, but no one really knew why. He was a skilled orator and his powerful blustering voice had over the years become almost physically penetrating.

He began to speak at once.

"The only thing I can do for you at the moment is to welcome you most warmly and give you a word or two on your way. Your task is an extremely delicate one and perhaps it will land you in some awkward situations. Don't expect swift or grandiose results—the situation is much too complicated for that. We expect nothing of that sort from you anyhow. What we do expect, on the other hand, is uncompromising loyalty and complete cooperation. Two things must be avoided at all costs: open military activity and incidents of a kind that arouse international attention. Otherwise you have a free hand. It is important that you get to your destination as quickly as possible. So an air force helicopter is coming to pick you up in twenty minutes. You should be able to get down there in less than five hours."

Zaforteza glanced at his watch, embraced him, heavily and powerfully, and then dashed out of the room.

Manuel Ortega stared in astonishment at the closed door. He had in fact not had the chance to say a single word.

"Yes, you can see how much help you can expect from that quarter," said Uribarri.

He was a small, neat man with a thin face and a narrow black mustache. Although he was wearing civilian clothes, his bearing bore traces of many and long years in various uniforms. He strode impatiently up and down the room.

"Manuel, what in the hell have you done?"

He said it suddenly and with unexpected violence.

"You've made a terrible mistake. The situation down there is horrible. They're all mad."

"I'm certain the problem can be solved."

"To hell with the problem. It's possible that you might get them to agree, but I don't care about that. What I'm thinking of is your personal safety."

"But the Federal Police . . ."

"The Federal Police are a collection of idiots—at their best. You saw the circus out there for yourself? Huge escorts with sirens to move one man three hundred yards on an empty airfield. The most logical thing would have been to let you come in as unobtrusively as possible."

"Well, anyhow, it's too late now."

"Yes—it's too late to withdraw—but not to save your life. Listen now. I've sent four men down there. They'll meet your helicopter. They're my men, the best I can find. Their only job is to look after you, and I promise you they know their job. Remember one thing: of all the people you'll meet, these four are the only ones you *know* you can trust. Don't trust anyone else, not the army, nor the police, nor anyone else."

Uribarri walked over to the window and peered out between the slats of the blind.

"Who's that woman?"

"My secretary."

"Where's she from?"

"The embassy in Copenhagen."

"Name?"

"Danica Rodríguez."

He pondered the name for a moment.

"Doesn't mean anything to me," he said finally.

Manuel Ortega smiled and looked at the clock.

"I must be going now, I suppose, Miguel. I can hear the helicopter."

"Are you armed?"

"Yes."

"What with?"

"An army revolver."

"Where is it?"

"In my case."

"Wrong place, Manuel, wrong place. Here! Here!"

He slapped the left side of his chest with the flat of his hand.

"You've always been so dramatic, Miguel. Are you quite certain that you're not exaggerating the risks?"

"No! No! I know I'm not exaggerating. They're mad. They're out of their minds. They'll try to kill you, if only for fun, or to be able to say someone else did it."

"Who?"

"Everyone. Anyone. Although no one here or anywhere else in the country thinks about it or even knows about it, they have been at war down there for eighteen months. Hard, bloody, ruthless war. Both sides are in despair, exhausted, finished, but neither will give way an inch. For fifty years those people have been pawns in the chess game of international politics. Now the pawns have gone mad. And still there are people who go on playing with them."

Ten minutes later the helicopter rose, humming straight up into the sky, wrapped in its own roaring swirl of air. Through the segmented plexiglass Manuel Ortega saw the white police cars break away and drive off. Only Uribarri remained on the concrete apron. He stood there, his feet apart and two fingers on the brim of his hat, quite still. He swiftly became smaller. Soon he vanished from sight.

Manuel Ortega wiped the sweat from his brow and looked at the woman sitting beside him with her book open on her knee.

"What fearful heat," he said.

"Wait till we get there," she said without looking up. "We'll have much more reason to complain then."

5

✳●✳●✳✳

"There's no proper airfield here," said the pilot, staring downward.

The country below them was without contours. It looked as if the sun had not only scorched all life out of it but also reshaped the whole of the surface of the earth into a hard rugged crust of stones and soil, yellow-brown flecked with gray.

"There is in fact nowhere in the whole province where one can land. The army fixed up a landing strip just south of the town for its own small observation planes. But even there it's very dangerous to try to land a plane."

Manuel Ortega yawned. He had slept for a while and had just woken up. The woman at his side appeared calm and composed. She was wearing dark sunglasses and was sitting with her elbow on her knee and her chin supported by her hand. Her fingers were long and thin. She was looking toward the ground.

"They say it's because of the heat," said the pilot. "The asphalt melts, and when they tried using concrete, the blocks swelled up and broke. Strangely enough, the nights can sometimes be very cold."

Manuel Ortega blinked and shook his head. But he still could not focus his eyes to get a clear picture of the desolate landscape below.

"You'll soon see for yourself. The provincial capital is just behind that ridge. We'll be there in ten minutes."

The helicopter rose a little to climb over the ridge with a

comfortable margin. The peculiar sun haze made judging distances hazardous.

All visual observations must be very uncertain, thought Manuel Ortega.

He had not even seen the mountain himself until the pilot pointed it out to him. Now they flew over it. He saw ragged, crumbling chunks of stone and scrubby bushes and suddenly a road with carts and a few gray huts. Then the first people, a great number of figures in straw hats and white clothes. They were walking in a long file with bent heads and woven baskets on their shoulders. More figures, a swarm of them, a great open gash and tracks and dark entrances into the mountain. More huts, a smelting works, tall and gray and sooty, and a plume of poisonous purple-yellow smoke which shot out of the tallest chimney and at once spread itself and sank like a membrane toward the ground.

"The manganese mines," said the pilot. "If it weren't for them, the whole damned country could be evacuated and given back to the mob that lived here in the first place. There's the town, by the way."

Manuel Ortega raised his eyes and saw a gray-yellow plain, diffuse and rugged and endless. In the middle of it he could see a group of square boxlike buildings, looking as if someone had happened to drop a collection of white-painted building bricks and then had not bothered to pick them up again. Diagonally down toward the town ran a dead straight gray-white ribbon which must be a highway. When they got nearer he saw that there was some sort of jumble of buildings around the tall white structures, and also a slope with villas and some tentative, dusty grass.

The helicopter droned in a wide curve around the western outskirts of the town, swept over the roofs of a row of large gray barracks and sank toward the ground.

The pilot let his machine down slowly and with infinite care, swearing all the time.

"If the Bolshies want to take this bloody country from us, then they'll have to use parachute troops. No sane person can land here."

"What Bolshies?"

"Well—the Bolshies," said the pilot, vaguely. "Down there."

He made an indefinite gesture toward the hazy mountains far away in the south.

"The government in the country you're alluding to was not Communist," said Manuel Ortega pedantically. "At the most it was Socialist and democratic. Moreover, it fell, as you perhaps know, three weeks ago and was replaced by a right-wing one."

"Thank God for that," said the pilot.

At last the helicopter was standing on the ground. The pilot switched off and the shrill whistling of the blades above was heard as the engine gradually turned over more and more slowly. He climbed out of his seat, opened the hatch, and jumped down to the ground, stretching out his hand to the woman. She took it and jumped down lightly. Manuel Ortega noted that she smiled swiftly and automatically as her eyes met the pilot's. He himself picked up his briefcase and rain-coat, put one hand on the pilot's shoulders, and jumped. His right leg gave way under him and he nearly fell headlong.

As he looked around he felt the hot, uneven asphalt burn through his thin soles. The heat was unbearable. He was already soaked through with sweat.

The airfield was very small and surrounded by a double row of barbed-wire fence. The ground was covered with coarse gravel and the buckled asphalt runway was perhaps a hundred and fifty yards long. At the far end of it lay the burnt-out wreck of a small aircraft which had crash-landed.

"Yes," said the helicopter pilot. "That was their Piper Cub. Now they've got only the Arado left."

In one corner of the enclosure was an arched corrugated shed. In front of it stood a gray sedan. It had evidently been

waiting for them; before the rotor blades had stopped whistling, the car began to roll across the bumpy field. It stopped,
and a tall man in a crumpled striped linen suit got out.

"My name is Frankenheimer," he said.

He put his hand in his pocket and produced his identity
card. Manuel Ortega recognized his brother-in-law's flourish-
ing signature.

The wail of a siren rose from behind the iron shed, and a
white jeep swung onto the field. The man in the linen suit
glanced at it and said: "Our car is a good one, though it's
small. I and my colleagues drove down in it. I suggest that you
use it while you're here." Then he said: "I think so. In fact,
yes."

The car was French, a CV-2 type Citroën. Manuel had
seen some like it in Sweden.

The jeep braked a few yards away from them, and two
police officers in white uniforms climbed out of it. The one
who had the most stripes on his sleeve saluted and said:
"Lieutenant Brown of the Federal Police at your service.
I bid you welcome. Unfortunately neither General Gami nor
Colonel Orbal was able to meet you personally. They have
asked us to convey their apologies."

"Are you the Chief of Police?"

"No. Captain Behounek is the Chief of the Federal Police.
He could not manage to come either, but he is prepared to
meet you later today. I've been detailed to take you to your
quarters."

"We prefer to use our own car. But perhaps you'd be good
enough to see to the luggage."

"Of course," said Lieutenant Brown, glancing at the man
in the linen suit.

He looked totally unconcerned.

"Aren't you going to come too and have something to eat?"
said Danica Rodríguez to the pilot, who was standing close to
her and shifting his feet.

"I'd like to of course, but I must be back at the base before it gets dark. But some other time . . ."

After a pause he added: "Anyhow, I'd rather get away from here before civil war breaks out or there's an earthquake or a volcanic eruption or something."

Manuel Ortega looked around with interest as they drove past the barracks. Inside the rusty fence he could see only a very few soldiers. They were half lying in the meager shade below the walls.

The man in the linen suit turned off the main street and drove in behind a stone wall along a narrow beaten track. To the right was a jumble of small tottering shacks. Most of them were clumsily put together with twine and planks; others consisted of rusty tin plates propped up with posts. Children were swarming about everywhere—dirty, ragged, half-naked, and emaciated. Women with faded strips of cloth wrapped around them were sitting on the ground. They were busy with iron pots and small charcoal fires. Others were walking along the street with water jars on their heads or buckets slung from yokes across their shoulders. Some of them turned their heads and stared at the car with apathetic, animal-like animosity. From the buildings rose a heavy rank stench of decay, sweat, and garbage.

Frankenheimer found an opening in the wall and swung back onto the main street.

"Have you ever seen anything like it? Excuse me for saying so, but this really is a lousy town."

Danica Rodríguez had not looked around once the whole time. She sat upright in the back of the car staring straight ahead of her.

They drove into the center of the town, past the monotonous dazzling white blocks of apartments, shopwindows behind locked grids, and a few bars which looked as if they were locked and bolted. Short, withered palm trees grew along the sidewalks. The streets were practically empty.

"It's still siesta time," said the man at the wheel. "And people don't dare go out either. Anyway, there aren't many people left here."

He drove across the square and stopped outside the Governor's Palace, which was large and white and looked fairly new, with its wide picture windows and rows of white pillars on the cornices. A policeman in white and a soldier in black flanked the entrance. The jeep was already there and their luggage had been taken out of it. Lieutenant Brown was sitting in the front seat smoking. He did not bother to get out or even turn his head.

As Manuel Ortega stood on the sidewalk he heard a faint humming noise and, looking up, saw the helicopter like a grotesque insect against the vapid pale-blue sky.

Pull yourself together, he thought.

"There goes your airman," he said jokingly to the woman.

She gave him a cold, tired look. "Yes," she said.

Then she dropped her cigarette butt, stepped on it and walked through the swinging doors behind the soldier who was carrying the luggage.

Manuel Ortega went into the marble hall. A sudden thought made him stop and look around.

"Mm," said Frankenheimer. "This is where it happened. Just here. The lad who did the shooting stood there behind the counter. We've said we don't want any more messengers here. The white chaps will have to put a man in here. I've told them about that too, but they haven't done it yet."

He looked tired and sweaty, and he wiped his forehead with a rolled-up handkerchief.

"Ye-es," he said. "I've told them. I've done that."

The offices were one floor up, a suite of rooms along the length of a white corridor. Most of them were empty and looked as if they had hardly ever been used. It was almost dark in all but two of them, for the shutters had been closed in order to keep out some of the heat. Nevertheless, the air in them was heavy and dusty and suffocating. A relatively young man in a black sateen jacket and dark glasses was sitting in one of the rooms. He had pulled out the bottom drawer of the desk so that he could put his feet up on it while he read the newspaper. When they opened the door and went in, he looked up, put down the newspaper, and stood up.

"I'm in charge of the chancery," he said. "But there isn't a chancery."

"Are you the only official here?"

"Yes. There were only three of us. The General and I and an ex-lieutenant who was the General's adjutant and secretary. He left immediately after the General's death."

"Probably given a medical discharge, yes, no doubt," said Frankenheimer.

Before they had had time to close the door behind them the young man had once again sat himself down with his feet on the desk drawer and was reading the newspaper.

At the end of the corridor was the room which Orestes de Larrinaga had used. It was large and light and bare, but at least there was an electric fan on the ceiling.

Danica Rodríguez stood by the window, smoking. She looked out over the square, and when the draft from the fan lifted her short hair, he saw that the slim nape of her neck was covered with tiny beads of sweat.

On a chair by the wall a short fat man was sitting with his legs apart and his hands on his knees, doing nothing whatsoever.

"This is López," said Frankenheimer. "He and I'll be on duty together and we'll always be near at hand. Twelve hours at a stretch from midday to midnight. Then the others change with us. You meet them tonight."

Manuel Ortega looked around. There were no files in the room, no books, no papers, nothing except the furniture. He pulled open one of the drawers in the desk. It was empty. He went out to the secretary's room. Equally empty. A green safe stood there, its door open. It was empty. He went back to the others.

"If you don't mind then, we thought we'd do it like this," said Frankenheimer, and then he fell silent.

"Like what?"

"You take this room and the lady sits in the other; don't you think it should be like that?"

The woman by the window looked dejectedly at him.

"One of us will always be in here. Where the other is— well, you needn't worry about that."

"You must have one of us here in the room because there are two doors," he added gloomily, as if complaining about the plan of the building.

Manuel began to feel tired and irritable.

"Hurry up," he said.

The man in the linen suit looked sadly at him.

"Then we've got the problem of where you're to live," he said.

He took a couple of long strides out into the corridor, glanced to the left, took out a key, and unlocked the door on the opposite side.

"Here," he said. "This way it's all right. Two rooms, one through the other, bedroom farthest in. There's a bathroom and shower too. When you're in in the daytime and in the evenings, then the one on close duty will be in the corridor."

"Close duty?"

"Yes, we call it that. It's usually called that. I'll put a chair here—a swivel chair will be fine."

He said this very thoughtfully.

"Couldn't we get all this over and done with a little quicker? I'm tired and would very much like to have a shower and change."

"When you're asleep or staying permanently in the inner room, then the one on close duty will be in here, in the outer room. Is that all right with you?"

"What do you mean by permanently in the inner room?"

Frankenheimer did not answer the question.

"Yes—well—that must be about everything," he said absently. "No, of course not. The girl."

He went back to the office. Danica Rodríguez was still standing by the window, smoking, and the fat little man was still sitting in his chair.

"You can live here too," said Frankenheimer, picking his nose. "We can fix it."

"Thank you."

"But if you don't want to, we've arranged for you to have an apartment in town. About three blocks from here. Two rooms."

"I'd rather do that."

"Yes. It'd be better. Then we've got you out of the way."

"In any case I'd prefer to have the apartment."

"We did it—so to speak—out of solicitude."

"Thank you."

"We haven't had any instructions about you. But it wasn't difficult. There are plenty of apartments. So many people have left lately," said Frankenheimer, staring at her breasts.

"Then I'll go there now, thank you."

"And change? Yes."

"No. I thought I'd blow the place to bits."

Frankenheimer's expression remained quite unchanged.

"What shall I do about my luggage?"

"Tell someone," said Frankenheimer.

That man will drive me mad, thought Manuel Ortega.

The telephone buzzed. Frankenheimer put out his hand and picked up the receiver. He seemed to listen for a moment or two and then put it down again.

"Who was it?" said Manuel Ortega.

"Well, it was someone who said he thought you ought to be rubbed out."

"In the future I'd prefer to take my calls myself."

"In this hole you can trace a call in ten seconds. . . . If you want to," he added.

The telephone buzzed again.

"Yes. Ortega."

"Good. Welcome to the town. This is the Citizens' Guard executive branch speaking. We want to remind you that you will be dead within two weeks, however many bodyguards you have. As we hope to avoid unnecessary executions, however, we are giving you this opportunity to leave immediately. This you must do by eight o'clock tonight at the latest. This is good advice, and we mean it. Good-by."

The caller was a woman. Her voice was clear and calm and businesslike, in no way unfriendly. She had stressed the word "unnecessary," and afterward Manuel Ortega thought that it was this particular detail which had made him tremble and fumble for the back of the chair.

When he looked up, his eyes met those of his secretary. She looked at him thoughtfully and frowned. Suddenly he thought that she was beautiful.

"Don't worry about them," said Frankenheimer.

Danica Rodríguez shrugged her shoulders. She picked up her suitcases and went out. They looked heavy, but she carried them without undue difficulty.

Three quarters of an hour later Manuel Ortega had had a shower and had put on a clean shirt and a light-gray suit. When he went out into the corridor, López was sitting on a swivel chair just to the right of the door, quite still, with his hands on his knees.

Manuel Ortega went into his office. As he was opening the door he felt his heart thumping, as if he were expecting something to happen. He sat down at the empty desk. Although the fan was whirring, the heat in the room was almost unbearable.

He sat still and thought: What if that fat pig were sitting in a chair in the corridor. What if he followed me in here.

I went in first and he was in no special hurry, and if someone had been standing in here he'd have had plenty of time to kill me ten times over before anyone could have done anything about it.

Then he thought: I must get the revolver. I must carry it on me.

He heard someone moving about in the other room and he rose to see who it was. Two steps from the door he stopped and looked at López, who was sitting immobile on his chair. Manuel opened his mouth to say something but at once closed it again.

This is sheer madness, he thought.

Anyhow there was someone out there. He took one quick step and whipped open the door.

Danica Rodríguez was sitting at the desk and sorting a pile of documents. Her legs were bare and she was wearing thonged sandals. Her dress was green and simple, made of some very light material, and she looked fresh and clear-eyed.

"You're quick."

"Yes," she said.

He felt his shirt sticking to his back and the sweat running down his neck and trickling between his skin and his collar. He went back through the office, across the corridor, into the outer room, took off his jacket, and opened his case. He took out the revolver, cleaned it carefully with a rag, opened one of the boxes of cartridges, twirled the chamber with his thumb, and put in six bullets. Then he fastened the strap over his shoulder, thrust the revolver into the holster, put on his jacket, and buttoned it up. It pulled a bit when he moved his arms, so he unbuttoned his jacket again and let it hang open. The fat man stood by the door all the time, watching. Or rather, not exactly watching, for his eyes were glazed and seemed to rest on some point much farther away.

Manuel Ortega felt somewhat more secure as he walked back to the desk and sat down. He opened his briefcase, took out the documents he had brought with him from Stockholm, and put them down in front of him. They had nothing to do with the matter. Nothing had anything to do with the matter. All resolutions and preconceived ideas could be scrapped.

For twenty minutes nothing happened.

Once or twice the chair under López creaked. The sun began to pour into the room and the heat became even more intense.

There was a bell on the desk, an ordinary one of black bakelite with a black button on it. He pressed it and wondered what would happen.

About a minute later someone knocked on the door and the youth with the thin jacket and the smoked glasses came into the room.

"How far did the General get with his contacts for negotiations?"

"As far as I know, he had no contacts."

"But hadn't he planned to make any in recent weeks?"

"I don't know anything about that."

"What have you been doing these last three weeks?"

"Me personally?"

"Yes."

"Nothing whatsoever."

"Were you present at the meetings?"

"There haven't been any meetings."

"Didn't anyone come to see the General?"

"A few."

"With whom did he negotiate?"

"I don't know whether he negotiated with anyone. But Colonel Orbal came here a few times. And a druggist called Dalgren. Perhaps some others, but no one I knew or recognized."

"What did the General do during those weeks? I mean while he was in the office?"

"He used to sit in here."

"Where are all his papers?"

"He didn't have any papers. But he did get a newspaper every day, which the cleaning woman threw away the next morning. She had orders to do that."

"And the mail?"

"There wasn't much. What did come, the adjutant had to read. If there were anything special he read it out loud to the General. Then he threw away the letters."

"In other words, you're suggesting that Orestes de Larrinaga didn't do a single thing during the whole of his time as Resident?"

"I'm not suggesting that. He was working on a proclamation."

"A proclamation?"

"Yes, a personal statement."

"Every day for three weeks?"

"I imagine he was very conscientious."

"Where is this proclamation?"

"It was never finished."

"But in that case the General must have left some papers behind, drafts and notes?"

"He never wrote things down. He dictated everything to his adjutant—sorry, secretary."

"Then this secretary should have left the notes behind, the draft of the proclamation, that is."

"Yes, the proclamation should be in the safe. It wasn't all that long. At the most one typed page. All the drafts and notes were destroyed."

"There's nothing in the safe."

"No."

"You knew that before."

"Yes."

"Where do you think that draft copy has gone to?"

"I don't know. The General did not take me into his confidence. He never spoke to me and never made use of my services. Perhaps the adjutant destroyed the draft when the General died."

"Then you know nothing?"

"No, unfortunately."

Manuel was silent and looked thoughtfully at him. The young man seemed intelligent but not very willing to cooperate. In some way their relationship had gone awry from the very start. Things had not begun well.

"How do I call my secretary?"

"Use the telephone—it's connected."

Manuel cursed himself for overlooking this simple solution.

"May I go now?"

"Yes."

He lifted the receiver and the woman answered at once.

"Get me the Chief of Police, Captain Behounek."

About three minutes later she opened the door and said: "It seems to be difficult. I just get through to someone who refuses to put me through to anywhere."

"Let me speak to him."

He lifted the receiver and heard someone mumbling.

"Hullo," said the voice. "Are you still there, beautiful?"

"This is the Provincial Resident. To whom am I speaking?"

"Duty officer."

"Will you put me through to the Chief of Police."

"He's at a meeting."

"Then get him. If you don't allow me to speak to him then it's at your own risk."

The duty officer hesitated slightly.

"One moment—I'll find out."

Silence for a moment. Then there was a click and someone said: "Behounek speaking."

"The Provincial Resident speaking. Manuel Ortega."

"Ah, welcome. Unfortunately I was unable to meet you today. But we'll meet this evening, won't we?"

"What do you mean?"

"Haven't you had the invitation? Strange. A party at Dalgren's. Particularly appropriate as it can be a welcoming party for you as well. You'll have the opportunity of meeting a lot of people and making a few contacts."

The man's voice was lively and forceful. He sounded at ease—forthright and humorous.

"I'd like to have a private talk with you first. Preferably with General Gami and Colonel Orbal too."

"Unfortunately I have to inform you that the General and his Chief-of-Staff will not be able to meet you for at least a week. They are much occupied with important military matters."

"Are they out of town?"

"I imagine so. To be quite honest, I don't know. But personally I'm at your service of course. When can you come?"

"I'd prefer to talk here in my office. In an hour. Will that suit you?"

"Yes, of course. I'll be there."

A moment later Danica Rodríguez opened the door and said: "We've had an invitation to some kind of party this evening. Do you want to go?"

"Yes. Accept it and find out the details."

"Don't you think it a bit unsuitable for me to go too?"

"Not at all. The Chief of Police is coming here in an hour. I think it'd be wise to note down in shorthand the gist of our conversation."

"Undoubtedly."

He looked at her in surprise as she went out. She still walked like an animal.

Captain Behounek arrived forty minutes late and seemed completely unaware of the fact. He was a heavily built man with a narrow black mustache, a rugged sunburned face, and a rumbling laugh. He threw himself into the visitor's chair and looked with amusement at López, who was sitting immobile in his chair.

"One of your specialists?"

Manuel Ortega nodded. The sun was very low and the heat almost intolerable. He felt sweaty and dull, especially in the presence of the police officer, who was lolling in the armchair, untroubled and good-natured, as he studied Danica Rodríguez's feet and long bare legs.

"Would you mind reporting on the situation in the province at the moment, from a police point of view. Only broadly, of course."

Behounek dragged his eyes with obvious reluctance away from the woman with the shorthand notebook, took out a cigar, cut off the top of it, lit it, and carefully put the match in the ashtray.

"It is calm," he said. "The situation is satisfactory. I have a feeling our problems will solve themselves in the near future."

"How many crimes of violence have been reported during this last week?"

"Practically none since the tragic death of General Larrinaga. Guerrilla activity in the countryside seems to be fading out. Here in the town we haven't had any incidents worth mentioning."

"How do people react to police action?"

"Very positively. In most cases with absolute confidence. The idea of the Peace Force has grown in everyone's mind. And it's an idea which has a certain validity. Thanks to our air patrols we have been able to cover the country districts pretty well, and our people work efficiently. Considering how quickly the force has been built up and organized, the behavior of the rank and file is astonishing. They have instructions not to use force except when absolutely necessary. As a result, the number of casualties is low and their own losses very slight."

"And the number of arrests?"

"Very few too. May I—yes, I must be quite frank with you. The fact is, in view of what happened before, my men have had orders not to be too zealous. The army's activities, guerrilla attacks, the perpetual killing. All our activities are based on common sense and persuasion. In general, people can be talked into things, both the poor and the rich. As a result, we have in many cases turned a blind eye to illegal activities. Personally, I'm convinced that this method will lead to success more swiftly than any other."

Manuel Ortega liked both the man and his reasoning. It was in pleasant contrast to the negative attitude he had so far come across, and to the hysteria he had in the federal capital, in men like Zaforteza and Uribarri. He glanced at the unmoving López, and Behounek, who followed his gaze, suppressed a smile. But the glint in his brown eyes was not so easily hidden and Manuel had to draw his hand across his mouth to prevent himself from smiling.

"I've been here for seven months now," said Behounek. "It takes time to get used to this country, but one does in the end. I thought we were definitely on the road to success when this unfortunate lunatic went and shot Larrinaga."

"Apropros of that, when does the murderer come up for trial?"

Behounek stared at him, and then said: "You can't try a dead man."

"Dead?"

"Do you mean you don't know what happened? Has the government really been too cowardly to publish a true version? Didn't you know that the assassin was court-martialed and executed less than half an hour after the murder? Anyway, you know now."

"Why didn't you intervene?"

The Chief of Police rose and said: "Because I didn't have time. The escort officer, a lieutenant, wounded the assassin with a pistol shot and then the man was taken by the soldiers in the escort and they took him off to the barracks of the Third Infantry Regiment. He was executed there almost immediately. I went there ten minutes too late to stop it. Perhaps I wouldn't have been able to stop it anyway."

"Who gave the order?"

"General Gami personally. That way it wasn't even illegal. General Gami is the Military Governor and after Larrinaga's death he was in every respect the highest authority. He condemned the murder as an attack on an officer and the situation was so serious that he could apply martial law. These army people! Do you remember the old saying about act first and think afterward? Even as a policeman I must deplore the whole thing. And what an opportunity we lost for interrogating someone who might be useful! One gets cynical in one's old age."

"Who was the assassin?"

"A young worker, God knows where from. Called something quite ordinary, Pablo Gonzáles, I think. I have the information from his Communist Party card. We managed to collect what he had in his pockets before they buried him, but that was all."

He looked at the clock.

"The army were naturally a bit touchy about the whole thing. General Larrinaga relied on the army, the way you do on your experts. Anyhow—are you coming to Dalgren's place this evening?"

"Yes, with pleasure. Who is this man Dalgren?"

"This man Dalgren," said Behounek calmly, "is the outstanding right-wing extremist and member of the Citizens' Guard. Perhaps its leader. It is presumably with him we shall negotiate, if anything is to be negotiated. No, don't ask me why I don't arrest him. Technically speaking, every single inhabitant of the whole province is a member of either the Citizens' Guard or the Liberation Front. I'd have to arrest two hundred and fifty thousand people."

"I wasn't going to ask you."

"Otherwise, Dalgren was originally a pharmacist, a druggist. He found the raw materials for certain medicines here in the province and began a pharmaceutical manufacturing concern. It's already earned him millions. Basically, of course, it's pretty squalid: impoverished Indians, women and children, climb all over the mountains for weeks and months collecting roots, or whatever they are, which he then buys from them with a shrug of his shoulders, and they get practically nothing. So he becomes a millionaire and they starve to death. But that's what it's like. We're not supposed to be able to change it."

"No, hardly. My life, moreover, was threatened by the Citizens' Guard today."

"I know," said Behounek.

Manuel Ortega started and opened his mouth, but said nothing.

Behounek glanced at the telephone and shrugged his shoulders slightly.

"The person who threatened you was arrested ten minutes later. A young lady who owns a perfume shop three blocks away from here. A rather exalted type. Full of talk. There are lots like her. Tomorrow we'll let her go again. But," the Chief of Police went on thoughtfully, "that doesn't mean that your position is not a very tricky one. We must hope that there'll be a relaxation of tension in a week or two. I'll keep an eye on you and then you've got your . . ."

He jerked his head toward the man in the chair.

They rose and shook hands. Manuel Ortega had collected his wits and was able to say: "One more thing. Will you send copies of your reports and your crime statistics over, so that I can let my staff work on them?"

Behounek thought for a moment.

"Yes, for the last seven months. You can have them in the morning. What happened before then will be in the military records."

They parted.

Manuel Ortega went in and had a shower and changed his shirt and underclothes. When he went out into the corridor again, López was sitting there on his swivel chair.

If he doesn't take his hands off his knees soon, I'll strangle him. I must send these orangutans back to Uribarri. Otherwise I'll go crazy. Nice not to have to look at that Frankenheimer anyhow.

As he put his hand on the doorknob and heard López's slothful movements behind him, the terror clutched at him. He thrust his hand inside his jacket and nervously gripped the butt of the revolver before pushing open the door to his office.

There was, of course, no one in there.

6

●●**

The villa was large and white and lay at the top of the artificially irrigated hillside. In front of it was a wide veranda with a grand colonnade of white marble. Dalgren was holding his party there. The darkness fell swiftly and the air seemed even thicker and hotter.

Manuel Ortega and Danica Rodríguez drove there in the little French sedan. López was driving and appeared later on on the veranda, where he sat on various chairs and ate tiny sandwiches.

Dalgren was a man of about sixty, thin and bald and dressed in a flimsy white dinner jacket. He gazed at his guests through rimless glasses, peering in a friendly way. Early in the evening while everyone was still standing in groups talking quietly, he walked up to Manuel Ortega, took him by the arm, and spoke to him. He talked calmly and informatively and in a strictly businesslike manner. He said, among other things: "I've identified myself wholly with the Citizens' Guard and if you'd lived here as I have for thirty years, or perhaps for only ten, you'd understand why. I'm telling you this at the start to clarify my position."

"Your organization has issued me a death sentence. One of its members threatened my life only today."

"I must point out that this organization can in no way, nor should it, be called mine. But I know the Citizens' Guard sometimes resorts to very stern measures. However, there is one thing that deserves noting. All the members, except a few schoolboys, are hard-working people, people who have families and positions to defend, who live here and who in many cases have lived here all their lives, and who as a result base their whole existence on this part of the country and this town. Do you think such people would resort to violence without very good reasons? Without feeling that they are forced to? Do you know that during the last fourteen months more than eight hundred of the best people in this province have lost their lives? You can imagine what that means, can't you? They are dead—gone. They don't exist any longer. They were farmers, teachers, technical men—all sorts—they are dead, but in many cases their murderers are still alive. And what kind of people are these murderers? Yes—half-crazy whining cretins who sleep in caves and creep about in the mountains—wild people with guns and knives and ammunition belts."

"It's horrible, but even so, I can't really see that it is sufficient reason to take my life."

"In point of principle, I can say that we don't know you. You might, from want of judgment, make sudden concessions to the pueblos which would give this so-called Liberation Front a free hand. Only a month ago such a concession would have been disastrous, would have lead to the whole province, yes, even this town, within a few days, yes, even hours, being flooded by plundering, murderous mobs. They'd have raped our women, tortured us and our children, everything that has been built up with tremendous sacrifices and infinite pains would have collapsed, mines, farms, factories, and workshops. Before the army could intervene, thousands of lives would have been lost and the greater part of all the invested capital would have been irretrievably lost. Finally it would have perhaps involved the whole country in a meaningless war."

Dalgren smiled in a friendly way and lowered his voice.

"Now fortunately the situation is no longer the same. So you needn't think that the Citizens' Guard's sentence cannot be revoked. Within this organization, as in most others, there are some wilder ones, youngsters who want to play dangerous games, just as you and I did at that age. The threat against you today almost certainly came from that direction. I can assure you that the Citizens' Guard is a well-organized movement. Of course it can't control what every individual member says and thinks, but it has their activities under complete control. I think that you, just by waiting and not doing anything too hastily, can feel secure as far as the Citizens' Guard is concerned. The real danger comes from another direction, as the case of Larrinaga clearly shows."

He beckoned to a waiter in a striped waistcoat and they both took a Martini from the tray. Dalgren raised his glass and said: "In a way, I admire your courage."

"I haven't come here to be brave. I've come here to be sensible and practical and to be of some use."

"Then you've got a good basis for a start. The new political situation smooths the way for common sense. What happened in our neighboring country to the south three weeks ago has saved us and perhaps the whole of the Federal Republic from a serious crisis. When the Socialist regime down there eventually fell after two years of misrule, the whole situation changed. All our troubles stemmed from there. Just think, night after night they sent rebels and armed bands of murderers across the border, day after day their press and radio poured out lying propaganda, directed against us. A considerable number of people came over from there in a steady stream. That's what made our soldiers into martyrs. How can one finally defeat an enemy who only has to withdraw over a boundary line when the ground begins to sizzle under his feet? And who can feel himself safe? But now it's different. In a week at the most the old administration down there will be out of the running. Then the border will be closed and all we need do is to take care of the last of these terrorists left on our side of the mountains. It's a job that'll be cleared up in a few weeks, or a month at the most. Everything that is evil comes from down there. They quite simply carried on a war against us without giving us a chance to hit back, a creeping war which gave all the trumps to one side. When you get to know the natives here in the province, you'll soon see that none of this really comes from them. They are poor and ignorant but in some way or other happy. They obey their own natures and like everyone else, all they want is to be left alone. They are like children. Unfortunately, like all children, they have to be punished sometimes."

Dalgren smiled and let his glance slide over his guests before he went on: "Well, now, I haven't asked you to come here just to give you a lecture. But I'll give you a bit of good advice. Stick to your common-sense line, don't rush into anything, and don't try to force any settlement. Then there'll be no danger from the Citizens' Guard. But you must be careful all the same, especially in the next few weeks. There are still terrorist groups about, the same kind of people as that madman who shot my old friend Orestes. The ground is shaking beneath their feet now. They'll be desperate and then they'll kill anyone, just to be able to kill."

He tossed down his drink, put his glass on the ledge of the balustrade, and said to a man standing a few yards away: "Dr. Alvarado, have you met our new Provincial Resident?"

Then he went away with his white dinner jacket and his smile.

Dr. Alvarado turned out to be the Medical Superintendent of the military hospital, and was slightly drunk. He said: "I heard those last words by chance; to kill for the sake of killing. He's right. It's the final consequence of hate and desperation. Personally I don't give a damn for their politics. I try to patch up those who come my way regardless of who they are and where they come from. When it was at its worst they came into the hospital and shot the wounded in their beds. Only six months ago, that was."

"Who did that?"

"A gang of crazy school kids with guns in their hands. I've seen a couple of them in the streets since. With schoolbooks in straps and gym shoes slung around their necks. The Citizens' Guard, that is. The others let loose their excesses in the country. And they shot one or two Provincial Residents too."

He took a drink and glanced at Ortega.

"Why don't you report them if you recognize them?"

"I'm a doctor. As I said, I don't give a damn for their crazy politics. Anyway they were mentally sick at the time. I certify them as unaccountable. They'll get better and become outstanding citizens of the country."

"But it could happen again. They could do it again."

"Yes, they could, or someone else could. But their victims didn't look so frightful as those I had in from the country. There are grades of corpses too."

He was silent and drank, but then said suddenly: "Are you thinking of pushing self-government and enforcing agricultural reforms? Well, of course you can't answer that sort of question, but if you are, then we're bound to meet again."

"The government is certainly thinking along those lines," said Manuel evasively.

"I think you should call up Radamek and ask him if he hopes to be President when the almond trees bloom," said Alvarado poetically.

The doctor was manifestly not on his best behavior. As if he had noticed that his companion was disturbed, he turned to Manuel Ortega and, gripping his dinner jacket lapel, he said: "Before you go, I'll just tell you a great and uncontestable truth. Orestes de Larrinaga was a stupid old fool. From every point of view he was a dolt. The stupidest thing he did was to try to do his job properly. I hope you're too clever to do the same thing."

An orchestra had begun to play dance music in the corner of the terrace. The sky was black and starry, the air heavy and filled with dust. When Manuel Ortega went looking for

the washroom he saw Danica Rodríguez standing at the cock-
tail bar with a tall officer in a black uniform. She was drinking
whiskey and she glanced fleetingly at her boss. Her eyes were
shining and she looked unsteady.

A moment later he saw her again. She was dancing with the
same officer and had taken off her shoes. As far as he could
judge she danced very well.

Then he met Captain Behounek, who thumped him on the
back and talked for a while. Finally he said: "Your secretary
is quite a piece though she's nothing much to look at. My
young officers here have gone quite crazy, I see. She gets them
like a knife through butter. But now an infantryman has got
hold of her. Well, well—these army chaps."

A little later he ran into his host, who took a flat container
out of his inner pocket and said: "You'll find it difficult to sleep
at first in this climate. These are excellent sleeping tablets
which my laboratories have just brought out. You'll sleep like
a child and wake up eight hours later—like a child, bright
and rested. But never take more than two at a time."

"Thank you. In fact, I am very tired, and I must be going
soon. I can see a hard day's work ahead of me tomorrow."

"Oh, don't overdo things too much. But I understand. I hope
we'll meet again under equally pleasant circumstances."

Manuel Ortega went across to López, who was sitting on
the balustrade ten yards away.

"We're going now. Do you know where the lady is?"

López pointed at the door near the orchestra platform.

Manuel opened the door and went into an empty room
containing comfortable chairs and potted palms. He went
straight across the floor and pushed open another door, which
was standing slightly ajar.

"Señora Rodríguez?" he said. At the same moment he saw
her. She was leaning against the wall inside the door, bare-
footed and with two buttons of her dress undone. The tall
officer was pressed against her and was kissing her. He had

one hand over her breast, under the material of her dress, and the other on her stomach, very low down. She had her hands in his hair.

The officer started and turned angrily toward Manuel Ortega. He had an ordinary, foolish face, and was quite young.

The woman freed herself and took a few nervous steps into the room, took out a cigarette, and lit it.

"I'm sorry. I was just going and only wanted to ask you if we could give you a lift into town."

"No," she said curtly and tonelessly. "I'm staying."

"I beg your pardon."

The officer grinned complacently and put his hand on her shoulder, but she immediately shook it off.

When Manuel turned to go, he found López standing only a few yards behind him.

"You don't make much noise, do you?"

"No."

On the way back he made another attempt at conversation.

"Your colleague, Frankenstein or whatever he's called, where has he gone?"

The man at the wheel shrugged his shoulders, stuck out his lower lip, and said nothing.

Even his attempt to strike a lighter tone had failed.

The main road was lighted by street lamps which stood fairly close together, but the slums on each side were mercifully hidden by the white stone walls. At the entrance to the center of the town a barrier had been set up across the road. A white jeep was parked to one side and a policeman was standing in the middle of the road holding a red lantern. López braked the car and the policeman shone his light on their faces. Then he saluted and stood to one side.

Somewhere behind them, three shots rang out and they heard a shrill drawn-out cry.

"What was that?"

"Don't know," said the policeman.

López put the car into gear and drove off.

Manuel Ortega was very tired but still not sleepy. He nodded once or twice in the car but jerked awake again immediately. He felt sticky and unhealthy and the revolver seemed to be weighing him down on his left side.

In his bedroom he strode up and down for a long time before taking a shower and putting on his pajamas. Then he remembered something and took out the container he had received from Dalgren, shook out two tablets, went into the bathroom, and filled a glass with water. He had all but got the tablets on his tongue when he stopped himself and put them down on the shelf. He went back into his bedroom and walked round the bed several times. Then he said: "No. It won't be like that. But just think—what a simple way . . ."

He got the tablets, swallowed them, and went to bed.

His last thought before he fell asleep was of the three shots and the long wailing cry from the native quarter.

The tablets fulfilled their donor's promise. Manuel Ortega woke up at exactly eight o'clock. The room was murky and very hot. The sheets were tangled and wet and his pajamas were clinging to his body like plaster.

When he had dressed he went into the other room; a man was sitting there. Manuel Ortega jumped and was fumbling for the gun inside his jacket before he realized that this must be the man who had taken over from López at midnight.

The man was called, quite simply, Fernández. He was small and ordinary and was reading a comic book. His colleague was out in the corridor, an older and coarser man but just as ordinary, called Gómez.

Like the fat López Fernández stood behind him as he opened the door and went into the office.

Manuel Ortega decided that he would have to take up the matter with the man in the linen suit. Then he realized he would be worse off with his back unprotected and that the chances of there being anyone in the room were very small, and anyhow the whole thing was absurd. Of course no one would try to kill him. There was no valid reason why anyone should.

He opened the door into the outer office and saw Danica Rodríguez, dressed as she had been the day before. She said: "Good morning. Captain Behounek has already sent over the papers."

The copies of the reports lay in stacks on the desk. He stood beside her and flicked absently through the papers. Then he shifted his glance to her. She looked fresh and bright and her dress was loosely buttoned. When she unthinkingly leaned forward to scratch her shin, he noticed two details. She was not wearing a bra and deep down on the inside of her right breast was an elliptical purple bruise.

He walked over to the window, looked out, and said:

"Were you late last night?"

"The party finished about two."

"Are you tired?"

"No. I didn't drink very much."

Manuel Ortega stood silently for a moment. Then he said: "Let the man look after this."

He went into his room, sat down at his desk, and waited.

Fernández made more noise than López. He rustled his comic book and chewed seeds of some kind which he apparently kept loose in his pocket. Sometimes he got up and roamed around the room. Once he opened the door and waved at Gómez, who relieved him for a while.

Right up to midday, Manuel Ortega waited for something to happen. It was absolutely silent in the building and the heat was appalling.

7

●●**

By ten past twelve López had come and Fernández gone.
Manuel Ortega suddenly realized that this was the only thing
that had happened during half a working day.

He picked up the telephone and called Captain Behounek.

There was a short wait before the Chief of Police came on
the line.

"How was last night?"

"Absolutely calm."

"And out in the country?"

"Calm."

"I heard cries and shots near the northern entrance when I
was going home last night."

"I'll investigate the matter. Probably nothing very serious."

There was a silence. Manuel was about to put a badly
phrased question but stopped himself. He thought for a
moment and said: "Have you, with your experience here,
any views as to what measures I should take first?"

"None at all."

"What do you mean by none at all?"

"Just what I say. Wait."

"You'll keep me informed if anything happens, won't you?"

"Of course."

He put down the receiver and rang for his assistant. The
young man came at once.

"Have you had a look at those reports?"

"Yes, but it'll take quite a while. I've almost forgotten what
one does when one works."

"It doesn't matter. I wanted to ask you one or two other

things. Do you know where the members of the reform committee and the legal experts are?"

"The whole committee went back to the capital when the troubles were at their worst a month ago. About the same time as General Larringa was appointed. They're working there now, I suppose. The only people left here are a group of surveyors. They're living at the hotel."

"Which hotel?"

"There's only one. Called the Universal. I'm living there myself now—since yesterday."

The last remark sounded bitter.

"Are they there now, do you think?"

"They were there yesterday."

"Another thing. Do you know if General Larringa has any relations in the town?"

"Yes. His widow lives here and so does his daughter. The girl who teaches at the Catholic school."

"Thanks very much. You can go."

Manuel Ortega got his hat. On the way he said to López: "I'm going out for a while."

He came out into the blazing heat of midday. There was no one to be seen in the square apart from the two guards at the entrance. Everything was blinding white, the sunlight and the buildings and the cobblestones. He thought: I must get a pair of sunglasses if I don't want to lose my sight.

On the main street he passed a shop that sold optical and medical goods. He looked into the window for a while and saw López's reflection as he stood on the other side of the street.

He went in and a few seconds later López was there, red-faced and panting. The curtains rustled and a woman came out into the shop. She showed him several pairs of sunglasses. He chose one, and just as he was about to pay, the woman said: "I know who you are. If I didn't have to depend on you to help us against the mob, I wouldn't sell you a corn plaster. Not for all the gold in the world."

When they came out onto the street again, López said reproachfully: "You mustn't do things like that. If you want to go in somewhere you must give me a sign first so that I can catch up to you."

There was hardly anyone on the streets; all he could see were a couple of police jeeps and a few cars, gray with dust.

In the lobby of the hotel a porter was fast asleep with a newspaper spread over his face. When he woke and stood up, Manuel saw that he was wearing a cartridge belt and an old American revolver in a holster on his right hip.

The chief surveyor, whose name was Ramírez, was in the hotel lounge playing billiards with two other men. He looked astonished as he put his cue to one side and went out into the lobby.

"But why . . . why didn't you call me? Perhaps I should have come on my own, but I didn't think of it."

"I need to get about myself sometimes too. Well, how many men have you got here?"

"Twenty now. We were twenty-eight to start with."

"Where are they at this moment?"

"Here at the hotel."

The man seemed surprised.

"Why aren't you working?"

"We haven't done any work for a month."

"Why not?"

"The police wouldn't let us. We had already lost eight men then, and the risks were thought to be too great."

"But the reform committee depends on your results, doesn't it?"

"I suppose so, but we've heard nothing from them. In fact, we've heard nothing from anyone for a month. But money is sent to us, so someone knows we're here. We just sit and drink away our pay. What else can we do?"

"How much of the work is completed?"

"About five per cent, perhaps. Probably not even that much."

"Have you enough men to complete the job?"

"Not within a reasonable time. I've always thought of this group as a token force."

"What happened to the eight men who are no longer here?"

"Four were shot by the farmers when they demanded access to their land, one was murdered by the natives—we know that because they wanted his clothes and boots—and three just vanished."

Manuel Ortega went back to the Governor's Palace. Despite the sunglasses, the glittering white heat was blinding and intolerable. As he crossed the square his head was buzzing and the sun burned his skin right through his clothes. It was like walking through liquid fire.

Before he opened the door to his office he put his hand on the butt of his revolver as usual.

He went up to the woman and said:

"Call Captain Behounek."

He was put through in two minutes.

"Behounek speaking. What's the trouble?"

"Why can't the surveyors get on with their work?"

"Risk's too great. And I've had orders from above too."

"From whom?"

"The highest. Ministry of the Interior."

"That order came a month ago, during the crisis. They've probably forgotten to countermand it."

"Don't ask me."

"Another thing. Why is there practically no one in the streets?"

"You've forgotten something. A state of emergency has been declared."

"And what does that involve?"

"Among other things, the natives are not allowed past the police barriers into the center of town."

"But that's absurd. They're citizens of the town too, aren't they?"

"The whites aren't allowed into the native quarter either. It's been done to protect both sides."

"But what if these natives, as you call them, want to buy something, what if they want food and so on?"

"They've got their own shops. What could they possibly want to buy anyway?"

"Who declared the state of emergency?"

"General Gami."

"Who has the right to end it?"

"General Gami."

"And the Minister of the Interior."

"Yes. I guess he can order the Military Governor to end it."

"Where is General Gami?"

"Away on active service."

"For how long?"

"For at least another week. I told you that before."

"How would you say the situation in the province was at the moment?"

"Definitely good."

"I'll get in touch with the Minister of the Interior."

"Good luck."

Manuel Ortega sat immobile for a long while. Then he picked up the telephone receiver and heard Danica Rodríguez answer.

"Get me the Minister of the Interior, Zaforteza."

Ten minutes later, she told him: "Can't get through to the federal capital. The line is down. But we can cable."

He pondered for half an hour what he should say in his cable and even then he was not satisfied with it. It ran: "Situation satisfactory. Order military commander end emergency. Arrange report on reform committee's results. Order survey to be continued. Ortega."

Danica Rodríguez sent the cable. The telephone exchange promised that it would arrive within an hour.

Manuel Ortega waited the whole afternoon for an answer. By five o'clock he had still heard nothing. The telephone exchange informed him that telephone communications were still broken off.

At half past five he tried to get hold of Behounek. He was told that the Chief of Police was out on an important mission.

At six o'clock he had an idea and called the headquarters of the Third Infantry Regiment. The duty officer informed him that General Gami was not with the regiment and neither was Colonel Orbal. Weren't they in their office at the Governor's Palace? The regiment's commanding officer, Colonel Ruiz, had gone home, but probably could be reached the following morning.

The operator at the switchboard in the Governor's Palace informed him that the Military Governor's offices were closed. General Gami and Colonel Orbal were away on active service for ten days and the office staff had been transferred to the headquarters of the Third Infantry Regiment.

At seven o'clock Captain Behounek had still not returned. A lieutenant who was on duty did not think he would be back until the following morning.

Manuel Ortega glanced at the immobile López. Then he rang for his assistant. No one came. The young man had evidently gone home.

I am alone in this fearful building with a dumb bodyguard and a girl with a mustache and a bruise on her right breast, thought Manuel Ortega.

He rose and went in to Danica Rodríguez.

She was sitting with her left elbow on the table, smoking, while she read a thick mimeographed report. Without looking up, she said: "In 1932 the infant mortality rate in this province was estimated at forty-eight per cent. Last year it went up to sixty-two per cent. In 1932 illiteracy among the Indians was ninety-eight per cent. A statement made just over two years ago put it at ninety-seven. A native mineworker here earns, contract and all, a tenth of what a coalminer earns in the northern province as a basic wage."

She stubbed out her cigarette and went on: "This is an official report made by sociologists at the university in the capital. It was completed last winter and was immediately classified secret by the Ministry of Justice. You should read it."

"Where did you get hold of it?"

"Stole it," she said calmly.

"Have you had anything to eat today?"

"No."

"Shall we look for a place to eat?"

She nodded without looking up. After a while she said: "Did you know you've got a large apartment in the town? Five rooms, kitchen, and servants."

"What's all that nonsense?"

"It's not nonsense at all. But a Mr. Frankenheimer inspected it just before we came here. He condemned it and dismissed the servants. Who landed us with that expert?"

He was about to reply but stopped himself. Why should he confide in his secretary?

"No idea," he said.

"Where's he gone anyway."

"Went back to the capital, I suppose. He's probably sitting in the shade in some sidewalk restaurant at this very moment, having a cool drink."

The telephone on her desk rang. He stood there waiting to take the receiver but then realized that the call was not for him. He heard her say: "Yes. Hullo. . . . Thank you, too. . . . No, not tonight. . . . No, I'm busy in fact, and I must get some sleep afterward.

"Yes, of course you can. . . .

"Yes, just call when you feel like it."

She replaced the receiver and brushed her fingers across her forehead. Her eyes looked tired and resigned and far away.

Manuel Ortega stood silently for a moment and then said:

"Will you put the phone through to me. I've a call to make before we go."

He went back to his room, shut the door, called the Larrinaga household, and asked to speak to the daughter. There was quite a wait before she came to the telephone.

"Yes, this is Francisca de Larrinaga."

"My name is Ortega. I have succeeded your father as Provincial Resident. I am calling partly to express my admiration for your father and his work and to present my condolences . . ."

He paused.

". . . and partly to ask you to do me the favor of meeting me personally."

She sounded hesitant and said: "Tonight?"

"Whenever it suits you, of course."

"Tomorrow morning at ten o'clock?"

"Where?"

"Here at my home. I don't like going out while we're still in mourning."

He went back to the secretary's room.

"Well, shall we eat?"

She nodded, arose, and picked up her bag.

As he walked behind her down the corridor he was very conscious of her physical presence so near to him.

They found a restaurant in a side street off Avenida de la República. It was small and practically empty, and they sat down in one corner and ordered wine, bread, and meat. López sat against the opposite wall. He studied the menu for a long time and for once did not look entirely indifferent.

"Let's gobble down our food and run out and then he'd have to leave whatever he's ordered," said Danica Rodríguez.

They both laughed.

The wine was flat, the goat meat tough and sinewy, and the bread badly baked, but neither of them had had anything to eat for a long time, so they swallowed the food ravenously.

"Well, I suppose one can't expect gourmet food in a country like this," said Manuel Ortega.

"And this would be a feast which eighty per cent of the people down here have never experienced."

She said this in a tone of voice he had never heard her use before. She must have noticed it herself, because she shook herself and said lightly: "That was a pretty banal statement, but it was what I was thinking. But one should never say what one thinks."

They were sitting opposite one another and they went on drinking the poor wine. All at once she put both elbows on the table and her hands against her cheeks. She smiled and said mockingly: "Are you interested in Orestes de Larrinaga? Or just in his daughter?"

"Do you listen to my telephone conversations?"

"Of course."

This exchange left him speechless and to save himself he took a large gulp of wine.

"But if you're interested in Orestes de Larrinaga, then I've one or two questions to put to you."

"What about, for instance?"

"For instance, the following: The assassin shot Larrinaga at a distance of three yards with a machine gun which had ninety bullets in the magazine. Two steps from Larrinaga there was a lieutenant whose name, I gather, was Martínez, and who was presumably taken completely unawares. As far as one can make out, it would have been a mere nothing for the murderer to have shot the lieutenant too while he was about it, wouldn't it?"

"I don't see what you're getting at."

"I don't really know myself either, yet. But the one who

carried out the assassination not only failed to shoot this Martínez—he also stayed where he was sufficiently long for the lieutenant to have time to take out his pistol and fire three shots, of which at least one hit the assassin and wounded him badly. And yet there was a door behind the counter which he could have fled through."

"One can't expect people to behave logically in that sort of situation."

"I'm certain that our friend over there eating tamales always behaves completely logically. Your explanation could be true, though. So I have another question, though this one is slightly vaguer."

She was speaking in a low voice and Manuel Ortega leaned over the table to listen.

"Despite the fact that at the moment there are definite regulations about how and where military vehicles and personnel may put in an appearance outside the barracks area, one of the army prison vans arrived at the Governor's Palace less than ten minutes after the assassination."

"What's strange about that?"

"It can hardly have been passing by chance. As you know, practically the whole regiment, or the garrison, or whatever you call it, has been confined to barracks since Radamek became President and played the soft line. So that the atmosphere should remain calm, only certain activities and routine guard duties have been allowed outside the garrison area. Larrinaga had a military escort because he was a general and had raised hell to get it. Even so the prison van was there seven or eight minutes after the murder."

"As far as I can see, that proves nothing. They telephoned for it, I suppose. Have you any more questions like that?"

"One more. The lieutenant wounded the assassin with at least one shot. He was hit in the pelvis and was obviously very badly hurt. He bled profusely and couldn't walk or even stand up. The soldiers who took him out to the van had wound a cloth around his head. It took ten minutes to transport him back to the army barracks—the distance is, in fact, so great that only prison vans can cover the distance quicker without previous warning. Only a few minutes after the murderer had arrived there, an execution order was produced, signed by General Gami. Five minutes later the firing squad dragged the man out to the execution place in the inner barracks square and shot him. He couldn't stand up but had been propped on all fours on the ground when they shot him, and he still had a cloth wound around his head. When he was dead the cloth was taken away and he was put on public view. He was lying like that when Behounek got there, and an hour or so later he was buried out there somewhere."

"Is this information really true?"

"I'm almost certain it is. What I want to know is roughly this: Why was there such a terrible hurry? And why did they have to hide the man's face when they let him be seen later?"

"And what do you think the answer is?"

"I don't know."

"Where do you get all these details?"

"Let's just say I've been assembling them."

Manuel leaned back in his chair, fingered his glass, and heard himself saying: "Is that why you sleep with officers?"

She sat up straight and irritably bit at the cuticle of one nail. Her eyes flickered.

"I'm sorry. That was a completely unwarranted question. I really didn't mean to say that. I do apologize."

She looked at him and now her eyes were firm and serious.

"You don't have to apologize. I'll even give you an answer. No, it isn't why I sleep with officers. It's not even the main reason. Not at all."

They sought distraction and gazed around the room. The only person left was López. He had already finished his meal. Now he was picking his teeth, philosophically staring around the room. It was pitch dark outside the window and very hot and stuffy inside.

After a while the proprietor came up to their table and said: "I'm afraid I must close now. Because of the state of emergency."

They walked together for a short distance until they came to the block where she lived. López followed in their tracks, six or seven yards behind. When they stopped at the entrance, his steps stopped too.

Suddenly she giggled.

"What is it?"

"Nothing. Sometimes I think such stupid things. I thought: If you come up with me, will he sit there with his hands on his knees, watching while we go to bed together? Or will he sit on a swivel chair outside the door and listen?"

She giggled again and began to rummage in her bag for her keys. As she did so, she butted him playfully in the chest with her head.

"What have you got there?" she said suddenly, fingering the revolver butt through the material of his jacket. "Goodness," she said.

It was the same old situation. He was being overcome and at the same time he felt that it was all very foolish. To hell with López and Behounek and General Gami. He took a step toward her and said: "Danica."

She stiffened at once, took a last drag on her cigarette, and crushed it out against the wall. Then she said: "I must go up and get some sleep now. Haven't had any sleep these last few nights, as you know. Good night."

He was still thinking about her as he crossed the square.

Then he heard an explosion a long way off and soon after that another. He stood still for a long time, listening, but he didn't hear any sirens.

When he got to his bedroom he felt unreasonably afraid and twice he peered around the door to see if López was still sitting outside. Only when he undressed did he discover that his clothes were soaked with sweat. He took a shower, but it didn't make him feel much better.

Then he took two of Dalgren's tablets, got into bed, and thought about a door he had to open though he did not dare to. He got out of bed and took the Astra from the bureau and put it under his pillow. Then he fell asleep.

8

●●***

At nine o'clock the next morning he called the police head-quarters. The officer on duty informed him that Behounek had not yet arrived. Manuel Ortega asked: "What sort of night have you had?"

"Calm."

"I heard a couple of explosions just before eleven last night."

"Just a blasting detail, I would think."

"What sort of detail?"

The duty officer did not reply to his question but said: "I'm sure Captain Behounek will be here by midday."

Half an hour later he went out to see General Larrinaga's daughter. Fernández drove and Gómez sat in the back. Fernández smelled of garlic, chewed his seeds, and was full of chatter. He also had difficulty in finding the way and drove badly.

Both at the exit from the center of the town and at the foot of the slope leading up to the villa area they were stopped at police barriers. Both times the engine stalled.

The road to the villa area led upward in long snaking bends, and as they had plenty of time, Manuel had the car stopped on a bend where there was a wide view out over the workers' part of the town. The area sprawled out below him was triangular and enclosed by barbed-wire fences and tall, crooked walls. Now he could see that not all the buildings were tin shacks and wooden huts, but that there were also a great many squat yellowish-gray stone houses with flat roofs. Between these ran a network of narrow streets and in the center of the district was a square marketplace. There were quite a lot of people moving about, and here and there he could make out white police cars. At least two were parked in the market-place. It was obviously a very old part of the town which had been built on to in the simplest way to hold about four times its original number of inhabitants. When he got back into the car he remembered that about half the apartments in the middle of the town were empty, and always had been, for people preferred to live within the artificially irrigated area.

The house which Orestes de Larrinaga had lived in was a very large one, almost a palace, and in front of it was a garden the upkeep of which must have required tremendous effort and enormous quantities of water.

A servant with a mourning veil tied in a rosette on his white jacket led them to a patio where there were stone seats, a spring, and beautiful flowers. The patio was covered with slate slabs, as was the bottom of the goldfish pond.

Manuel Ortega sat down on one of the stone seats and waited. Fernández cleared his throat and pondered at some length on where he should spit, and in the end decided on the goldfish pond. When one of the goldfish came up to the surface to look at the gobbet of spit, he laughed, quietly and heartily, for a long time.

Manuel decided quite definitely that this was the most objectionable member of his bodyguard, especially now that Frankenheimer had gone.

After a few minutes the servant came back with two glasses of chilled almond milk on a silver tray. Fernández sniffed at his suspiciously and put it to one side on the stone seat. Then he took out his revolver and twirled the magazine with his thumb as he slowly took out bullet after bullet and looked at them. Manuel thought that this was in no better taste than taking out one's false teeth and adjusting them at the table, and he was driven to saying: "Remember that we're in a house of mourning."

Fernández glowered at him in an offended and uncompre-

hending way. Then he sighed and put away his revolver, very
meticulously and ostentatiously adjusting his gun in its holster.
Manuel thought: I must get rid of this tribe of apes. And
I'm sure they're useless anyway. Behounek will have to arrange
something from tomorrow on. Aloud, he said: "When the lady
comes, move over to the other side, out of earshot."

Five minutes later Francisca de Larrinaga came down the
stairs from the floor above. Manuel Ortega rose and went to
meet her. She was dressed in full mourning and was undoubtedly very beautiful, but in some way it was an im-
pregnable beauty which did not excite him.

They sat down by the goldfish pond and the servant brought
more almond milk. Manuel glanced at Fernández, who was
looking at his two glasses with a confused and unhappy
expression.

It took Manuel no more than two minutes to find out that he
could come straight to the point. The woman listened politely
to his conventional phrases. Then she said sharply and coldly:
"What do you want?"

"During his tenure as Provincial Resident, the General must
have undertaken certain measures . . ."

"My father never spoke of his work at home, neither when
he was in the army nor during this last period."

"Nonetheless, he seems to have been working during these
last three weeks on a proclamation, a personal statement."

"It is possible."

"This proclamation was never completed but seems to have
been almost ready."

"And?"

"The text of it was not found after his departure."

"Will you kindly explain what you mean?"

"Let me be quite honest. I have succeeded your father in
this difficult post and want to carry on the work in the spirit
in which your father would wish and with the same intentions
with which he began. The enduring contribution your father

wished to make was obviously bound up with this proclamation. I think it would therefore be very valuable to get some idea of its contents and the views it expressed. Best of all, of course, I would prefer to see it."

After a short pause, he added: "In fact I believe the text was destroyed at the time of the General's death by someone who didn't want it to be known. Either by the murderer or by his employers."

The conversation ceased. The only noise was Fernández chewing and scraping his feet on the other side of the fish pond.

Francisca de Larrinaga looked at her visitor. She was frowning slightly and her face was hard and serious beneath her mourning veil. Finally she said: "You are wrong. If the murderer or his employers had known the contents of the proclamation, my father would still be alive."

Manuel said nothing. He thought feverishly but could think of nothing to say.

After a while she said: "You are surprised. Well, let me say this at once. There does exist a copy of the draft of my father's statement. By sheer chance I found it after his death. In the pocket of his smoking jacket. He must have taken his papers home with him to study in the evenings. This was contrary to his usual habits and in itself shows how much importance he attached to this . . . proclamation. On the other hand, he never spoke of it. I had no idea at all of his work, just as little now as before, when he was on active service."

"And you've read it?"

"Yes. I have read it and kept it. The views he expresses in it would surprise many people if they were published. I was astonished myself. My father was a man of strict principles, everyone knew that, but lately he seemed to have changed his opinions on quite a few points."

"In what respects?"

She did not answer the question but said: "I was very close to my father. He found that with me he could relax and be himself more easily. I went in the car with him practically every morning. On one of these occasions he talked to me about his mission; not exactly to me but more to himself. He did that sometimes, in the company of someone he knew very well and could trust implicitly. I was one of these people, perhaps the only one. Anyway, I received the impression that the government had demanded that he call and lead a conference, some kind of peace negotiations between the so-called right-wing extremists and the Communists. He refused, partly because he —as he expressed it himself—was a soldier and not a shifty-eyed diplomat, and partly because he thought it degrading and preposterous that men like Count Ponti and Dalgren and General Gami should sit at the the same conference table with Indians and mountain bandits and partisan chiefs, El Campesino, and whatever they are called now."

Again she paused. Then she said: "If I hand my father's statement over to you, what will you do with it then?"

"Publish it, whatever it contains. In my capacity as his successor, I would consider it my duty."

"And in my capacity as his daughter and closest friend, I regard it as my duty to consider very carefully what should be done with his effects."

Where does she get it all from? thought Manuel Ortega, humbled. But he collected himself at once and resumed: "For various reasons I am interested in the circumstances of your father's death. Does it pain you too much to talk about it?"

"I can talk about anything," she said.

"As you were present at the time . . ."

He broke off.

"Yes?"

"I have been told that the murderer was carried away with his head covered."

"That's true. I was sitting in the car outside and heard the shots. When I went in, my father was already dead. He had been hit in the chest with about fifteen or twenty shots. The escort officer, a young lieutenant, had shot the murderer. The man was badly wounded in the pelvis and was lying on the floor behind the counter. He was shouting curses and abuse like a wild animal. A captain who came shortly afterward gave orders for him to be silenced, and some soldiers took a tablecloth and wound it around his head and tied it up with a belt."

"Could you make out what he was saying?"

"I was, as you can understand, deeply upset. And the man was badly wounded too. In fact I think his wounds were fatal. In any case, he would have been a permanent invalid. He was probably in great pain, for his voice was blurred and it was hard to catch his words. As far as I could make out he was cursing the man who had shot him, the generals, the government, and the Citizens' Guard."

Manuel Ortega looked at the young woman. Her face was calm and her voice controlled. She was using the same tone of voice as that of the person who had threatened him two days earlier.

"Thank you for your kindness in giving me this information. Will you also allow me to see your father's statement?"

She replied at once: "I cannot decide that now. But I shall give you my answer within four days."

"Forgive me if I ask you one more question. Who other than yourself knows that this document exists?"

"You."

"I think it would be wise if you refrained from letting anyone else know."

"The moment," said Francisca de Larrinaga, "when I shall be in need of your advice is, as far as I can judge, very far away. Should it arise, which I doubt, I would take up the matter on my own accord. To be more precise: I don't know you, sir, and neither have I any opinions about you. The information I have given you, and might eventually give you,

I am putting at your disposal because I think you have a right to it in your capacity as my father's successor."

They rose from their seats.

"Who is the man with the sunflower seeds?" she asked.

"My bodyguard."

"Really? Good-by."

"Good-by."

In the car, Fernández said to López, who was slightly dazed with sleep: "What a bird! Jesus Christ, what a piece! You should've seen her. I could almost feel my cock rising on the spot. Quite a different kettle of fish from that bearded scarecrow up with us."

He drummed his fingers on the wheel and said unhappily: "Sorry. My manners aren't very classy, I know. I can't help it."

"Drive on," said Manuel Ortega.

He felt physically and psychologically exhausted, as after a tennis match or an important business deal. Just before Fernández had begun to speak, he had thought that Francisca de Larrinaga was one of those women whom he could not imagine undressed.

Well, he said to himself, there are different views on most things.

Then he thought: Why have I begun to think about those things so much?

As they drove through the dismal screened-off workers' sector, it struck him that anyone lying behind the wall with a rifle could easily fire and no one would be able to do a thing about it.

To his own mortification, he hunched up behind Gómez and tried to keep his head as low as possible.

At two in the afternoon he got in touch with Captain Behounek.

"How is the situation?"

"Calm."

"And out in the country?"

"I've just come from there. Made a little personal inspection."

"And?"

"Calm."

"No attacks?"

"Hardly any. I think our patrols have pushed the partisans up into the mountains."

"I'd like to go with you sometime on a trip out into the country."

"There'll be a very good opportunity tomorrow. A sanitary patrol is visiting one of the bigger Indian villages. It'll have a safe escort."

"Will you arrange the matter for me?"

"Certainly."

"One question. What is meant by a blasting detail? One of your subordinates used the term as if it were quite an ordinary event."

"Well, it's quite an unpleasant story. Roughly speaking, it's like this: the youngsters in the Citizens' Guard have learned to use plastic bombs. It was a European idea to begin with, I gather. You get a tough mess of stuff which you stick onto something, and then you put in a fuse with a flint in it. Well, at night, small groups go into the native sector and stick plastic bombs here and there. During the worst disturbances we had a great deal of trouble with them. The streets there are badly lit—mostly not lit at all. It's difficult to keep an eye on them at night."

"Does this still go on?"

"To a limited extent."

"Was there a raid of that kind last night?"

"Yes."

"And the damage?"

"Trifling. These bombs have an open explosive effect and the damage is usually not very great. I shudder to think what would happen if they ever think of putting the stuff into iron pipes for instance."

"Was anyone killed last night?"

"No, I don't think so."

"Think?"

"I mean that nothing has been reported. Some of the natives are pretty peculiar, you see. They won't or daren't report damage and casualties. But their faith in us is growing steadily."

"Have you caught the raiders?"

"Not yet."

"Well, let's hope for the best."

He put down the receiver, rang for Danica Rodríguez, and was surprised when he saw her. She was dressed as on the previous day, but her face was pale and resigned and her eyes very serious.

He could not help saying: "How are you feeling?"

"Very well, thank you."

"You hadn't come in when I left this morning."

"No, I'm sorry."

"Oh, well—do you know if the telephone lines are in order yet?"

"They're still cut."

"Have you asked whether there's a reply to my cable?"

"It hasn't come yet."

"Send a reminder then. No, don't—send a copy of the text and point out that there is some urgency."

"Yes."

When she reached the door, he said: "Come back for a moment, please."

He tried to smile at her, but either it was an unsuccessful attempt or else there was no way of breaking her seriousness.

"I've got some information for you. About the assassination."

He repeated all the details of the murder that he could remember from his conversation with Francisca de Larrinaga.

She listened with interest but made no comment. Then she said seriously: "Did you find that out for my sake?"

"Well—partly."

"Thanks."

When she walked away he stared at her thighs and hips. Earlier he had tried to decide whether she was wearing a bra but had been unable to come to any conclusion.

A moment later he turned to the fat man who was sitting against the wall, his hands on his knees.

"López, are you married?"

"Yes."

The conversation was not prolonged. He had thought for a moment of asking a question such as "Have you any children?" or "What do you think about it then?" but he decided not to.

Manuel Ortega sat and felt the heat become thicker and thicker, filling the room more and more. Despite the fan he was soaked with sweat, but he did not bother to go and shower.

When he tried to analyze why he did not bother he discovered it was because of fear. He did not want to have to open the door to his room unnecessarily and go in while López was still sitting on the chair behind his back. But after a while he went in after all, to shower and change his clothes, trying an experiment by leaving the door ajar. When he opened the door to his living quarters there was some kind of draft, probably caused by the fan, and the door slammed shut.

He returned, as usual, with his hand on the butt of his revolver.

This thing with the door had become an *idée fixe*. Common sense told him that there were many situations in which he had equally good or better reasons for being afraid—but what use was common sense in a situation like this? He repeated the question to himself.

What use is common sense?

Then he sat down and thought over the situation. He was

trapped by a string of foolish circumstances and abandoned to the arbitrary decisions of others.

As long as the Ministry did not answer his cable he had no idea how to go about his present job.

As long as General Gami and Colonel Orbal were pleased to stay away he could not carry out any discussions at the highest level.

As long as the girl in the big house on the hill had not decided what she was going to do with the famous papers he would know nothing about what General Larrinaga's work had really involved.

All this tied him down and forced him into inactivity.

He also accused himself of being too official, too lacking in initiative, too bound to conventional points of view on how an assignment should be carried out. And worst of all, his single-mindedness was turning his assignment into a simple office job.

And also, he was afraid.

He thought he ought to make an extensive trip around the town, but could not make himself do so. The town frightened him and he did not want to become involved in its violence any more than he already was. Also he was certain that the picture that he had built up of the atmosphere in the community was correct. At least in its essentials.

He went to the window and looked out over the great deserted square and the white cobblestones on the other side. In some way he found this empty, sizzling, desolate plaza more repugnant than the rank odor of destitution and privation in the native quarter.

At six o'clock he went in and asked the woman in the green dress to go out and have dinner with him.

"I'm afraid not," she said, "not tonight."

He borrowed her copy of the sociological report and went back to his room. He switched on the radio and listened for two hours to the local program which consisted almost entirely of screeching records and advertisements for various more or less meaningless goods. A routine-type appeal from General Gami, asking for calm and order, was repeated three times. The General's voice was supercilious and dry.

Once a news bulletin was read; indifferent and meaningless reports from distant countries where something had happened and where people at least seemed to know what was happening.

At nine o'clock he took López with him and ate a wretched meal.

When he got back he went straight to bed.

He began to read the sociological report and that kept him occupied until he heard Fernández relieve López in the room outside.

At that, part of his relative feeling of security vanished too. He ascertained with a certain surprise that he had evidently relied more on the one than the other although he really did not know either of them.

He got up and took two of Dalgren's tablets, looked under his bed, put the light out, and went back to bed.

His last conscious action was to see that the Astra was in its place underneath his pillow.

Manuel Ortega fell asleep with his hand on the walnut butt.

9

✳●✳●✳✳✳

The sanitary patrol started out from the plaza at eight o'clock the next morning, two hours after the prescribed time.

In the first vehicle, a large white Land-Rover with a searchlight and a canvas cover, sat the escort officer and three policemen. Manuel Ortega and Danica Rodríguez went in the army-type medical car, equipped for rough ground with coarse-treaded rubber tires and red crosses on the rear doors. Then came Gómez and Fernández in their gray Citroën, and last an ordinary police jeep with two more policemen in it. Captain Behounek was obviously not a man to leave anything to chance.

The convoy drove diagonally across the square and continued southward between the dusty palm trees along Avenida de la República. The sidewalks were almost deserted, but outside the great new church at the corner of the Avenida and Calle San Martín there were quite a few people who were evidently on their way home from mass.

The town looked white and dead and very hot.

They passed the police barriers and the barracks, which looked almost equally dead. Only a couple of sentries could be seen at the iron gates and a few idle soldiers were scattered about the great dusty barracks square.

A mile or so farther south, the highway came to an end. A barbed-wire barrier had been erected across the road and behind it they caught a glimpse of great heaps of stones, one or two skeletons of trucks and a bulldozer, solid with rust. The work seemed to have been broken off at very short notice and quite a long time ago, as if those engaged in it had suddenly lost interest in the project and just walked away.

"I gather the highway was to have gone all the way to the border, but then the government fell and nothing came of it," said the doctor.

He was young, scarcely more than twenty-five. He was driving. Manuel Ortega sat farthest to the right with his elbow resting on the open window. Between them, on the car's wide front seat, sat Danica Rodríguez. She had crossed her legs and was staring straight through the windshield. It was impossible to catch her eye behind the dark glasses.

There was one more person in the car, a middle-aged orderly in a crumpled gray linen uniform with brass buttons. He was sitting on a pile of blankets behind the driver's seat and smoking a thick yellowish-brown cigarette.

"It'll be pretty uncomfortable from now on," said the doctor. "The road isn't much."

They swung off the highway onto a narrow stony gravel road which climbed up between the ridges in long snaking bends.

"That road was built for strategic reasons," said Danica Rodríguez. "By a military government who thought that the army needed a route southward."

"It's possible," said the doctor. "Anyhow it was never finished and it doesn't make any difference. As little as this kind of trip does."

"Why not?" asked Manuel Ortega.

"Everything is meaningless here. You'll soon notice that."

The landscape around them was grayish yellow and dismal. The hilly land looked dry and desolate and there were no trees, just a few scattered scrubby bushes between the crumbling chunks of stone.

The convoy drove through a little village consisting of about twenty low mud huts. They saw no one, only a thin donkey which ran zigzagging across the village street, frightened and clumsy. Manuel Ortega said: "Is this place uninhabited?"

"I don't think so. Probably the people hid when they saw the cars up on the ridge. They're afraid."

"Of us?"

"The police car," said the doctor laconically.

For about a quarter of an hour he concentrated all his efforts on the road. Then he said: "The people here are very hard to reach. South of the provincial capital there are only Indians except for one or two landowners. But they are few and far between. The estates are huge, and for that matter most of the owners prefer to live in the town. They have foremen on the farms and are content to go out to inspect once or twice a month. The foremen are usually half-breeds."

He paused before adding: "They're not particularly popular."

"How long have you been here?"

"Almost two years. At first I minded very much. There's almost nothing one can do. The people are unfathomable, as I said. They seem to stand outside everything, looking on. You can't get really near them. They are frightened and ignorant, and if you speak to them they answer in monosyllables and always with some meaningless phrase, just to keep you happy. If someone is very ill and in great pain and you ask if it hurts, he usually answers no. He thinks you'll be angry otherwise. And our resources are very limited. The medical supplies don't cover five per cent of the need. And neither is there any possibility of teaching them to use the drugs. Usually they're scared and throw away the medicine as soon as your back is turned."

"But there are teachers in the villages?"

"Yes, of course. You'll be meeting one soon. Do you see those little fields up there?"

"Yes."

"They're a good illustration of the problem. There was quite a lot of forest up here before. But the Indians burned it all down in their ignorance and sowed in the ash. After a few years the fields were ruined by erosion. In this way the forest goes to hell and all the cultivable land left is in the hands of the landowners, who know how to look after it. The food situation is already hopeless. Practically everyone who lives here is undernourished and the children die like flies."

"What's the name of the village we're going to?"

"Pozo del Tigre—in Spanish. I've forgotten the Indian name."

The conversation came to an end. The engine roared harshly in low gear. Manuel Ortega stared at the stony landscape shimmering in the heat. Danica sat silently smoking. In front of them the white jeep climbed farther and farther up the steep sharp bends. Once they met a police patrol on its way down and several times they caught a glimpse of low huts below the hillside, but nowhere did they see a single human being.

An hour or so later the cars drove into Pozo del Tigre and stopped in the marketplace. Children, pigs, and dogs ran in all directions. Several old Indians with sunken cheeks stared resignedly at the men in white uniforms.

"How big is this village?" asked Manuel Ortega.

The doctor shrugged his shoulders, but Danica Rodríguez answered the question.

"There are about sixty households here—four hundred people in all."

"Have you been here before?"

She nodded.

Manuel Ortega thrust his hand inside his jacket and felt the Astra. Then he got out onto the hard ground and looked around.

The village consisted of about fifty squat huts with mud walls and dirty gray thatched roofs. Each hut stood in a fenced-in plot and there appeared to be three parallel village streets, all surfaced with uneven, sun-baked clay. By the marketplace stood the village's chief building, a large white church with an annex which must have been for the priests and their servants.

On the opposite side of the marketplace stood another white stone building; it was long and low and across its façade was the word ESCUELA in tall brown letters. Above the brown wooden door was a piece of paper on which was written CUARTEL DE LA GENDARMERÍA and on the steps leading up to the school building sat two policemen with no caps on and their uniform jackets unbuttoned.

In the middle of the marketplace was a well with faucets and rusty iron pipes. A bit beyond stood a little group of people looking timidly at the cars. The men were dressed in straw hats, white shirts, and white trousers with broad red belts, the women had coarse strips of material wound around their waists and were wearing some kind of triangular blouses tied at the nape of the neck. They were all dirty and their clothes hung in rags.

Danica Rodríguez looked around, thoughtfully chewing her lower lip.

"They build schools and use them as police stations," she mumbled. "Nothing changes."

She said this very quietly, but Manuel Ortega was sufficiently close to her to catch her words. He asked: "Is this your home village?"

She shook her head and took a few steps across the marketplace.

"Come," she said.

Manuel Ortega hesitated. He was disturbed by the people and the surroundings, and the feeling of alienation made him reluctant to move far from the policemen and their cars.

"You needn't be afraid," she said. "It's quite safe here. No one will recognize you and I doubt that they even know that such a person as the Provincial Resident exists."

He realized she was right. Besides, he was armed and had

both Gómez and Fernández less than ten yards away from him, not to mention the men in the white uniforms.

They walked across the marketplace and the people drew silently aside.

Behind the church lay a low, primitive stone barrier below which was a steep slope deeply scored by a ravine. At the bottom of the ravine they could see a slimy green pool of water, still and stinking, and beyond the slope the landscape widened into scorched furrows between gray-white ridges.

"You see the road down there? If you follow it for about twelve miles to the south, you come to the village where I was born. It's about a third as big as this. Behind the mountains there."

She pointed, and he looked out over the monotonous landscape.

"As I say, I was born and grew up there. The huts looked the same as these here, and there was a church there too and a Catholic priest who lived by practicing blackmail on illiterates. I remember that he sold candles to people and then omitted to light them. The next day he would maintain that their sacrifice had pleased the Holy Virgin and the saints, and then he sold the same candles again. That way he could keep the price down and still do good business."

"And your family?"

"My father died down here more than ten years ago. He was a doctor, although he had broken off his studies rather early."

She lit a cigarette, put one foot up on the stone wall, and adjusted the straps of her sandal.

"He was crazy, of course. A naïve idealist who was doomed to failure in everything he undertook."

Manuel Ortega said nothing, but he looked at her legs and feet. Again he felt a vague disturbance, as if he were a little afraid of her, but yet not afraid.

"It's silly," she said, "but true. He met a girl in the provincial capital and married her. Had a child by her and then another and then moved down and built a hospital there. After a year or so she tired of it and left him, but he stayed. With us."

"For how long?"

"He stayed till the end. During his last years he drank quite a lot and then he died. By then his hospital had already fallen to pieces. He lived with some Indian woman and I believe they had a child."

"And you?"

"I went off when I was fourteen."

"Why?"

She did not reply at once but remained standing for a moment, her eyes fixed far away. Then she said:

"I realized even then that it was meaningless to stay here if one wanted to do any good."

Manuel Ortega said nothing and he wasn't in fact thinking about anything in particular. She must have misunderstood his silence, for a moment later she drew in a deep breath and said violently: "Don't you see? What had happened? At thirteen the boys began to sleep with you. In that respect they were no different from any of the others. Then you would have become pregnant and acquired a handicap which you could not overcome and so . . . yes, then you would have been stuck here."

"Yes," said Manuel Ortega.

When they got back to the marketplace, the police had organized a line outside the school. Most of those standing there were women, and nearly all of them had their children with them. They were standing, relaxed and apathetic, without moving or speaking. The children did not even cry or whimper, although many of them were encrusted with dirt and had large running sores on their faces.

As Manuel Ortega made his way past the waiting line, he smelled once again the rank odor of dirt and poverty.

In one of the rooms the doctor had set up a temporary surgery. He had laid out his instruments and hypodermic syringes on a wooden box. Behind him stood the orderly in the gray linen uniform sorting ampules in a box. There was also a woman there; she was quite young with dark eyes and brown skin. She was the schoolteacher in Pozo del Tigre. Now she was helping with the injections, clumsily wiping the children's arms with a pad soaked in antiseptic and then putting a patch of lint and strips of adhesive on afterward.

The doctor looked tired and irritable. He searched around with his stethoscope in the rags which hung on the little girl standing in front of him, glanced at Manuel Ortega and said: "They've an epidemic here. Measles."

Then he turned his attention to the child again. The girl was perhaps seven or eight years old. As he examined her, the mother stood to one side, calm and resigned with her arms hanging loosely down.

"This child has pneumonia," said the doctor, as if to himself.

Then he turned to the mother and went on: "She must have an injection from the schoolteacher here every day for a month. That is, thirty days. Do you understand."

"Yes, yes."

"Every day for a whole month then."

"Yes, yes."

"Once or twice isn't enough. You must bring her every day."

"Yes, yes."

"When will you bring her next?"

The woman thought.

"Tomorrow," she said.

"And then?"

"Next time you come with the cars."

"No! The day after tomorrow. Do you understand?"

"Yes, yes."

"And you must give her this medicine every morning and every evening. Do you understand that too?"

"Yes, yes."

He waved her away and turned to the next patient.

"We're short of medicine," he said in passing. "And they throw it away. It's all hopeless."

Manuel Ortega walked across the room and leaned against the wall. After a while the schoolteacher came over to him.

"The doctor is wrong. The child had another sickness. Not what he says. A dead person is lying in the house next to hers and the chill has spread to the child. Of course that's what it is, isn't it?"

Manuel Ortega stared at her.

"What kind of training have you had?" he said.

"I know Spanish," she said. "I believe in the one true God. I've learned to read. I went for a hundred and three days on a training course in the provincial capital. In the big building, with the soldiers."

She went back to her antiseptic pads.

Manuel Ortega looked at his secretary. She pushed her sunglasses up on to her forehead and met his eyes.

In the background he heard the next Indian woman say: "Yes, yes . . . yes, yes . . . yes, yes."

On the way home, five hours later, the doctor said: "Measles isn't a very serious disease. It's just that they die of it. Tonight ten children will die out there. One mustn't mind. If one minded one would go mad."

"But it shouldn't be all that difficult to do something about it," said Manuel Ortega.

"No, of course not. Give us more money, more medicine, and more people. Give us people who will teach them to eat their eggs instead of giving them to the priest; who will teach them not to take water from the pool because someone has persuaded them that there are evil spirits in the well; who will teach them to use the latrines, to use soap, to get rid of lice. Give us more instruments. There's a shortage of money, to put it briefly."

"And the will to do it," said Danica Rodríguez.

"Yes," said the doctor. "Exactly. What does it matter that their kids die. I want to live."

10

●●**

It was the morning of the fifth day and Ortega did not wake like a child. He was awakened by someone leaning over him and shaking his shoulder. At first it was a nightmare and then misinterpreted reality. Desperately he thrust his hand under the pillow and tried to throw himself onto the floor. And then a voice: "Calm down, calm down, for Christ's sake. It's only me."

Eventually he sat up again and stared at the man who had awakened him. It was Fernández.

"Something has happened and I thought I'd better wake you."

"What's happened?"

"I don't know, but there's a hell of a row going on in town. It's already been on for some time. Gómez has had a look out front and says it's to the right somewhere. There was a whole string of explosions at first, a long way off, almost like an air raid; more than two hours ago. Now they're shooting away like mad. You can hear yells and screams too, Gómez says."

"Get out while I dress."

He did not bother to shower, although he was soaked with sweat and still dazed by the sleeping tablets. He rinsed his hands and face, however, but the water only trickled spasmodically out of the faucet. He dressed and strapped on the Astra, shrugging on his jacket as he went into his office. For once he forgot to be afraid of the door and this time there happened to be someone in there. But it was Gómez.

He lifted the telephone receiver and looked at the clock,

which said twenty-five past five. He had to wait a long time before getting through to the switchboard, but police headquarters answered immediately. An excited voice said: "The chief? No, he isn't—yes, just a minute—he's just going past."

There was a clatter.

"Hell—yes. Behounek speaking."

"What's happened?"

"The dirty rats have blown up the pumping station and the mains at the waterworks. The buildings up there are on fire and the whole town's without water."

"Who did it?"

"A Communist sabotage group—about two and a half hours ago. Nearly all the men who work up there have had it, and one of my men too."

"But what's all that shooting?"

"The Citizens' Guard has got its emergency forces out. They're trying to get into the—for Christ's sake, can't you see I'm talking to the Resident—yes—into the workers' sector at the north end. Excuse me—I must go now."

"The north end, did you say? I'll go on up there."

"No, for God's sake don't. Please don't. No one can be responsible for anyone's safety up there at the moment."

"I'll take the risk."

"You're the last person on earth who should go there now. But if you must, then at least come in my car. I'll pick you up in ten minutes."

The Chief of Police was gone but he must have flung the telephone receiver down onto the table, for footsteps and shouts and telephone signals could still be heard.

Ten minutes later a white Dodge, its siren wailing, drove straight across the square.

"Get in the back. No, I've no room for your gorillas. They'll have to go in their own car."

He sat in the front seat next to the driver and turned

the knob of a short-wave set which crackled and hissed. In the back sat the deputy from the airport, Lieutenant Brown.

"Hope to hell we won't need the army's help."

"Is it so critical?"

"So-so. If we survive the next two hours, the danger is over. They started this at the worst possible moment."

"Who?"

"The Citizens' Guard. Before half past five the mineworkers haven't gone off to work. That means that nearly four thousand able-bodied men are still inside the barricaded area. They're the dangerous ones. There's a risk of a coordinated break-out. I can't cope with that."

"How do the workers get to the mines?"

"They walk. It takes about an hour and a half for them to get there."

Manuel Ortega thought that this must be a considerable crowd of people and he wondered why he had not seen anything of them, not even in the evenings. Behounek promptly solved the problem for him.

"They walk along a special road in a curve southeastward around the town."

"But to blow up the waterworks," said Manuel. "That affects everyone in the same way."

"No, it's better calculated than that. The native quarter isn't dependent on the waterworks. It's in the old part of the town where there are several wells. Not very good ones, but all the same. But the whole of the center of town and the villa district will be without water. It'll be sheer hell."

The car drove at a tremendous speed down the middle of the road between the stone walls, its siren wailing and its warning lights on. There were a great many people on the road and police jeeps were parked along the walls.

They swung up toward the villa district, around a few bends, and then stopped at exactly the same place where Manuel had parked for a moment the day before.

Behounek got out of the car. He had a pair of binoculars hanging around his neck. The driver was trying to adjust a portable short-wave transmitter. A large open American car crammed with men wearing yellow armbands rolled past them going downhill. Most of the men were armed with rifles and had cartridge belts slung over their shoulders.

"The Citizens' Guard," said Behounek. "They're beginning to rally round now. Not sending kids out any longer."

"Do you let them through the barriers?"

The Chief of Police did not answer the question, but said: "If it gets too awful I'll swear them in as militia. I've done that before now. The problem now is to keep the natives inside the barricaded area and the whites as much as possible outside it."

From the triangular section of the town below rose a cacophony of shrieks, shots, and unidentifiable sounds of violence.

"D'you see?" said Behounek. "There—you see the smoke over the ridge there?"

"Why did the trouble break out here?"

"Most of the Citizens' Guard live up here," said Behounek laconically.

He had got the walkie-talkie working and had made contact with someone.

"Clear the square," he said.

Manuel tried to concentrate his gaze on the open space in the middle of the jumble of houses. It looked filled to bursting, but only a few minutes later several white jeeps drove up to it and one could see how the crowd was scattered and driven into the side streets.

"You must stop those idiots from shooting at the road," Behounek shouted into the transmitter. "What have you got there? Yes. Yes. Send them. Send everyone you've got. At once. Make sure the road is opened and people get moving along it. Listen! There's a bunch of kids from the Citizens'

Guard in the field west of the road in square 14. They're shooting at people on the road. You must get them to stop it. Now. At once.

"This is madness. They're preventing them from getting through to the mines. There's a standstill on the road already. They must be stopped! And see that people keep moving along the road. The quicker we get the workers away from the town, the better."

Against his will, Manuel was fascinated by what he saw. The distance made the drama more or less abstract; made it hard to believe and to realize that every dot down there represented a separate individual.

Nor did he escape the infection of Behounek's dynamic direction of operations, just as he had been similarly affected by the chief's fear when the Citizens' Guard had aroused the wrath of the workers by shooting at them on the road to the mines.

"Disperse the crowd by the wall in section 3. Immediately!

"Barricade the road from the square to the eastern well.

"Four extra men to the north gate. Is the loudspeaker system working? Good."

Aside he said: "We've got a loudspeaker system down there. They'll get orders now to go indoors and stay there."

Half an hour later the shooting had practically ceased. Behounek's orders became more positive in character.

"Clear section 1.

"Clear section 2.

"Are the loudspeakers still working? Good. Tell them that everyone who has to get to work has free access through the east gate. And that they must go quickly.

"I think it's over now, for this time," he said to Manuel Ortega.

He wiped his forehead with his sleeve and took his right foot down from the low stone wall.

"Would you lend me your binoculars?" said Manuel Ortega.

"Yes, yes, of course. Here you are. But I warn you, you're not going to like what you see."

As he focused the lenses, Manuel realized the extent of the tragedy of which he had been a passive spectator for the last hour or so. In the square alone he counted eight bodies. He let his glance slide on, along stretches which were more or less clear. He lost track of the number by the time he reached twenty. Only policemen in white uniforms could be seen down there now. In some places he saw people bending over prostrate figures and then walking on, as if they had not found what they were looking for. Then he turned the binoculars to the east and saw clumps of people walking diagonally across a scorched field toward the road which led to the mines.

He had a sudden attack of shivering and nausea, and he lowered the binoculars.

The Chief of Police glanced at him.

"Yes. There it is. Quite a few lives lost for this."

"How many do you think?"

Behounek shrugged his shoulders.

"How should I know?"

Then a little later: "All I know is, it could have been worse, much worse."

I stood and watched them die, thought Manuel Ortega in confusion. I stood up here as if on a platform and watched people being maimed and killed and all I thought about was how long it would take for the police to clear the streets and disperse the crowds.

"I stood and watched them die," he mumbled.

"Yes, well, we managed all right," said Behounek, and he peered up at the sky. Then he added absently: "It's going to be a hot day. Otherwise this week's been a good one."

"Do you think so?"

"Yes. It's just that you're not used to it yet. These last few days have been fine and fresh. It'll be worse today."

He turned to the police car.

"It's all over down there now. Shall we go and have a look?"

Manuel Ortega looked absently at him. Behounek frowned.

"Perhaps it would be better not to after all. They probably don't think much of you at the moment, and someone might take a pot shot at you from one of the houses. You don't look too good either."

He looked at his watch.

"Eight already. I must go over to the pumping station. It doesn't look too good either. You'll tackle the water question, won't you? Damned nuisance that General Gami should be away."

"Who is his deputy?"

"Colonel Orbal."

"And his?"

"C.O. of the regiment, Colonel Ruiz."

"I'll contact him."

Manuel Ortega went back into the town in the little French car with Gómez and Fernández. On the way they saw several army ambulances, and at the breaks in the walls, police stood on guard together with members of the Citizens' Guard in their yellow armbands.

"Something doesn't fit," said Manuel Ortega to himself. "Doesn't fit at all."

He felt tired and ill, and as soon as he went into his bathroom he was violently sick. When it was over, he saw that someone, probably the cleaning man, had put two earthenware jars of water there. After lying on the bed for a quarter of an hour, staring apathetically at the ceiling, he pulled himself together and went into his office. When he opened the door, and saw that someone was standing in the middle of the floor, he jerked back as if from a blow or a sharp jab of pain, although he must have seen who it was immediately.

Danica Rodríguez looked at him, seriously and searchingly, before she said: "Have you been over there?"

"Yes. It looked appalling."

"It is appalling."

"The worst thing was that no one really seemed to mind much. When it was all over, the men went off to the mines, just as if nothing had happened. And there were at least thirty people lying dead in the streets and the square."

"These people are fatalists," she said. "They have to learn to be. They think it's the only way that pays. It's always been so."

"How can you be so certain?"

"I was born here."

He went over to the window and looked across the blinding white plaza. A group of men with rifles and yellow armbands was marching across the far side.

"The C.O. of the regiment has called you three times."

"Contact him."

He got through right away. Colonel Ruiz spoke in a high voice and very quickly, as if we were trying to sound efficient.

"The position is precarious but we have put all available forces in to clear it up. I have ordered a company of engineers to the waterworks. As soon as the fires have been extinguished, they'll begin repairs."

"Have you any idea how long it will take?"

"Hard to say. Forty-eight hours perhaps. Could take less, but could also take longer. We can't estimate the damage yet."

"How will water supplies be maintained until then?"

"We have three army tankers and private companies have put twelve more at our disposal. That's fifteen altogether. They'll have to do a forty-eight-hour shuttle service. I think we should be able to get going in a couple of hours at constructing temporary reservoirs in the town. We need volunteers for that. When you speak on the radio it would be appropriate if you would urge volunteers to report either to the plaza or to the main entrance gates."

Manuel Ortega had had no idea that he was expected to

speak over the radio. In fact he had forgotten that the radio was an available means of communication. He said: "Can't you get detachments from the army to construct the reservoirs?"

"I'm short of men," said Colonel Ruiz briefly.

He went on smoothly: "But I can contribute overseers and a few engineers. My position is not entirely agreeable. The Chief of Police has, for example, requisitioned sixty thousand yards of barbed wire. I've only half that much."

"What does he want so much for?"

It was a spontaneous question which of course should never have been asked.

"To strengthen the barricades, I presume," said the colonel suspiciously. "It's probably necessary. Moreover, I should inform you that I've given the Citizens' Guard authority to take over responsibility for order in the center of town."

"The Citizens' Guard is an illegal organization, isn't it?"

"We-ell, illegal. It's useful and reliable anyway. And even Captain Behounek is short of men. The Guard has also promised to take over responsibility for water rationing. On this matter I should advise you to contact the leader of the executive committee of the Citizens' Guard."

"Who is that?"

"Dalgren—didn't you know? No, of course, you're new here. You and I should get together on how we shall organize the giving of orders and sharing of duties."

"From now on we can surely put our minds to finding reasonable and workable solutions as things crop up."

"That sounds all right but usually doesn't work out in practice. I can't stand disorganized reasonableness."

At that the conversation ended. Manuel Ortega at once called his assistant.

"Do you know anything about military matters?"

"A little."

"How big is a regiment?"

"About two thousand men."

"How many vehicles suitable for transporting water do you think they might have?"

"Well—thirty at least, probably more. I suggest you call the C.O. and ask him."

"Thanks for your advice."

He put down the receiver. The cooperation of the army seemed to leave a great deal to be desired.

"The military are all loafers—tramps in uniform," said Fernández philosophically. He was standing by the window, chewing at his seeds, his hands behind his back.

The heat in the room now surpassed all previous records and when Manuel rose to his feet, a dark patch of sweat had already begun to form on the seat of his chair. Despite this he felt as if he were just beginning to hit his stride. In front of him lay a list of things to do, none of them especially interesting but they were at least urgent. He adjusted the gun under his jacket, and went into the other room to dictate his radio appeal to his secretary. When she had typed it out, he read it through and she said, as if in passing: "Shouldn't this so-called Citizens' Guard be condemned more forcibly?"

"As far as I can see, both sides have behaved most irresponsibly. The trouble this morning was at least of a spontaneous nature. To blow up the waterworks, with the people in it as well, was, on the other hand, a planned outrage."

"No, it wasn't very nice, was it?"

"Besides, we seem to have arrived at a situation in which the whole town is dependent on the help of the Citizens' Guard. In such a position one must be reasonable."

"Your radio appeal is undoubtedly reasonable," she said dully.

"Besides, it in fact condemns the proceedings this morning."

"Yes, it does."

When he was back at at his desk he saw that she was right. His speech was just as routine as the speech by General Gami which he had heard the day before. It urged all political organizations and all sections of the population to be calm and dignified, condemned violent measures, and appealed for solidarity and reason. After that it finished up with information as to where people should report to help in the emergency.

The speech contained no personal views or opinions, no anger, sorrow, or bitterness. He had quite simply copied it from memory from hundreds of similar appeals he had heard over the years. Manuel Ortega was conscious of this, and each time he read through the text, the worse he thought it.

At a quarter past twelve he went to the radio station with López and read his speech. It was broadcast live without rehearsals, which made him acutely nervous, and his voice was tense and unnatural. At the same time they took recordings on a tape which could be broadcast at half-hour intervals. The radio station, which was new and situated in the western part of the town, was guarded by both the police and members of the Citizens' Guard.

When Manuel Ortega got back to the Governor's Palace, Danica Rodríguez had taken a radio into her room and was listening to the first repeat of his speech. She gave him a tired, indifferent look. He went into his room but at once turned back and, standing in the doorway, he said: "I don't like it either."

She looked up in quick, cool surprise but said nothing.

Five minutes later Dalgren telephoned.

"Your speech was excellent," he said. "May I be the first, on behalf of the Citizens' Guard, to express my regret over the impetuous events of this morning? Youthful imprudence and a spontaneous desire for revenge got the upper hand for a while. You were right to condemn such behavior. You'll be glad to hear that the whole executive committee is in agreement with me on this."

Then he went on to the subject of maintaining the water supply.

"We've twenty large tankers now in use. I assume that's enough. I've put my own people to work figuring out what quantities should be dealt out to each household. You can leave those details to us. But I should be glad if you would keep an eye on the work on the reservoirs. Otherwise we might find ourselves in a situation where the tankers would be immobilized because we haven't enough collecting places."

Soon afterward an unidentified citizen called and said: "I hope you haven't inadvertently overlooked the situation we villa owners find ourselves in. We've invested very large sums in laying out our gardens and in this climate they'll burn up in a few days if we can't water them. Some of the transport must be detailed for this purpose."

"You must understand that we must first see to the people's drinking water requirements and after that make provision for matters of hygiene."

"Yes, yes—I see I'll have to talk to Dalgren personally. You don't seem to understand what I'm talking about."

A moment later Colonel Ruiz was on the line again.

"I've just had the first reports from the officer in command of the engineers' company. He thinks the business at the waterworks should be fixed up to a limited extent in about two or three days."

"Can you possibly put a few more vehicles at our disposal?"

"Not at the moment."

"The construction of the reservoirs is going too slowly, especially in the southern sector."

"I'll try to send a few more men there."

Later on in the afternoon, even Behounek made his presence known.

"Behounek speaking. Just wanted to tell you that peace and quiet reigns in all sections of the town."

"What's the atmosphere like? Rebellious?"

"No. Not at all."

"Not in the workers' quarter, either?"

"No. Your appeal has had a calming influence. We put it out over the internal loudspeaker system."

"And it was well received?"

"Yes. Especially among the natives. Most of them are decent peaceable creatures. Like children. Believe what you tell them."

"Have you counted the casualties?"

"Yes. At the waterworks one policeman was killed, two slightly injured. Of the Citizens' Guard one man was killed, only a youngster by the way, and seven injured, one seriously."

After a moment's silence Manuel asked: "And the natives?"

"That's not certain. At a rough estimate, about thirty-odd people were killed, no more, I don't think."

"By the police?"

"My men reported six."

"And injured?"

"About ten have been taken to the hospital. But that figure is of course neither reliable nor final."

"How many arrested?"

"None so far. But you'll be pleased to hear that the saboteurs will probably be tracked down tonight. They were brought in a small truck. An hour ago we found the truck wrecked in a sector which is well known to us. I think I even know where they are."

Behounek's voice was cold and hard.

No one called for the next ten minutes, and Manuel Ortega took the opportunity to think out a few points. At least thirty people had been killed in the workers' sector, and according to Behounek, only six of them were victims of police bullets. The others had been killed by an organization which was in all respects illegal. In other words, there had been twenty-five murders and none of the murderers had been arrested or even taken in for questioning. No one seemed to expect the police to make any arrests, not even the next of kin of the murdered men. The appalling injustice of this filled him with cold rage and without another thought he picked up the receiver and called Behounek.

The conversation that followed was heated.

"I refuse to accept your failure to arrest people who commit murder under the cover of an illegal civil-military organization."

"You saw for yourself, for God's sake! Everything was just one great shambles. Can *you* say who shot whom? Do you think we've time to carry out police investigations of individual cases in time of war and revolution?"

"In that case you should arrest Dalgren as responsible for the Citizens' Guard and its members."

"You're crazy! Whom should I arrest for the death of one of my men who was shot down there?"

"Whoever killed him or whoever gave the order."

"Man, can't you hear what I am saying? I don't *know* who killed him. I don't know who was responsible! That's why I haven't arrested anyone."

"In that case it is your duty to find out about it. If you take sides in a conflict like this then you've misinterpreted your duties. It is possible that you're a good officer, Captain Behounek, but you're a bad policeman!"

"That's enough insults. What did you yourself do during the whole mess? I'm just asking. What did you do? Stood and gawped a quarter of a mile away. And besides, you had an opportunity to watch me working all the time."

"I maintain that you saw thirty people murdered without lifting a finger to find those responsible. You haven't even bothered to count the casualties."

"You can go to hell with your moralizing!"

"Do you call thirty dead men moralizing? Have you no respect for human life? You're a monster!"

"What are you then? What are you doing here? You're

a completely meaningless figure, a nobody sent here to . . . well . . . at least I know my job."

"No, I repeat. You do not know your job. And if you do then you hide the fact damned well. You're either a rogue or a bungler, Captain Behounek. You should resign or give yourself up to the police!"

There was a silence for five seconds, then Behounek said with dreadful acerbity and concentration: "You are upset because today you've seen something new and frightening. I am tired because I've been working without sleep for forty-eight hours. For the sake of both of us, therefore, I refuse to continue this conversation."

Manuel Ortega slammed down the receiver in the middle of the last word.

He got up and raged backward and forward across the floor. His heart was thumping and his eyes glistening. He breathed heavily and unevenly and the sweat poured down his face.

Never before had he experienced anything like it. It was years since he had found himself in such a state of emotional upheaval. He was used to carrying out both his work and his private affairs in a rational and businesslike way. Now he could not even see the people around him, neither the totally unmoved López nor Danica Rodríguez, who had come into the room just as he had slammed down the receiver. Obscurely he realized that it was Behounek who had drawn the longest straw, who had succeeded in keeping cool and had had the presence of mind to collect himself for his final rejoinder. But despite this he was convinced in some way that it was he himself who was right and that he had followed a clear line throughout. In other words, he had acted correctly.

Manuel Ortega tramped backward and forward once or twice more. Then at the door he suddenly stood still and remained there for perhaps half a minute with his head lowered. Then he banged his fist on the doorpost, turned around, and looked at the others. López was sitting on his chair with his hands on his knees. With his short legs and fat arms he looked like some Oriental idol.

Danica was standing by the desk, smoking and holding a piece of paper in her hand. She stood absolutely still and looked at him and her gray eyes seemed to glitter. She put the paper down on the desk, took the cigarette out of her mouth, and smiled a narrow, avid smile. Then she turned around and went back into the other room.

Manuel Ortega stood still and watched her go, gripped by a wild impulse to fling her over his shoulder, carry her into the bedroom, throw her down on the bed, and tear off her clothes. He crushed the impulse and went back to his place behind the desk.

Most remarkable, he said to himself, shaking his head.

At dusk their work was far from completed. The telephones went on ringing and reports flowed in. Through the window they could see people in the plaza working by the headlights of cars on the construction of a water reservoir of planks and tarpaulins. It was soon finished and half full of water. The situation was under control.

At half past eight the telephone rang for about the fiftieth time. It was Behounek. His voice was calm and formal.

"I want to emphasize," he said, "that I still think it more important to track down and put out of action a bunch of irresponsible terrorists who might even tonight appear again and blow up the hospital or the power station, than to go from door to door asking decent citizens what they were doing at six o'clock this morning."

"I'll admit that, but I still don't think that the one duty should override the other. Anyhow, I apologize for the tone of voice I used in our earlier conversation."

"I do too. We were both exhausted, and for my part it looks as if there'll be no sleep for me tonight either."

"I wish you success in your search."

A little while later Manuel Ortega at last went out to the woman in the other room.

"Are we eating together tonight?"

"No, I'm afraid not. I'm sorry, but I've another engagement. I'm afraid I can't."

"I suppose it's not much to cry about."

At about ten he got López to drive him around the town. The reservoirs were ready and well filled, the streets mostly deserted, and only in a few places could the patrols with the yellow armbands of the Citizens' Guard be seen.

As they were standing in front of the Governor's Palace again, all the lights suddenly went out.

The whole world became utterly silent. The only sound Manuel could make out was the gentle trickling of water from the temporary reservoir. The darkness had not brought the slightest cool breeze with it. The heat was heavy and oppressive and the night as black as asphalt.

Ten seconds later López switched on a flashlight and went ahead into the building. Manuel went into the office and called police headquarters.

"Just a fault on the line," said the duty officer. "A not infrequent event."

Manuel Ortega lay on his bed, abandoned to the room's absolute darkness. He was both psychologically and physically exhausted, but for the first time he felt a certain satisfaction with himself. He was also aware that he had something to look forward to tomorrow, something positive and meaningful, which would give him cause to test his strength and throw in his lot wholly and completely.

Soon after that he fell asleep, free of fear.

He woke at about two. The light was on and he heard Fernández moving about in the outer room. He got up and undressed, looked under the bed, and put the gun under his pillow. Then he lay down, but it was some time before he fell asleep again.

Manuel Ortega lay on his back with his eyes closed and let the binoculars glide over the sun-baked dirty-yellow stones as he counted the outstretched bodies. One—two—three—four—five—six—seven—eight.

All the time he remembered the metallic voice giving the order: "Clear the square."

11

✳●✳●✳✳

It was half past seven. Manuel Ortega opened the door and saw Fernández seated on the swivel chair. He took two steps across the corridor, laid his left hand on the doorknob, and thrust his right hand inside his jacket. He felt the security of the revolver butt.

Fernández had not yet begun to rise. Manuel opened the door and went into the room. It was empty and the cramp in his diaphragm loosened its grip at once. He went over to the window and looked out over the town, the large blinding white square, the white cubelike buildings on the other side, the tall dusty palm trees, the reservoir of planks and tarpaulins, and in front of it a little line of people carrying metal pails and clay water pots, and two members of the Citizens' Guard.

These two were women, wearing yellow bands diagonally across their breasts, and they had rigged up a sun shelter of canvas. Beneath this stood a little table which everyone getting water had to pass; the women were busy with some kind of rationing control and despite the distance he could see one of them stamping the papers as each person went by.

"See if my secretary has come," said Manuel Ortega.

For some reason Fernández was the only one of his bodyguards to whom he could bring himself to give orders or send on errands. It seemed absurd to him that he should be able to give orders to López or the huge Gómez, not to mention Frankenheimer.

Manuel watched Fernández as he opened the door. At first

the man took a short step onto his left foot, leaning slightly forward, pulling his head down between his shoulders as he kept the weight of his body on his right leg. His whole body looked tense and watchful. He reminded him of a cat walking into a strange house. Manuel Ortega shuddered with distaste and then Fernández pushed open the door, relaxed, and said indifferently: "Yes, she's sitting in there."

"Señora Rodríguez!"

She was wearing a thin white dress and certainly no bra, for the lines of her body looked soft and natural and he thought he could make out her nipples beneath the material. Her expression was different from usual. It had never before seemed so open and expectant.

"The answer to your cable has come," she said. "A policeman brought it here two or three minutes ago."

He held the folded piece of grayish brown paper in his hand before opening it. It looked very official, with EXPRESO, PRIORIAD and SERVICIO OFICIAL stamped on it, and he thought resignedly of the long time he had already had to wait for it. Then he read:

KINDLY REFRAIN FROM INTERFERING IN GOVERNMENT AFFAIRS STOP FIRST TASK SOONEST POSSIBLE ARRANGE ARBITRATION MEETING BETWEEN AUTHORIZED REPRESENTATIVES OF CITIZENS GUARD AND LEADERS OF COMMUNIST LIBERATION MOVEMENT STOP SAFE CONDUCT FOR ALL STOP POLICE AND ARMY INFORMED SEPARATELY STOP RECOMMEND COOPERATION WITH BEHOUNEK WHO IS YOUR SUBORDINATE UNTIL FURTHER NOTICE ZAFORTEZA

Manuel Ortega was aware that the woman was watching his face as he read, and he made an effort not to move a muscle.

"Thank you," he said.

Danica Rodríguez could not entirely hide a certain disappointment, which for some reason pleased him. She went out but turned at the door and said: "Next time you talk to your friend Captain Behounek, you might ask him what the Peace Force was doing in the village called Santa Rosa last night."

"Could you explain that a little more clearly?"

"Unfortunately not."

The cable lay on the desk in front of him. His first reaction to the preliminary reprimand had been impotence and rage, but after reading it a second time he realized that the fundamental point of Zaforteza's message was that the government had given him a constructive and positive assignment. The instructions were clear and concise, in fact orders, and he could think of no other order which he would rather carry out. To arrange a conference between the opposing sides would be anything but easy, but on the other hand it really was a task worth tackling. He had thought so much earlier, perhaps even in Stockholm and he had been aware that discussion at the highest level between the two sides was the only way that would lead to a peaceful solution.

Even the final piece of advice in the Minister of the Interior's cable seemed sensible. To reach the right people he would be to a large extent dependent on the resources of the police and on Behounek's personal experience and general view of the situation.

Just as he put out his hand to call police headquarters, the telephone rang.

"Yes, Ortega."

"Behounek. Morning."

"I was just about to call you about an extremely important and urgent matter."

"I think I know what it's about. Ten minutes ago I had a certain telegraphic communication from the Ministry. And a friendly exhortation to cooperate with you."

"Do you think the government's plans can be realized in the relatively near future?"

"Yes, why not? The difficulty will be enticing certain gentle-men out of their holes in the mountains."

"I suggest that we meet for personal discussions sometime today. By the way, how did things go last night?"

"According to plan."

"You mean . . ."

"Yes. We surrounded the saboteurs, six men, in the sector I told you about before. Unfortunately we couldn't get them alive."

"None of them?"

"No, not a single one. One of them was still alive, but he died on the way here. There was some wild shooting out there. One of my men was killed and another wounded in the leg. That's three dead in less than twenty-four hours. Nothing hits so hard as when my men have to sacrifice their lives on duty."

"I understand."

"I'm afraid you probably don't. I brought most of these men with me from other parts of the country. They have homes and families which they ought to be able to return to. They're not soldiers and haven't come here to die but to create security and order. Oh well, those saboteurs hardly ever let themselves be taken prisoner. They're well armed and usually put up a stiff resistance to the end. It was like that this time too. Just as well we managed to surprise them, other-wise our losses would hardly have been only one man."

"And they were all killed?"

"Yes."

Manuel Ortega again thought of that caustic order: Clear the square.

Aloud he said: "Congratulations on your rapid progress."

"Thank you. What's more, it'll save us quite a bit of trouble in the future."

"And how are things here in town?"

"Calm, or near enough. That was what I was calling about,

actually. The northern native district is reported to be in somewhat of a state of unrest. It seems that some kind of delegation from there is trying to get permission to see you. At the moment I gather they're on sitdown strike at the police barrier."

"Do you know what they want?"

"They maintain that the water in their wells has been poisoned."

"Can that be true?"

"I don't know. It sounds unlikely. Poisoning wells is a method which I can scarcely imagine an organization like the Citizens' Guard using. But one of my lieutenants who is in charge in the northern sector says that the water does seem mysterious. Yes—that's his own word—mysterious."

"Send a sample of water to the hospital for analysis. Dr. Alvarado's laboratory staff should be able to settle the matter quickly."

"Yes, that's an idea. I'll get it done immediately."

"And I'll receive the delegation, of course."

"Ye-es. How many shall we let through?"

"Can't they decide that for themselves?"

"If you don't give them definite instructions you'll have about two thousand people in your room within half an hour."

"Oh yes. Well, three should be enough."

"Three then. All right. And what time?"

"Let's say eleven o'clock. Perhaps the analysis of the water will be done by then."

There was a moment of silence during which Behounek seemed to be making notes. Then Manuel said: "One more thing. Someone has asked me to put a question to you."

"What about?"

"The question is: What was the Peace Force doing in a village called Santa Rosa last night?"

Behounek didn't answer right away. Finally he said: "Who asked that highly remarkable question?"

Manuel almost answered truthfully but collected himself at the last moment. "I don't know. It was an unidentified voice on the phone—a man as far as I could make out."

"Hmmm. Oh yes, on the phone . . ."

"Yes,"

"You see, whoever asked seems to be suspiciously well informed. Santa Rosa is the name of the place near where our patrols succeeded in surprising the Communist saboteurs last night."

"And the village itself?"

"It's abandoned. No one lives there."

Manuel Ortega went in to the woman in the next room and, standing by her desk, said: "The Communist terrorist group who blew up the waterworks was wiped out near Santa Rosa last night. The village itself is abandoned. No one lives there."

"No," she said, without looking up. "That's quite true. There is no one living there."

He stayed for a while, looking at her black hair, which was short and untidy. She nervously bit on a nail and did not raise her head. Suddenly she said: "You made a mistake when you said it was an anonymous telephone call. He can immediately check on it at the listening-in post."

Manuel Ortega started.

"Listening in," he said acidly. "And you . . ."

Then she raised her head and looked at him, calmly and seriously.

"Yes, I've told you that I listen in."

Manuel Ortega did something completely unpremeditated. He raised his right hand and slapped her across the face. Her head jerked sideways, but otherwise she did not react at all. Then she looked at him again, with the same look as before, and said: "You must understand one thing—I'm on your side, now, to some extent anyway."

"I'm sorry . . ."

He said this confusedly, and made a movement which as far as he could make out was not intentional. He raised his hand again and stroked her gently across her cheek. She did not move and her eyes were firm and positive.

He left the room, got the cable from his desk, went back, and put it down in front of her.

She took her time reading it. Then she said in a low voice: "This implies very great possibilities."

She lightly brushed the backs of her fingers over his hand.

They said no more and soon afterward he went back into his room.

He was on the telephone for the next two hours, talking to men like Dalgren and the man in charge of the waterworks, mostly about transportation and water rationing. He also thought of sending the twenty idle surveyors up to the pumping station and immediately put the idea into action.

Promptly at eleven o'clock the three-man delegation of workers arrived. They were escorted by a policeman in a white uniform who demonstratively stood on guard at the door. Manuel's first thought was to tell him to leave, but then he changed his mind after a glance at the sharp, resigned, rancorous faces of the three men. The delegates glared darkly from the policeman at the door to Fernández, who had unbuttoned his jacket and swiftly eased his way over to an unoccupied spot by the wall. Fernández's gait was reminiscent of Danica Rodríguez's, but only on certain occasions. This was one of them.

The three men stood in a row in the middle of the floor. All three held their hats in their hands and were wearing the usual floppy white clothes. Two of them were older than the third and were obviously Indians. These two bowed deeply and humbly. The third gave no sign of greeting. He looked fairly young, somewhere between twenty-five and thirty, and appeared to be a half-breed of indeterminate origin. It was he who spoke for them.

"We've come here because our wells have been poisoned," he said. "The people have asked me to convey this to you."

His voice was shrill and aggressive.

"When was this supposed to have happened?"

"Last night all the lights were turned out for more than half an hour. Men came into our district in the dark and poisoned our wells."

"Are you certain the water is poisoned?"

"It smells bad and is red in three wells. In the fourth it is blue. No one dares drink it. Perhaps we cannot wash in it. They say a dog which drank some died in terrible torment."

"And who would be guilty of this?"

"Those so-called citizens. Those who live on the hill in the big houses."

"The men with the yellow armbands," said one of the others.

"If the water has really been poisoned, we shall, of course, help you in every way. As you know, even we here in town are without water after the Communist sabotage yesterday."

"I've also been asked to say that it is unjust that the people in our parts of town should be punished too. Most of them are not Communists. All the same, they were punished yesterday for something which not they, but white men, did. Forty-two people were killed by the citizens and the white policemen. They were buried early this morning. Now, however, we want water."

"Let us first find out what is wrong with your wells. We have sent the water for analysis—for examination. Wait a moment."

Without waiting for instructions Danica Rodríguez, who had been leaning against the doorpost smoking, went into her room, telephoned Dr. Alvarado, and put the call through to the other room.

"Aha—good morning. We met on Dalgren's terrace, didn't we?"

"Yes, and today I've had some samples of water sent to you. . . ."

"Yes, we've looked at them. The water is contaminated with one or a number of chemicals, God knows which, but it is not exactly poisoned. In one case we can say that something as simple as methylene blue was used—seems almost like a boy's prank. I remember from my own schooldays, putting it into chocolate and then getting some poor sucker to eat it. He'd be scared out of his wits when he both spat and pissed blue for a couple of days afterward."

"The water is drinkable then?"

"My dear chap, that water has never been drinkable. Before this muck got in, it was deficient in iron and contained every possible impurity. I was just about to say every impurity one could think of, but that of course would have been an exaggeration."

"But everyone seems to drink it all the same."

"Yes, and the infant mortality rate is sixty per cent. Well, that isn't only due to the water—but it means that those who manage to survive the first five years are really tough. They tolerate most things. Almost anything except certain nickel and lead alloys."

"I have a delegation from the mineworkers here at the moment. They say that no one dares use the water. What do you think I ought to say to them?"

"I think you should say this: The water is no more poisonous than it was before. They can use it for baking and washing and they can boil things in it too. They can even drink it, though I would spew up my whole stomach if I tried. But the best thing would be if you could arrange to provide them with drinking water from the town's reservoirs. That seems just, I think, and it can't be a question of exorbitant quantities."

He repeated word for word what the doctor had said, apart from his personal comments. The three men looked at him suspiciously.

"Will we really get water to drink?" asked one of the older ones, as if refusing to believe what he had heard.

"Yes, from tankers."

"When?"

"We should be able to arrange it today."

"The citizens water their trees and flowers with fine water," said the one of the trio who had hitherto not spoken.

"That has nothing to do with the matter," said the young spokesman loftily.

The other one looked crushed.

Manuel Ortega asked them one question, directed at the spokesman: "What's your name?"

"Crox."

The delegation trooped out.

Two minutes later Behounek rang. His voice was hard and rough. "Have you time to come with me for an hour?"

"What's it about?"

"I want to show you something. You'll meet a few people."

"Yes, of course, if it's important."

"I consider it very important. I'll come for you at twelve sharp."

The Chief of Police was undoubtedly very tired. His eyelids were sore and red, his eyes bloodshot, and his white uniform wrinkled and grubby. He had several bits of plaster on his right hand, which seemed swollen and hurt. But his voice was cold and his movements precise and resolute. He brought to mind an exhausted boxer who goes into the last round firmly determined to knock his adversary unconscious.

"This house belongs to a young real estate agent from the town, Alfonso Pérez," he said.

They were standing outside a house set somewhat apart, below the artificially irrigated area, half in the country and about as far from the workers' quarter as from the upper-class villas. It was a low house, of white roughcast with blue shutters, and was surrounded by low yellowish gray stone walls. Outside the entrance stood one of the white police jeeps.

"I want you to meet Pérez and his family," said Behounek. "They've something important to tell you."

They opened the gate and walked up the flagged path through the garden. A couple of yards behind came López, who had relieved Fernández twenty minutes earlier. The house was neat and well cared for. In front of it stood a swing and a little farther away a child's bicycle.

"What a humid day," said Behounek, looking up at the sky, which was hidden in a woolly white mist.

Manuel took a step toward the door.

"No! Wait a moment! Don't go in yet. As you've evidently not understood the situation, I must warn you that what you're going to see is very unpleasant. Let me go in first."

Despite this, Manuel Ortega was almost totally unprepared when he went into the house only a step behind the Chief of Police.

Behind his back he heard someone draw in his breath sharply and he realized it must be López.

They were standing in a large room with cane furniture and whitewashed walls.

In the middle of the stone floor lay a dead man in striped pajamas. He was lying on his side and his throat had been cut with such force that his head was thrown back almost perpendicular to his torso. His tongue had been driven out through the gaping slash. His pajama top and the floor all around him were covered with congealed blood.

"This is just the beginning," said Behounek, taking the other man's arm.

On a sofa in the room lay the corpse of a woman. She was naked and had a towel bound around the lower part of her face. It was knotted behind her head and pulled very tight. Her stomach and thighs were covered with blood and her legs lay at such an angle that they seemed to have been broken off from her body. It was impossible to imagine what she had once looked like.

"She was twenty-three," said Behounek. "The man was twenty-six."

He was still holding Manuel's arm, as if to keep him upright.

"That's not the end yet. They had a child too."

"I can't stand any more."

"No, I understand. Neither can I."

They stopped on the steps, outside. Behounek lowered his eyes and looked to one side, beyond the stone wall.

"Sometimes," he said, "even I need to explain what I mean."

López was standing immobile beside the steps. He had gone out before the others.

"Well, Mr. Bodyguard," said Behounek, slapping him on the shoulder. "What d'you think? Not bad, eh? Or d'you just like nice corpses in suits, with three bullets in their bodies?"

A moment later he added: "I'm sorry. I'm very tired. Come on, let's go."

A long while later, he said: "Well, what did you think of Crox? A charming young man, isn't he? . . . if it weren't so hard to differentiate, I'd say he is one of the worst rogues I've ever met. He can read and write and isn't badly off for money. He's paid for everything. His role as lawyer today certainly cost them a pretty penny. . . . He's also my most reliable informer from that part of town. But unfortunately the Liberation Front people spotted him early. Strange that he's still alive."

Manuel Ortega was sitting in the back. He said nothing.

When they had left the Chief of Police and were going up the white marble stairs, López said: "It's odd, but I've been a policeman all my life and there are still certain things I can't get used to."

12

●●**

"Yes," said Danica Rodríguez, "I understand. It's horrible. Almost everything that happens here is horrible. It's the same in many places."

"So brutal, so animal . . . and meaningless."

"That's true. That was meaningless."

"To destroy the water mains yesterday morning was also meaningless. And it was even worse, of course, to shoot forty-two innocent people afterward."

"No, on that point you're wrong. Both those events were horrible, but not quite so meaningless as the murder of the Pérez family. One side demonstrated that they still had resources and the will to fight, and the other demonstrated that they know how to take revenge. In all this there is a kind of calculation. Blowing up the pumping station was a show of strength on the part of the Liberation Front, and the Citizens' Guard retaliated with the only kind of show of strength they are capable of."

"But it is the innocent who suffer."

"Of course. But when the Liberation Front blew up the water mains, that contained a threat too: If you go on murdering our people, we shall blow up your power stations, your hospitals, your barracks, your roads. And when the police and the Citizens' Guard immediately afterward kill forty people, that too is a threat: If you go on sabotaging, we shall arrange for more and even worse massacres."

"But this is madness."

"Of course. It's a sort of balance of terror, which is vile but which is inevitable in a situation like this. It's also very unstable. In some cases it can lead to neither side doing anything at all. It'd be a kind of cold war, in other words, on a well-known pattern. But it can just as easily lead to all barriers of reason being broken down and everything being turned into a chaos of terrified people who kill one another blindly and mindlessly."

"This is what we must avoid. If I only . . ."

She looked searchingly at him and said: "Your friend, Captain Behounek, who undoubtedly has a great deal of experience in this district, could have given you some good advice. He evidently failed to do so. He should have said: This is a horror scene and you'll never forget it. But for you yourself to survive, you must realize that these people are no business of yours except from a technical point of view. Therefore, you mustn't involve yourself with them except to try to create a state of affairs in which they can stay alive in a tolerable and not too degrading way. When they, in spite of this, slip out of your hands, then you must forget them, not think about how they might still be living, and working, and loving, and sleeping, and cooking breakfast, and—yes, anything."

"Your cynicism is astounding."

"Cynicism is astounding in itself. In a sane society it lacks authority, but for people like you and me, in our time, it enables us to exist. Have another glass of cazal. It won't hurt you."

It was half past two. They were sitting in a deserted bar on the far side of the square drinking black coffee. They had already been there for an hour. Manuel Ortega was still pale and his eyes uncertain and flickering. López was standing not far away from them with his back to the bar.

"We should take the siesta," she said. "It's crazy to try to work or even to be up at this time of day."

"The state of emergency applies to us too. Behounek certainly doesn't take a siesta either."

She looked thoughtfully at him.

"Apropos of that," she said. "I think I must tell you about several things which I happen to know of, so that you won't imagine that you understand the psychology of people like Captain Behounek."

She stopped speaking.

"Yes?" he said questioningly.

"Well, as I was saying. The latest outrages,—that is, the ones that have occurred since we came here,—are part of a long chain of events that goes back too far to be traced. The day before yesterday a so-called blasting detail from the Citizens' Guard, presumably schoolboys, got into the workers' sector. How they got past the police barriers we can leave for the moment. This is something that has been re-peated two or three times a week for a long time and Captain Behounek is quite right when he says that plastic bombs in general have not done much damage. But this time they blew up two metal boxes which were evidently crammed with scrap iron and dynamite. Eleven people were killed or badly hurt. Among others a three-year-old child who had one leg torn off above the knee. The Federal Police did nothing whatsoever, according to reports, because they didn't want to provoke either side. On the other hand, the barrier guards, possibly out of stupidity, held up several people who wanted to take the child to a doctor. They were delayed so long that the child bled to death, but perhaps it would have died anyway. That the pumping station was destroyed the next night can partly be seen as a result of this incident, as can the rioting the next morning."

"How do you know all this?"

She did not reply, but went on: "Captain Behounek is quite right when he says that no one lives in that village I asked you to question him about. Santa Rosa was a very small village. About twenty people lived there. The saboteurs, who wrecked their vehicle, took to their heels and the inhabitants hid them.

Soon afterward the police came. The saboteurs fled but were overwhelmed, as you know. Then the police returned to Santa Rosa and executed twelve of the thirteen adult villagers. The children were taken away somewhere, God knows where. One of the saboteurs was taken prisoner, but Captain Behounek personally is supposed to have maltreated him to such an extent that he died."

"How do you know all this?" said Manuel Ortega once again.

"There were thirteen adults in Santa Rosa. One of them got away. He even came here into town."

"That person is an extremely important witness."

"Yes. And he has already been taken to a place which is supposed to be safe."

"Is all this the truth?"

"On that point, I naturally can't give any assurance. I can only sit here and tell you about it. And in doing that I'm taking a certain risk."

"If this is true, then Behounek should be arrested."

"By whom?"

Manuel Ortega looked helplessly at her.

"Anyway," she said, "he's not altogether without official and legal backing. There's a military emergency regulation which states that anyone hiding people who are manifestly a danger to the security of the state, or anyone helping them to flee, can be tried by court-martial and sentenced to death."

"There must be a way out. This can't be allowed to go on. What you tell me, and what I saw today . . ."

"I know nothing about what you saw today," she said.

"Obviously there are active elements on both sides, and it ought to be in everyone's interest to restrain them."

"But they are restrained," she said. "It's obvious. Practical leaders like Dalgren and his confederates stop most of the more meaningless ventures. It's the same on our . . . yes, the same on the Liberation Front side. No one really wants things like the sabotage the day before yesterday and the murder this morning. At least that's what most people think."

"But evidently anything can happen at any time."

"Yes, that's true."

"The solution still lies in peace negotiations then."

"Yes, that's a possibility."

"The only one, I would think."

"As long as we can rely on the President and his government."

"The government is the only thing we can rely on."

Manuel Ortega raised his glass and swallowed the aniseed brandy, which was sour and raw and burned his throat.

"Come," he said. "We must do some work."

They stepped out into the devastating afternoon heat and walked across the square. All around them everything was shimmering white, the ground, the buildings, and the sky.

In the middle of the square, Manuel Ortega said: "I had a shock today. You've given me another one, but you've also been a great help."

"That's a good thing. I want to be a help."

Manuel Ortega sat at his desk and López by the wall. Danica Rodríguez stood in the doorway. Everything was as usual. He looked at the woman and felt nothing of the desire for her which had irritated him the last few days. All he felt was the heat and the sweat which ran down his chest and stomach and soaked through his shirt and underclothes. And all he heard at that moment was an echo of the dull muffled buzzing of flies in the low house with its blue shutters and its dead woman on the sofa.

Now, he thought, now there's only one thing to do. To work. To negotiate. To arrange the conference. To be reasonable, even if all the others, including my bodyguard and my secretary, are mad.

He phoned Colonel Ruiz.

"The colonel is taking a siesta."

"Wake him up."

"He's not to be disturbed."

"I'm not asking you to do this. It's an order."

"Yes, sir."

While he was waiting he took a cigarette out of the pack on his desk and pressed the ends so that the bits of tobacco would not fall out. He seldom smoked and his cigarettes were as dry as snuff by the time he bought another pack.

After three minutes Colonel Ruiz came to the telephone.

"Have you begun to take the water to the northern sector?"

"No. Not enough trucks."

"How are the vehicles distributed?"

"There's a reservoir in the square, one at each entrance to the center of town and two in the villa area. Each one is served by three vehicles. One is being repaired."

"But you've got twenty. Where are the other four?"

"Busy in the villa area."

"Doing what?"

No reply.

"Doing what, I said!"

"Irrigation."

"Get them to take drinking water to the northern sector at once."

"I can't. I simply haven't got the authority. The vehicles are private property and I've no right to dispose of them."

The colonel sounded dismissive but somewhat uncertain. Manuel broke off the conversation and called Dalgren.

"Señor Dalgren is at a meeting."

"Interrupt it."

Dalgren came.

"Is it true that you're using four tankers for watering the lawns although there's no drinking water in the northern sector?"

"My dear fellow, it's at the demand of the villa owners

up there. And they're using their own vehicles too. And they say that the water in the wells is quite drinkable."

"I've promised the people in the northern sector drinking water and it's a promise I mean to keep. Are you refusing to release those four vehicles?"

"My dear fellow, as I said before, the vehicles are privately owned and I can't do much. Remember that thirteen other privately owned tankers are being used too."

Manuel Ortega got a wet towel, put it around his neck, and called Behounek.

"Dalgren, and with him the Citizens' Guard, refuse to release four tankers which are being used for watering gardens in the villa area, despite the fact that the northern sector has still not got its drinking water."

"Oh yes."

"Under present circumstances I have the right to requisition private property for official use, haven't I?"

"I presume so."

"Then I'm requisitioning the seventeen vehicles already in use. You must implement my decision. From now on four of them will begin serving the northern sector."

"I must have a written order."

"Send a man over here at once to get it."

"It'll be done."

"And another thing, Captain Behounek. I understand you applied military emergency regulations in a village called Santa Rosa last night? Is that true?"

"Yes."

"I hereby give you definite orders that, from now on, under no circumstances whatsoever are you to apply that or any other military ordinances, but strictly follow police regulations."

"Your right to give me orders can presumably be discussed."

"I shall immediately send you a certified copy of the cable I received today from the Minister of the Interior."

"That's not necessary."

"Do you submit to the order then?"

"Yes."

"Do you want it in writing?"

"Yes."

An hour or so later the first tanker arrived at the northern sector. Somewhat earlier Behounek had called.

"The order about the vehicles has been carried out."

"Did it present any problems?"

"Not at all. They've got more vehicles."

Manuel Ortega phoned Dalgren, who laughed and said: "Well, you got your vehicles."

"As you see."

"Good. A bit of initiative here and there won't do any harm."

"I have a more important question to discuss with you. Today the government has requested me to arrange a conference between representatives of the Citizens' Guard and the Liberation Front as soon as possible. All participants are guaranteed safe conduct."

"There've been rumors before about some kind of action like that from the government's side," said Dalgren evasively.

"What do you think about the idea?"

"Personally, I am not entirely in favor of it. But I shall take up the matter with the executive today."

"I would like to emphasize that, as far as I can see negotiation is the only means of creating law and order in the province."

"I shall pass that on. You'll hear from me sometime tomorrow."

"I'm also counting on you, Señor Dalgren, to do all in your power to stop any reprisals occasioned by the murder of the Pérez family."

"As I said, I'll let you know something tomorrow."

His voice was cool and impersonal.

Manuel Ortega looked at the clock. Half past six. The sun was low and it was hotter than ever in the room. The fan made practically no difference. He began to understand what Behounek meant when he said that the weather had been fine and fresh during the last few days, for this heat was different, clinging, cruel, and crippling. He was breathing heavily and unevenly and his heart was thumping.

He went in to Danica Rodríguez and saw that her white dress already looked soiled and was sticking to her back.

"Shall we have dinner together?"

"Yes, I'd like to."

Manuel went over to his living quarters and changed his clothes. Then he went through the usual procedure, with López at his back and the door in front of him, and although he was certain nothing could happen today, he had his hand on the butt of the revolver as he stepped through the doorway.

At that moment the telephone rang. It was Behounek.

"We've got them," he said.

"The ones who murdered Pérez?"

"Yes."

"Alive?"

"I've got them here now. Come down and have a look at them if you're interested. Then we can talk about the other thing at the same time."

"I'm coming."

"Don't forget your bodyguard. I've got only eighty men here. Is it the same one as last time?"

"Yes."

Manuel Ortega went to the girl.

"Would you like to come too?"

"No, I'd rather not."

"I'm sorry, but I must go. Partly to talk to him and partly because I want to see to it that he's not too hard on them. I'm really very sorry."

"It's not really much to be sorry about. Anyway, I must do some washing tonight. As long as there's some water."

The police depot and headquarters were in the western part of the town, not far from the radio station—several long, low buildings surrounded by a white stone wall with barbed wire along the top. The Chief of Police was sitting in his office, talking into the telephone. He had unbuttoned his collar and tunic, and his belt with its holster was hanging over the back of a chair. On the wall was a large map of the province with a great many white, red, and black pins stuck into it.

"The white ones show where our patrols are or should be at the moment," said Behounek when he had finished his phone call. "The red ones mark the places where groups of partisans have definitely been seen during the last three weeks."

"And the black ones?"

"Show where terrorists, singly or in groups, have been caught or put out of action since we came here."

Manuel Ortega studied the map. The white pins were all over the place but with distinct areas of concentration in the southern part of the province and around the capital.

The red pins, perhaps forty of them, were almost entirely in the mountain districts in the south. Only five were placed in the town or the immediate vicinity.

The black ones were evenly distributed over the whole of the province, from the border in the north to the mountain range in the south. The map gave a good idea of how the partisans had been pressed southward since the Federal Police had taken over the responsibility for dealing with them.

"That's where Santa Rosa was," said Behounek. He put his thick brown forefinger on the head of a black pin about twelve miles outside the town.

"That pin means eighteen dead then?"

"Nineteen. Six terrorists, a policeman, and twelve villagers."

Manuel Ortega looked at the Chief of Police's plastered,

bruised hand but said nothing. López gazed at the map indifferently.

They went down an iron spiral staircase, along an underground passage, and through a guarded barred door. Behounek stopped in front of a steel door. Before knocking on it he took a cigar out of his breast pocket, bit off the top, and struck a match against the wall.

Manuel felt an excitement which could only be explained by the fact that he had never to his knowledge seen a murderer before, in any case not one who could be linked to a definite crime. All the time he was thinking about the terrible things he had seen in that white house, the man on the floor and the woman on the sofa, and worst of all, the child whom he did not see. He thought also, with a certain distaste, of the state of mind the murderers might be in, but at that moment that did not particularly disturb him.

A policeman opened the door. The room inside was large and bare, with benches fastened around the walls and a few small apertures high up near the ceiling.

Against the far wall sat three men in ragged white clothes. Their dirty wide-brimmed straw hats lay on the floor in front of them.

"Get up," said Behounek.

The men rose at once. Manuel Ortega looked at them. They might well have been the three men who had stood in his office eight hours earlier.

"They're mineworkers," said Behounek. "Did it on the way to work this morning. Then they carried stones for ten hours and were caught on the way home."

"How?"

"We received some information. They took quite a lot from the place. Alarm clocks, small change, the woman's rings, a tin trumpet, several other toys. Pérez's pistol too for that matter, with his name plate on it and all . . . yes, this and that."

"Did they try to use the pistol?"

"No, they didn't know how to. Couldn't make out where the safety catch was. They thought it was no good and threw it away."

"What do they themselves say?"

"Confessed. What else could they do? That one on the right has even got blood on his trousers. These people hardly ever deny things anyway."

The three men stood there with their heads bowed.

Again Manuel Ortega saw before him the woman on the sofa and her husband on the floor and the child's bicycle in the garden. Suddenly it was as if a wave of blood rushed through his head. His brain throbbed behind his forehead and buzzed at the back of his head.

"What have you done to them?"

He found it hard to control his voice. The first words sounded like a hoarse croak.

"Arrested them. Questioned them a bit. Let them put crosses and squares on a statement."

Manuel again looked at the police officer's right hand.

"Wasn't it a temptation to use . . . other methods?"

Behounek shook his head.

"You don't understand. These are the ones who are led astray."

He took a puff at his cigar.

"Interrogation," he said, shrugging his shoulders. "It's hardly worth it. Just listen to this."

He pointed at the man farthest to the right. He was a little man with a round face, a black mustache, and melancholy brown eyes.

"You there, take a step forward. That's right. Are you married?"

"Yes, señor."

"Have you any children?"

"Yes, señor."

"How many?"

"Two, señor."

"Which of you murdered Señor Pérez?"

"Juan, señor."

He pointed at the man nearest him.

"Why did he murder Señor Pérez?"

"Don't know, señor."

"Who killed the señora?"

"Don't know. She wasn't dead when we left."

"No, but she died soon afterward," said Behounek aside. Then he said: "Who cut the child's head off?"

"I, señor."

"Why?"

"It was crying."

"Don't your children cry?"

"Yes, señor."

"Well, why did you kill Señor Pérez and his wife and his child?"

Silence.

"Which one of you said you were going to do it first?"

"I, señor."

"When?"

"This morning, when we went past the house, señor."

"Have you killed anyone before?"

"No, señor."

"Did you suggest it as a joke? That you should break into the house?"

"Yes, señor."

"Did you know Señor Pérez and his wife?"

"No, señor."

"Had you seen them before?"

"No, señor."

"Had you said before that you ought to go and kill someone?"

"Yes, señor."

"Why didn't you do it before then?"

"I didn't want to go alone, señor. No one would come with me."

"Was it only white men you wanted to kill?"

"Yes, señor."

"Why?"

"They kill us, señor."

"Has someone said that you must kill white people?"

"Yes, señor."

"Who said so?"

"The Liberators, señor."

"The Liberation Front, you mean?"

"Yes, señor."

"Are you in the Liberation Front?"

"No, señor. I wanted to be in it, but I wasn't allowed to. Neither was Juan."

"Then you weren't joking when you said you ought to go and kill Señor Pérez?"

"No, señor."

"Why did you steal the trumpet?"

"It was pretty, señor."

"Do you regret what you've done?"

"I don't understand, señor."

"Do you regret killing the man and the woman and the child in the white house?"

"I don't know. I don't understand, señor."

"Why are you sad?"

"I want to go home."

"How old are you?"

"Don't know, señor."

"What do you think we'll do with you?"

"Kill me, señor."

Again Behounek shrugged his shoulders.

"Sit down," he said. "Come on, let's go."

"What will you do with them?" said Manuel, out in the corridor.

"Keep them under arrest. Then they'll appear before a federal civil court and will probably get a life sentence of hard labor without the prerogative of mercy. Without understanding why."

As they were going up the spiral staircase, he said, presumably to himself: "On the edge of the precipice. So near. So very near."

"I'm convinced that your extermination tactics only make matters worse," said Manuel Ortega. "And it's wrong."

"Everything is wrong," said Behounek. "Where shall we eat?"

They ate at a private club for businessmen and officers. It was at the top of one of the blocks in the middle of town. The rooms were large and bleak with tubular furniture and fans on every table and on the ceiling. There were quite a few guests, but the food was bad, even worse than in the little place near the square. It was very expensive too, even in comparison with the luxury restaurants of the federal capital. Both Manuel and Behounek ate listlessly and meagerly, and they did not say much.

Not until the coffee came did they talk briefly of matters relevant to the future.

"Which leaders of the Liberation Front are known by name?" said Manuel Ortega.

Behounek stared stiffly into his brandy glass and remained sitting like that even as he spoke.

"Most of them. First and foremost, the one called El Campesino, the leader and organizer of the partisan activites. He's a Cuban, I gather. He has taken the name of some legendary Communist in Catalonia during the Spanish Civil War. Next, Dr. Irigo, who was the leader of the Communist Party in this country before it was disbanded. He's from the north and has some kind of legal qualifications. He used to live in a place just south of the border, but now he's probably somewhere abroad, either Cuba or Chile. Then a woman,

Carmen Sánchez, who looks after the propaganda. She's only twenty-seven and is supposed to be beautiful. And then a certain José Redondo, called El Rojo. He's a partisan hero and holds a prominent position in the organization."

"These are evidently the ones we need to reach with a message about the conference. I assume that one can get hold of them through the radio and the press or by dropping leaflets."

"Yes. And the bush telegraph."

"Have you any more names?"

"Will have eventually. But those four must be in on it. El Campesino, Dr. Irigo, Carmen Sánchez, and El Rojo Redondo. I'll send you a list of names with all the data early tomorrow morning."

It was half past eleven when Manuel Ortega undressed. He felt ill and frightened and found it hard to breathe. He put the Astra under his pillow, took three of Dalgren's tablets, and went to bed.

When he switched off the light, the darkness descended on him like an ancient black-velvet curtain, thick and fluffy and dusty and suffocating.

13

●●***

It was morning again, his seventh in this frightful town.

Fernández, sunflower seeds on the carpet, the smell of sweat, the two steps across the corridor, and his hand on the revolver butt.

The faucets were still not working. The officer in charge of the engineers complained of a lack of materials and demanded twenty-four hours more.

On his desk lay a gray-brown cable covered with official stamps: SOON AS POSSIBLE MEANS AT LATEST WITHIN ONE WEEK STOP SIX DELEGATES FROM EACH SIDE ZAFORTEZA.

Beside the cable lay a letter from police headquarters with the promised names and information.

On the telephone: Behounek.

"Everything calm."

"No casualties?"

"No."

"No blasting details?"

"Nothing at all."

Ten minutes later: Dalgren.

"The Citizens' Guard is prepared to negotiate."

"When?"

"As soon as you're in a position to get the two sides together."

Danica Rodríguez in her green dress and thonged sandals on her bare feet.

Gómez, who relieved Fernández. Large, heavy, and unshaven, with streaks of sweat on his face.

The rays of the sun which hurtled straight to the ground like a cloudburst of white fire.

At ten o'clock Manuel Ortega sat behind his desk and began to write out a rough draft of his speech. The effects of the third sleeping tablet began to slacken.

The text seemed disorganized, and soon he went into the next room to give his secretary some instructions.

"Reserve a spot for me on the radio at five o'clock."

"Find a printing plant which can begin printing ten thousand leaflets today."

"Investigate distribution possibilities and find people to do it."

"Get some ice and another crate of lemonade."

"Don't bite your nails."

Then she laughed. It was the first time she had laughed while on duty. She was pretty when she laughed, he thought. And she was not wearing a bra. Today her nipples could clearly be seen beneath the material. Perhaps it was because of the heat.

He felt very peculiar and went back to his draft.

At eleven o'clock Fernández came back, slinking into the room like a cat.

At half past eleven Danica Rodríguez stood in the doorway and said: "You've a visitor. A lady."

"Show her in."

It was Francisca de Larrinaga. Manuel rose to his feet in confusion. He discovered that he had forgotten all about both her and the proclamation as well as the General.

She was dressed completely in black with a mourning veil over her face, but she moved swiftly and energetically. Despite this, she seemed cool and fresh, quite untouched by the appalling heat.

"May I speak in the presence of your staff?" she asked.

Danica Rodríguez was still standing in the doorway and Fernández was rooted by the wall.

"Certainly."

"Good. I just wanted to be sure on that point. I promised you a definite decision within four days. Well, I've decided."

She opened her handbag and took out a long white envelope with a monogram embossed on it.

"This envelope contains the draft of my father's speech. I have also enclosed a certificate in which I confirm on oath the genuineness of the document."

Manuel Ortega took the envelope with two fingers as if he were afraid of soiling it.

"I'm handing it over to you then, for reasons I explained to you earlier. What you will now proceed to do with it is something with which I do not want to be concerned."

She closed her bag.

"That I've come in person is partly due to the fact that I consider this document much too important to be entrusted to a servant, and partly because it is not the kind of business to be dealt with over the telephone."

"Of course. Listening in . . ."

"Yes, it is very efficient. At one time it even saved people's lives. It would perhaps interest you to hear that five people called me up after your visit of condolence with the single intention of finding out what you had come for. You ought to know at least two of them. Señor Dalgren and Captain Behounek."

Before Francisca de Larrinaga left the room, she looked at Danica Rodríguez in an amused way and said: "Terribly hot, isn't it?"

Then she left.

In comparison with the woman who had left the room, Danica Rodríguez looked undressed, sweaty, and excited.

Fernández stared after the General's daughter as if he had just experienced a revelation.

Danica Rodríguez shrugged her shoulders.

Manuel Ortega wiped the sweat from his forehead with a

handkerchief which was already drenched. Then he sat down, picked up the letter opener, and slit open the envelope.

"Come here," he said. "This might be interesting."

She walked around the desk and read over his shoulder.

The proclamation was spread over two quarto pages. It was typed and divided into numbered paragraphs like a military order of the day, but here and there the General had crossed words out and added notes in his spiky handwriting which was hard to read. One could see that the changes had not all been made at the same time, for he had sometimes used ink and sometimes pencil.

PROCLAMATION

1. I, General Orestes de Larrinaga, at present Provincial Resident and authorized representative of the government in this province, hereby wish to state my views on the situation here.

2. These views are based partly on the conclusions I have drawn from my knowledge of the country and the people, and partly from the experience I have accumulated during a long and varied career as an officer of high rank.

3. The disturbances in the province are caused by two political extremist organizations competing for power. One of these (the Citizens' Guard) wishes to retain the established order. The other (the Liberation Front) wishes to destroy the present order. Both these endeavors are equally erroneous and must be utterly condemned; not only the aims but also the methods which are used on both sides.

4. In recent years, in most parts of the world, and even in most parts of the states in our Federal Republic, there has arisen a new concept of the citizen as an individual (human being). This point of view has not been applied in our province. The majority of the inhabitants live in great material and spiritual poverty; nor are they given opportunities for education. This, in the present day, is indefensible.

5. The Citizens' Guard is wrong when it tries to retain by force the old system, which from several points of view is out of date. Through it the majority of the people are forced to remain in wretchedness. This could lead to a catastrophe.

6. The Liberation Front is wrong when it tries to seize power by violence. It is also wrong when it believes it can use that power without support from other groups of people.

7. The Citizens' Guard is right when it tries to protect and retain the enterprises and material culture which have already been created in the province. They are also right when they, within reasonable limits, wish to represent the interests of the landowning classes.

8. The Liberation Front is right when it asserts every person's right to employment and education, tolerable living conditions, and wages which are more or less in reasonable proportion to the work done and likewise are roughly comparable with the wages of workers in other parts of the Federal Republic and in other countries.

9. In view of the foregoing, neither side has the support of the government or the armed forces.

10. Nevertheless, both sides should be awarded the legal right to represent the interests of their own respective social classes, on condition that armed activities are suspended.

11. Because of the people's low level of education, it is too early to institute universal suffrage. An interim government should therefore be set up with an equal number of representatives from each side and an equivalent number representing the federal authorities.

12. The education system should be expanded immediately. Also the health services. New living quarters should replace the present substandard housing around the capital of the province.

13. The wage system for mine, estate, and industrial workers should immediately be adjusted according to the

standards outlined above. Likewise regulations for working hours should be instituted.

14. The inhabitants' demand for land of their own should be met at once; not a difficult task. On the other hand, any idea of rapid and comprehensive agricultural reforms would be premature.

15. The Federal Police should be withdrawn and in the future should be used only for purely police purposes.

16. The army should take over responsibility for law and order, but not until the present Military Governor and the present High Command are removed and replaced by non-political officers.

17. The present situation in the province is degrading, both for the people who live here and for the country as a whole. The measures suggested in points 10–16 should therefore be carried out immediately.

Orestes de Larrinaga
General. Provincial Resident

There was an eighteenth paragraph in the text too: All political ideologies should be permitted. Similarly every person's right, regardless of color, creed, or class, to a basic education and a decent standard of living should be secured by law.

It had, however, been garnished with several question marks and finally struck out altogether.

"But this is magnificent," said Danica Rodríguez. "Elderly reactionary discovers the majority of the human race and produces a three-point plan. This is dynamite."

"Yes, it's dynamite," said Manuel Ortega.

"What are you thinking of doing with it?"

"Publishing it," said Manuel Ortega.

"Now?"

"Yes, as soon as possible."

"They'll take any measures to stop you."

"Which 'they'?"

"The Citizens' Guard, the army, the police, the lot."

"Let them try."

"How are you going to publish it?"

"We'll have to think of a way."

"Yes," she said. "We must think of a way."

She stood behind him and scratched her short black hair.

"One even sweats in one's hair," she said. "It really does feel damned awful."

Manuel drank a glass of lemonade and wiped his face again with his soaking handkerchief.

"Francisca de Larrinaga didn't appear to sweat at all," he said.

"No, if one lives here all one's life one gets used to it."

Quite unexpectedly she added: "D'you think she's beautiful?"

"Not very."

"But attractive?"

"No, not at all."

The incorrigible Fernández let out an astonished grunt.

"Give me the papers and I'll make a few copies," said Danica Rodríguez. "Otherwise something idiotic might happen to us."

"You think of everything."

She leaned over his shoulder and picked up the General's proclamation. As she did so she brushed her lips over his ear and he felt her nose against his temple.

"Yes," she said. "I do think of all sorts of things, but even so, I'm mostly wrong."

She went out and he watched her go. When he shifted his look he saw that Fernández was watching him with a mixture of doubt and pleased consternation in his eyes. At that moment López came in, hung up his black hat, and sat down on the chair by the wall.

It must be twelve o'clock then.

Two hours later he had finished his speech and he went in to the next room to get it typed.

"I don't think they'll accept this," said Danica Rodríguez.

"Who won't?"

"The Liberation Front. The guarantees aren't good enough. They daren't trust the government and first and foremost they don't trust you."

"They should," said Manuel Ortega.

"Yes, I think so."

"Well, the main thing is to get in contact with them."

"You can easily do that."

Half an hour later she had finished the typescript and brought it in. At the same time she brought two copies of General Larrinaga's proclamation.

"I made three," she said. "I'll keep one myself."

He nodded, folded one of the papers up, and put it in his pocket. As he took out his wallet he noticed that the leather was soft and damp and had begun to acquire a slightly pungent smell. He put the other copy in an envelope, sealed it, and went over to the man in the chair.

"Will you keep this for me until tomorrow?"

López nodded and put the envelope into his right inner pocket.

Manuel Ortega sat down at his desk and thought. The heat and the low air pressure worked against even his ability to think. Now and then it was as if whole sections of the system of cells in his brain turned numb and were put out of action. It was a long time before he succeeded in coming to a decision.

In the meantime Behounek called.

"Everything calm?"

"Yes, but the Communists are dropping a leaflet signed by the Liberation Front. It's a long time since they did that."

"What do they say?"

"It's well put together, I must say. That damned Carmen

Sánchez . . . Yes, they've got it all, the blasting details, the wells, the riots the day before yesterday, the Santa Rosa affair . . ."

"I think you should keep very quiet about that, Captain Behounek. Later on you'll certainly have to explain yourself further."

"Yes, yes, but what worries me is how it ever got out at all. Someone must have been careless somehow. Perhaps . . . yes, I'll have to check up on it."

He sounded as if he were talking to himself.

"Where do they get their leaflets printed?"

"Here somewhere, God knows where. You see, they don't need a printing plant, but just set the text by hand and print it on one of those little hand presses—proof presses, I think they're called. We've found and confiscated eight or nine of them, but there are evidently several more around. They're small and easy to hide."

"I'm broadcasting at five o'clock."

"Good. I'll listen to you."

"Would you check that the broadcast goes out over the loudspeakers in the workers' quarter?"

"Of course. I'll see that the loudspeakers up at the mines are switched on too."

Manuel Ortega thought for a moment.

"I'll be giving a more detailed speech tomorrow."

"Good."

"Apropos of that, is the telephone working?"

"Only locally."

"I've noticed that. But why not further out?"

"The line is cut somewhere up north. The fault doesn't seem to have been found yet. The line is evidently cut somewhere near the border anyway, perhaps not even on our side. I've sent a cable about it."

"Could it be due to partisan activities?"

"Possibly."

The conversation ended. Manuel finished his glass of lemonade, looked out at the deserted square and went in to Danica Rodríguez.

"Reserve broadcasting time for ten tomorrow morning. And inform the Chief of Police that I'll be making another important speech then. Tell him that the loudspeakers in the workers' quarter and at the mines are to be switched on."

She looked questioningly at him.

"Are you thinking of . . ."

"Yes," he said, tapping on the pocket containing his wallet.

She smiled and stuck out the tip of her tongue between her teeth.

Mischief, he thought conventionally.

Then he said: "But that's not enough. Do you think there's a printer who can be persuaded to do a couple of thousand copies?"

"No," she said. "Definitely not."

He looked at her legs and feet. She followed his gaze and smiled. The same smile as day before, narrow and eager and with a glitter behind her half-closed eyelids.

You damned little . . .

His thoughts were broken off by the telephone and he left her at once. It was Colonel Ruiz, who carried on a long and involved conversation about the transport of the water. He spoke very formally and what he said was almost totally lacking in interest. Manuel asked only one question.

"How many vehicles are working at the moment?"

"Twenty-five. Three army, sixteen requisitioned, and five more private. One being repaired."

Manuel said "thank you" and replaced the receiver. Behounek had been right as usual.

But then he thought: No, not as usual. Behounek had not been right. Behounek had *not* been right. Behounek must not be right. Behounek had never been right. In essentials Behounek had never been right.

A short while later Danica Rodríguez came in with a cable which ran: HOW IS CONFERENCE GOING STOP COMPLETE GUARANTEES GIVEN STOP COOPERATE CLOSELY WITH BEHOUNEK ZAFORTEZA.

He threw the paper into a drawer in his desk and went to change his clothes. He noticed that five jars of water were standing in the shower. He was being looked after in spite of everything. When he went back, he thought: This time I won't be afraid. This thing with the door is a foolish complex which I must get rid of.

But he still automatically thrust his hand under his jacket as he turned the doorknob. The room was hot and white and terrible.

He went to the radio station at half past four. Just as he was on his way out he was stopped by Danica Rodríguez.

"I've had an idea," she said. "I've found an old duplicating machine in one of the rooms. I think it'll work. We could do a couple of thousand copies on it."

"Tonight?"

"Of course. I'll get some ink and stencils and paper."

"Then you'll be here when I get back."

"Of course."

The temperature in the radio station was beyond belief. The technicians were working in shorts and had put wet towels on the backs of their necks. The woman at the controls was sitting with her feet in a bowl of water. The announcer, who had great red heat patches on his face and arms, shook his head and said: "We're all from the north and haven't been here long. Most of their own people were wiped out in the rioting in March last year when the right-wingers blew up the old radio station and set fire to it."

"I didn't know that. Why did they do it?"

"There were a couple of Communists on the staff here, I think. They fixed up ghost broadcasts for the Liberation Front several times a day. That was before the government crisis and before the Federal Police came here. It seems to have been pure Wild West then."

"But it's better now."

"Yes, it's fine now. But one never gets used to the heat. This place is faultily built, like everything else in this rotten part of the country. The idiot who planned it forgot the ventilation."

Manuel looked around the studio. Although the building was brand new, the ceiling had cracked and the plywood had warped in the heat.

"We've thrown away the thermometer. If we could actually see how hot it was in here we'd have a stroke. Well, we're lucky they haven't television here, with its lights and all that jazz," he said philosophically.

Manuel Ortega was forced to take off his jacket. He sat at the table with its green felt cloth, dressed in a shirt with the collar unbuttoned and sleeves rolled up, striped suspenders and a revolver in a shoulder holster.

The anouncer stared incredulously at the Astra.

As Manuel waited for the red light, he looked at López and felt utterly foolish.

The light went on and he began to read. It was all over in two minutes.

"That sounded fine," said the announcer nonchalantly. "Though we'll adjust your *s*'s down a little next time. In fact, we can do your new recording direct and take a bit of time over it and then we'll know once and for all what adjustments are needed for your voice. Then we'll put that tape out over the air every hour."

The man was obviously quite indifferent to the political implications and hardly conscious of the seriousness of the situation.

"That's good," said Manuel Ortega to himself. "He'll do."

When he got back to the Governor's Palace, he asked Danica Rodríguez: "Did you hear the broadcast?"

"Yes. The guarantees are still not good enough."

His announcement had been very simple. He had said that the government had assigned to him the task of arranging a meeting of reconciliation between the Citizens' Guard and the Liberation Front, and that complete guarantees were being assured for the delegates' personal safety. Finally, he had urged the two parties to make themselves known through authorized messengers.

"Well, we'll see," he said.

Danica Rodríguez did not reply. She had gotten paper, stencils, and tubes of ink. The materials were all lying on her desk, and at the side stood the duplicating machine, a dusty old-fashioned model which no one seemed to have used for the last ten years.

A moment later she said: "It doesn't work properly."

She had typed a few sentences on a stencil to try it out. The result was scarcely encouraging.

Manuel Ortega looked dejectedly at the machine. He was not mechanical-minded and felt nonplused. As if that were not enough, the woman shook her head and said: "I'm no good at all with mechanical things."

He turned the machine again, looked at the unreadable script, and crumpled up the paper.

"Damn," she said.

"Excuse me."

They both jumped, and Manuel thrust his hand under his jacket.

It was López who had spoken.

"Excuse me," he said again. "When I worked in the aliens' department we had a machine just like that."

They stared at him. He was sitting as usual by the wall with his hands on his knees.

"I was convalescing then," he added. "Shot in the foot."

"Then perhaps you can help?"

"It's possible," said López.

Ten minutes later the machine was working, but after a hundred or so copies the first stencil tore. Manuel stood by the wall and looked on while she typed another. She worked swiftly, apparently enthusiastic and happy, and her breasts moved beneath her dress. She had a spot of ink on her temple, and when she raised her hand to wipe the sweat from her forehead, the ink was rubbed into a long black streak.

She brushed by quite close to him, softly and supplely. Like an animal. She fixed the stencil and adjusted the paper. She brushed past him again. When she came back, he put out his hand and held her arm.

"Danica."

"Yes."

Her eyes were large and dark gray and questioning. At first. Then she nodded and put the pile of paper down.

"Yes," she said. "I'm coming."

He held her by the arm and led her through the other room, across the corridor, unlocked the door, and went in.

He did not think. Not about López. Nor about Behounek. Nor about anyone. Or anything.

He turned on the light.

She looked at him seriously and pushed aside the hair on her forehead with her wrist.

"Yes," she said.

He took her by the shoulders and kissed her. Her lips were thin and soft and alive. Slowly she moved her head and opened her mouth. He felt her tongue. She was with him, next to him. Her body soft, melting against his.

Then they let go. He took off his jacket and shoes and unfastened the gun.

She unfastened the top two buttons of her dress and then stopped.

He reached over and unfastened the third. The fourth. He pulled the dress down over her shoulders. Touched her naked breasts. Looked at them. Small and well formed. The mark had almost vanished now, only a faint blue shadow. Her nipples were dark brown and hard.

He began to take off his shirt.

She looked at him. Suddenly she said: "Hell. No. It's no good."

He was utterly dismayed.

"Why not?"

"The usual. How could I forget?"

He stared at her.

"It's no good. It's not good for me. Hurts."

She seemed just as dismayed as he.

"It sounds quite crazy," she said, "but I really had forgotten."

"But later?"

"What do you mean, later?"

"Well, when it's over. Then?"

"Of course. At once."

"Sure?"

She laughed and put two fingers against his mouth.

"I swear," she said.

He laughed too.

"You realize, I really do want to," she said.

"Undress."

She gave him a questioning gray look.

"I'll give you a shower. There's lots of water in there."

He pulled down the zipper of her dress.

She was wearing only two garments apart from her sandals and was ready before he was. They looked at each other.

"You're naked," she said.

"So are you."

"You're awfully hairy."

"So are you."

"Only there," she said.

She drew her fingertips through the close black hair.

Above the hairline was a circular bruise.

She stood in the shower, at first with her hands on her knees. He slowly poured two jars of water over her.

"My hair too," she said.

"Then it was his turn. He shivered and thought that the water could not have been all that cold.

They dried themselves and went into the bedroom. She lay down on the bed and looked at him as he shut the door and came back.

"You've a fine body."

"So have you."

"I've long legs and good feet. Otherwise I'm not much."

He leaned over the bed and kissed her.

"Sometimes I get an inferiority complex," she said. "Me, who's supposed to be so tough and hardened."

"When?"

"When I see people like that woman today. Silly."

They looked at each other again.

"Do you want me to do something to you?"

"I can wait," he said.

"I didn't ask you what you can do. I asked you what you wanted."

He lay down beside her and raised his arm.

"No," she said. "Don't turn out the light."

Soon afterward she said: "I'll lie on your arm."

He lay still, with her wet hair against his shoulder. Her body was cool and pleasant after the shower. Clean.

He thought: When you are lying down you seem tall and fully grown, but when you are dressed you seem so small. At the same time slender and firm as only boats and certain women can be.

He said: "How many pulls will a stencil stand, by the way?"

"A thousand, but hush. Don't talk about it. Don't even think about it. Not now. Think about me. Think about yourself. This is our only chance."

She pushed her fingers through his hair, and laid her hand flat on his stomach.

"Well," she said. "Do you want to?"

"Yes."

She lay still, immobile . . . After a while she said: "Good?"

He said nothing. He gripped her. Her shoulders. Her breasts. Her stomach. Thrust his fingers through the tight hair. Came nearer.

"You're a little afraid of me, aren't you?" he said.

She raised her left leg a little and laid it across his. Knee to knee. Foot to ankle.

"Only a little," she said.

"Yes."

"I'm lying on my right arm. It hurts."

She sat up.

"Can you see me now?" she said.

"Yes."

"I can see you too."

He nodded.

"Look then, because I'm going to turn the light out now."

She knelt up and put out the light. She bent down in the darkness and kissed him with her open mouth. He stroked her lightly from hip to neck with his right hand, feeling her skin. He lay with his hand on her head without holding on to her. She began to move, at first imperceptibly. She slid the tip of her tongue over his lips and chin. His throat and on down his chest.

"You're fine," she said.

He took hold of her hips and raised her. She was light and lay astride now, on all fours. Over him. He held her feet firmly. He let go. Slowly he stroked her calf and thigh with his right hand. She moved her knees. More comfortable, she thought, with her heels against his ribs. So open, and he stroked her, his fingertips moving in an elliptical curve.

Searching for the sensitive place. Finding it as one finds things in the dark.

"Good?"

"Yes," she said.

"Really good?"

"Yes," she said. "Really. You'll soon see."

Near to breaking point. Very near. Very very near.

Breathing. Lying still. A long time.

She moved and changed her position in the dark. She put on the light. She half lay, propped on her elbow, looking at him. Stroking his lips with her fingertips.

"It must have been a long time ago for you," she said.

"Yes, quite a long time."

"What do you mean by quite?"

He had to think.

"Nine or ten days. But not so long for you?"

"No, not so long ago."

"How long?"

"Three days ago. No, four."

"The officer?"

"No."

"Then who?"

"No one you know. He's called Ramón."

"Do you know him? Well?"

"Fairly."

"It wasn't the first time?"

"Not at all."

"Was he good, Ramón?"

"I like him. That's the main thing."

"Did he make that bruise?"

"Which one?"

"On your stomach."

"Yes."

"And the officer?"

"Yes, but that was earlier."

"Was he good too?"

"I don't know. I didn't exactly like him."

"But you slept with him?"

"Yes."

"Then it was all wasted then?"

"It's seldom completely wasted when you sleep with someone."

"Do you always live like this?"

"More or less. Not always. In spasms. Do you disapprove?"

"Yes. Very much so."

She lay down, putting her head on his shoulder and her hand on his chest.

"It wasn't like that before," she said. "Not in the beginning. But it's become like that. I've become involved twice, seriously you know, and all that. But it didn't work. Always ended with me hurting those I really liked. So I was scared of getting involved, and to avoid it I began to live like this. Now I don't think I could get involved again. But I don't know and that's why I've been hesitant in this case, the Manuel case."

She said this in an intentionally comical tone of voice and he could not help laughing. Then she said: "That's what I'm like. What are you like?"

"Little different."

"Are you unfaithful to your wife?"

"As you see."

"Often?"

"Now and again, but not often."

"With a lot of women?"

"No, definitely not with a lot. And I don't like talking about it."

"You're fine," she said, "anyhow."

"So are you. How do you feel, though?"

"Awful."

"What are you scrambling about for?"

"Cigarettes."

She lay still beside him, smoking. She said: "Do you feel awful too?"

"Yes."

"Nothing to what we'll feel the day after tomorrow."

After a while: "Listen—we must get to work now. Mustn't fall asleep."

"I'd almost forgotten."

It was true. He had almost forgotten.

He rose and dressed, and she said: "Haven't you a thinner suit than that one?"

He shook his head.

"Then I'll get hold of one for you tomorrow."

He fastened on the gun and picked up his jacket. She was still lying naked on the bed, stretched straight out.

"Aren't you going to get up?"

"Yes, but do me a favor will you?"

"What?"

"Go and get my tampons out of my bag."

López was sitting in the revolving chair. Manuel took the two steps across the corridor, gripped the doorknob, and turned it. Then he got scared and jerked back. He put his hand on the walnut butt and pushed open the door carefully. Then he thought how foolish he must look from behind and he straightened up and walked in. He took the bag with him. She was still lying on the bed.

She looked for the box in the bag, went into the bathroom, and came back. She walked up to him and kissed him on the cheek. Thirty seconds later she was dressed and had even had time to pull a comb through her hair.

At half past two, fifteen hundred copies of General Larrinaga's message to the people were stacked in the safe.

Fernández was there, slinking around the walls in his rubber-soled shoes, like a caged wild animal.

They had worked hard and were tired, the heat still heavy and oppressive.

"Come on, let's go home," she said. "I mean, you can come home with me. If you want to, of course."

Manuel hesitated for a long time.

"No," he said at last. "Someone must be here."

"Yes, of course. I'm a bit haywire sometimes."

"Can't you stay here?"

Her turn to hesitate.

"No, not really. I can't. No."

"Good night. Listen—it's late. Wouldn't you like the revolver? If you're scared?"

"I'm not afraid."

14

●●**

It was the morning of the eighth day and Manuel Ortega was again awakened by Fernández leaning over him with his hands on his shoulders.

He had not taken any sleeping tablets the night before and awoke at once.

"The lady is here and says it's something important."

"Which lady?"

"Her, ours, Señora Rodríguez."

"Let her in then."

Danica came in. She was smoking and wearing the white dress.

"Hullo," he said. "Thanks for yesterday."

"Thanks to you too. Sixto wants to meet you."

"At this time? And who is Sixto?"

It was half past five. Neither of them had slept for more than two hours at the most.

"He's the regional leader here in the Liberation Front."

"What does he want? To shoot me?"

"Hardly. But I've no idea. Just got a message about it twenty minutes ago."

"Why didn't he come himself? Or phone?"

"He's still on the wanted list and doesn't dare use the phone. Hurry now."

Ten minutes later they were on their way. Danica Rodríguez drove and Manuel Ortega sat beside her, with Fernández in the back. They passed through the police barrier at the southern entrance, drove past the barracks, and turned off onto a gravel road which led across a stony littered field to the so-called southern sector.

Danica drove very well, swiftly and with intuitive skill. Manuel looked at her sideways and saw that a tiny wrinkle appeared just above the ridge of her nose when she was concentrating on the uneven road.

"How deeply are you involved in these circles?" he said.

"Quite deeply."

She braked at the opening in the stone wall. In front of the radiator stood a policeman with a machine gun held at the ready.

"It was nice of you not to begin asking about that sort of thing when you were playing truth and consequences last night," she said.

He looked reproachfully at her, and she shook her head and said: "Sorry. I'm feeling generally rather ragged today. I get nasty then."

They produced their identity cards for the policeman, who saluted and said: "Do you want an escort?"

"No, thank you," said Manuel Ortega.

Then he thought that an escort was in fact exactly what he did want.

She drove along a crooked street between grayish-yellow stone houses. In the spaces between the leaning walls there were all kinds of temporary dwellings for human beings, from old metal drums to overturned truck bodies on trestles and ancient wheel-less buses. The street was seething with children, pigs, and dogs, but there were not many adults about. Danica used the horn incessantly and the children's curses rained down on the car.

They came out into a large triangular marketplace which was relatively empty except around the well, where several women with clay jars in their hands were pushing and chattering. The square was not paved but covered with trampled clay, sun-dried and yellow and cracked into an uneven checkered pattern. In the middle, pigs, children, and vultures rooted in the heaps of garbage. The vultures were frightened by the car and rose, flapping their wings heavily. They landed again ten yards away.

"We'll stop here," said Danica. "We can walk the rest of the way."

She turned off into a narrow alley and went on down a few steps. It stank of urine and rotten garbage, and Manuel almost held his nose but manged to restrain himself. Instead he turned around and looked at Fernández, who was walking three yards behind them, hunched up, with long gliding steps, and his right hand resting on his hip.

Danica stopped at a low wooden door and knocked. The knocking was obviously some kind of signal but was hard to interpret since it was so short.

Someone pushed back the cover of a peephole. Soon after, the door swung open.

Danica stepped to one side and let Manuel go in first. Fernández followed. They stood in a bare windowless room with rough stone walls. The daylight that seeped in through the hole and the cracks in the door filled the room with a grayish, unreal light. The man who had opened the door was perhaps a little younger than Manuel and was dressed in rubber boots and carelessly buttoned overalls with a leather belt fastened tightly around his waist. His face was sunburned, with strong, heavy features, and his hair was brown and curly. His eyes were blue. Danica had shut the door and bolted it.

"Hullo, Ramón," she said, patting the man on the cheek in a light and comradely way.

Manuel Ortega felt a faint twinge of jealousy, but it died away at once. They went up some stairs and into the next windowless room. On the far side stood a long table and two long wooden benches. Behind the table sat a man cleaning a gun. He was heavily built, powerful and had short, rather fair hair.

"This is Sixto," said Danica. "He's the regional leader."

"And head of the Liberation Front politburo," said the man, rising. "Please sit down."

They shook hands and sat down.

Fernández retired at once to the wall. His glance flickered back and forth from one man to the other. The short-haired one looked at him, pushed the magazine back into the gun, and put it to one side.

"You sit down too," he said. "There's not going to be any shooting here. Only talking."

"Sit down, Fernández," said Manuel Ortega.

Fernández sat down eventually but hesitantly and on the very end of the bench.

"To be brief," said Sixto, "we're ready to negotiate. It's what we've always wanted. But we demand real guarantees. First and foremost we want to negotiate on neutral ground, out of the country."

"That's impossible. We simply haven't the time. The conference must be held within six days."

"Where then?"

"Anywhere. In the town here."

"That's impossible for us. Perhaps some place out in the province with a six-mile demilitarized zone in all directions. No police or army within six miles."

"That can be arranged, of course. I can't believe the other side will have any objections."

"If only we could agree on that," said Sixto. "What's the general position otherwise?"

"The first condition is that all acts of violence cease immediately. A truce will be declared from the moment it's decided the conference will take place. All participants have the government's guarantees of safe conduct to and from the meeting place."

"How can we rely on that?"

"I am the representative of the federal authorities and you'll have to trust me. This is a binding promise from the government's side. I officially represent the government, and I guarantee that the promise will be fulfilled. Otherwise I'd hardly be here."

"We don't know you," said Sixto.

"You must trust me and the government. Otherwise all cooperation is impossible."

"Listen. We find ourselves in a very difficult situation now that the supply route across the border has been blocked. That's no secret, so I might just as well say it. So we can't afford to take any risks. Anyhow, with whom shall we be negotiating?"

"The leaders of the Citizens' Guard. With me and a couple of assistants, probably Señora Rodríguez here and someone else as presiding chairman. What I consider vital is that it should be a meeting at the highest level, between the real leaders within the respective organizations. So I had thought that each side should nominate three or four of their adversaries' delegates."

"That's very unorthodox. Is it your own suggestion?"

"Yes."

"Very unorthodox, as I said. But you're right to the extent that if there is to be a meeting at all, it must be at top level."

"Are you prepared to agree with this suggestion then?"

"We aren't agreeing with anything. We can't rely on you personally as a guarantee for the government's promises. We must have further guarantees."

"You will be receiving a detailed written document in which all conditions for negotiations are carefully laid down. If you like, signed by members of the government. As you don't trust me personally."

"Yes—well—by way of example," said Sixto.

"How can I keep in contact with you?"

"As soon as we've come to a decision—and that decision is

dependent on the guarantees you have to offer, for the government and for you personally—well, then we'll place a contact-man with you, a kind of liaison officer."

"Who would it be?"

"A man called Ellerman, Wolfgang Ellerman."

"Is he around here?"

"Yes, he's around here."

"I must point out that the most important condition is that all acts of violence cease and that the more active element is kept in check."

The man behind the table gave him a tired look.

"We've been keeping a quarter of a million people in this province in check for a year and a half now, just to prevent them from being butchered by the army and the police."

"The army has gone now."

"And the police serve as shock troops instead. As recently as the day before yesterday the whole population of a village was wiped out. Three days ago, forty-two people, most of them unarmed, were murdered by the police and members of the Citizens' Guard in the northern sector. The day before, eleven by one of the so-called blasting details. Before that —well, there's no point in going on. Do you think it was the police who stopped the rioting three days ago? No, it was we. We who calmed the people and held them in check. Otherwise we'd soon have had a general bloodbath."

Suddenly he clenched his fist and crashed it down on the table.

"But," he said, "if we'd seen an opportunity of making some progress, then we wouldn't have held them back, we'd have led them into the fight. As it was, the only result would have been a pointless sacrifice of human lives."

Manuel Ortega looked straight at him and said: "We know about most of that. So certain measures have also been taken on our side. One result of the events in Santa Rosa is that the police have orders to act in the future in accordance with the Federal Police regulations and they have been forbidden to apply military emergency regulations."

Sixto glanced at Danica Rodrígeuz, who nodded in confirmation.

"You speak well, but the time when talk made any impression on us has long since gone by."

He gripped the edge of the table to get up. Manuel said at once: "One moment. Two more points. A representative of the Citizens' Guard has already been in contact with me . . ."

"Who?"

"Dalgren . . . and I have had certain discussions with him. To gain time, it would be to great advantage if you would not only suggest a meeting place but also provisionally nominate the four delegates from the Citizens' Guard whom you would like to see at the conference."

"Well," said Sixto, poking at his gun. "A place—yes."

He looked at Ramón, who nodded assent.

"Mercadal," said Sixto. "Mercadal would be a good place It's a little place about sixteen miles south of here. There's a good building there too—an army post which could easily be evacuated."

Manuel looked at Danica Rodríguez.

"Make a note of it," he said.

"Then the four delegates—yes, that's not difficult. Count Ponti, Dalgren, José Suárez, and of course Colonel Orbal."

"Colonel Orbal?"

"Yes, he's the founder and organizer of the Citizens' Guard. Didn't you know that?"

"No. I certainly didn't."

"And remember one thing. We may be fighting with our backs to the wall, but we're far from being powerless."

"I know that."

"Those who betray us do so only once. We did not, despite

all the assertions to the contrary, kill the previous Resident, but that doesn't mean . . ."

"I know all that, and you'll gain nothing by threatening me either."

"What do you know?"

"That you didn't murder Larrinaga. But you've murdered plenty of others instead, if I'm not misinformed."

Sixto seemed to be speechless. He frowned and rose to his feet.

"Will I be able to get in touch with you here?" said Manuel Ortega.

"Nothing in the whole wide world would persuade me to stay here ten minutes after you've gone."

They shook hands. Sixto pocketed his gun. Ramón came with them to the door.

Later in the car Manuel Ortega said: "What kind of people are they? They're not Indians."

"Most of the regional leaders are poor whites or half-breeds who for various reasons have grown up here in the slums or in the villages out in the country. Ramón was born in the same village as I was."

"Bematanango?"

"You've a good memory."

"And Sixto?"

She drove diagonally across the square and stopped in front of the entrance.

"Sixto . . ."

She stopped and laughed a short, rather cold laugh.

"Ask me next time we sleep together. Then I'm defenseless."

Ten minutes later Manuel Ortega had his first conversation of the day with Behounek.

"With the Communists? Who was there?"

"A certain Sixto."

"Good Christ. Sixto Boreas. Just think—only three days ago I'd have surrounded that whole part of the town if I'd known he was there. Well, I'll have to leave it now. He's not a really top man, but he's dangerous."

"Who is José Suárez?"

"A journalist, chief editor of the newspaper here, *Diario*. A friend of Dalgren's, a great gun in the Citizens' Guard."

"How were things last night?"

"So-so."

"What do you mean by so-so?"

"Two people killed in the northern sector. One in the eastern. All found shot this morning. A partisan raid farther south, four people killed. That's all I know at the moment."

We must have a truce, thought Manuel Ortega. We must have a truce. Now. Today. At all costs.

Then he remembered the proclamation and what he was about to do.

He went over to the window and looked at the empty plaza and the palm trees and the square buildings in the distance.

The town had looked like this every morning at this time, and every time he had wondered whether he was looking at it for the last time.

15

✳●✳●✳✳

It was five past eight. The heat stood like a wall outside the window, close and awful and blinding.

The faucets were not working. The officer in command sounded tired and resigned and demanded twelve hours more.

The telephone lines to the north were still cut. At the exchange they said that the break was near the border of the province in a blockaded zone in which army maneuvers were taking place.

The headquarters of the Third Infantry Regiment informed him that General Gami and Colonel Orbal could not be counted on to return within the next three days.

Colonel Ruiz had come down with dysentery and had been taken to the military hospital. His chief of staff reported that eight tankers out of twenty-five were in the workshops being repaired.

An unknown person said on Dalgren's behalf that the question of a meeting place for the conference and the nomination of delegates would be taken up immediately by the executive of the Citizens' Guard.

Manuel talked to Danica.

"Call the station and tell them my speech is to be broadcast every five minutes from now on."

"Yes."

Her face was hard and tense.

"How shall we get the leaflets out?"

"I've fixed that. Better if you don't know how."

"It can't take more than four minutes to read the proclamation. Do you think they'd have time to cut me off?"

"Depends on who is quickest to the phone."

"How do you feel, by the way?"

"One breast hurts like hell."

"I'm sorry about that."

"It hurts all the same."

Manuel Ortega was sitting at his desk. His heart thumped and his hands shook. He had to go to the bathroom although he had been there only five minutes earlier.

Fernández was chewing. Outside the world was white.

It was quarter past nine. Then it was twenty past nine. No one telephoned, not even Behounek.

Twenty-five past nine. He would go in ten minutes. He went to the bathroom. The steps of terror across the corridor. The Astra was like a lead weight against his heart.

Danica had switched on the radio. The announcer's voice was fraught with routine solemnity: We are about to broadcast an important message. At exactly ten o'clock the Provincial Resident will speak to the people. We urge everyone to listen.

Music: brassy and shrill.

When he laid his hands flat on the desk, wet prints appeared on the brown blotter.

Fernández yawned and picked at his nails.

A drop of sweat fell from Manuel Ortega's forehead onto General Larrinaga's proclamation.

He wiped his hands on his trousers and large dark patches appeared on the material.

We are about to broadcast an important message. At exactly ten o'clock the Provincial Resident will speak to the people. We urge everyone to listen. We are about to broadcast an important message. At exactly ten o'clock the Provincial Resident will speak to the people. We urge everyone to listen.

He got up. Folded the proclamation and put it in his left inside pocket. Moved it over to the right one. Put on his sunglasses. Picked up his hat. Said to Fernández: "The radio station."

A woman in a white dress looked seriously at him. She said nothing and made no sign.

Manuel Ortega walked along the white corridor, down the white staircase, through the white hall, past the white counter and a policeman in a white uniform, drove through the white town. He looked straight ahead and thought about nothing whatsoever.

The same studio and the same announcer with red patches on his forehead and on his pale arms. The walls were wavy in the heat. Two technicians behind the glass wall. They had religious medals hanging on silver chains around their necks and they were talking to each other. One had hair on his chest and kept drinking out of a tin mug.

The lights dead like blind eyes. Fernández by the wall. The announcer saying: "When the on-the-air signal comes through, I'll stay here and announce you and then I'll go. What kind of music would you like afterward? A march?"

His heart thumped, heavily and unevenly, and the quivering in his diaphragm would not stop. He thought his voice had gone and he cleared his throat several times. The papers rustled in his hands.

Green light. The technicians behind the glass were still talking to each other, but they were looking at something in front of them. Red light. The announcer leaned over his shoulder and said easily:

"Hello. Hello. This is an important message to the people. Over to the Provincial Resident, Don Manuel Ortega."

While he was saying this, Manuel Ortega stared at the green felt cloth. A sunflower seed lay just beside the microphone. He was now quite certain that his larynx had ceased to function and that his voice would break down into a hoarse and inaudible croak at the first word.

So he was surprised when he suddenly heard himself speaking, calmly and clearly and convincingly.

"This is Manuel Ortega. As your Provincial Resident it is my duty to create peace and security in the district. It is also my duty to give all citizens in this area every opportunity for a richer and more worthwhile life, materially and spiritually. This task I shall try to fulfill to the best of my ability. My predecessor, General Orestes de Larrinaga, was a great and broad-minded man. Before his death he composed the proclamation which I am now about to read to you. It is directed to all of you, without exception, and it lays down the principles for my and my successors' work. This is General Orestes de Larrinaga's message to you, written in his own hand."

He read the seventeen paragraphs slowly and emphatically, the whole time in a state of unreality and isolation. The only things that existed were the letters and words and a little yellow spider which slowly, slowly crept diagonally across the paper.

The moment he read out the words "Orestes de Larrinaga, General, Provincial Resident," he knew he must say something more. He extemporized: "To this I must add that I have a sworn certificate from the General's daughter, Doña Francisca de Larrinaga, which attests to the genuineness of this document. I must also stress that a great deal of evidence points to the view that this proclamation was the reason for the death of the General. My personal view is that he was killed so that he would not have the opportunity of publishing the seventeen points that you have just heard. From this it follows that the organization accused of his death is in fact not guilty of that particular crime."

He paused for a moment. The red light was still on.

"The government has given me the task of following up General de Larrinaga's plans for peace and reforms. The tense and difficult atmosphere will shortly be dispersed—will be

dealt with at a peace conference. Details of this will be sent
out in an extra communiqúe at midday today."

All the colored lights had gone out.

Manuel Ortega remained sitting at the table with his head
lowered. His hands on the green felt looked small and weak
and ineffectual. The drops of sweat from his face fell onto the
sheets of his script.

Fernández was sitting by the wall with his legs outstretched,
indifferently picking at his teeth with a broken match.

The technicians behind the glass were gesticulating and
talking excitedly to each other. Now and then they threw
timid, curious glances at the man sitting at the green table.

Manuel raised his right hand, placed his thumb over the
little yellow spider, and squashed it. Then he rose slowly,
leaving the papers on the table.

The announcer came in. His face was excited. The heat
spots on his cheeks flared angrily red.

"Well . . . I couldn't make any final announcement," he said.
"We were cut . . ."

"When?"

"I couldn't tell you the exact moment."

Manuel Ortega took a paper out of his jacket pocket.

"This is an important announcement about the peace conference," he said. "It's to be put out at midday and after that
every hour."

"We must record it," said the announcer nervously. "Nothing is to be broadcast direct from now on. That's a new order."

"Who gave this order?"

"The Military Governor, General Gami."

The little gray car drove through the empty town, oozing
its way through the dazzling heat. There were very few people
about. The streets between the dusty rows of palm trees were
deserted. On each side stood the great white blocks of apartments, their white shutters closed.

At the intersection of the Avenida and Calle del General

Huerta stood four men with the yellow armbands of the Citizens' Guard. They looked like middle-aged family men. One of them raised his rifle and aimed it at the car. Manuel Ortega saw him and thought: Now I'm going to die. He heard a long gurgling gasp and knew that it came from himself.

"Don't bother about stupidities like that," said Fernández calmly. "It won't be like that. He didn't even bother to put the safety catch off his blunderbuss."

In the back Gómez sat with his short machine gun on his knee. Manuel wondered where he had come from.

A white square with white monumental buildings, the white vestibule and counter and the patch on the floor where General Larrinaga had lain with his shattered chest and blood on his white uniform. The staircase and the white corridor and the white door of his fears. He dared not open it but turned and went through the other office, where there was nothing but a pile of statistical tables on the desk, and then on into the woman in the white dress.

"They cut us off," he said.

"Yes, but not until the next-to-last sentence."

Fernández rustled with his seeds.

The telephone rang.

"One moment—I'll answer."

She put her hand over the mouthpiece.

"It's Dalgren's secretary. Do you want to take it?"

He picked up the receiver. The girl connected him. Then Dalgren was there. His voice sounded very near, piercing, as if he were standing close to Manuel Ortega or had already stepped into his consciouness. It was dry and hard and rasping, like emery paper on rusty tin.

"Young man, you have made a devastating mistake. I cannot protect you any longer. I don't even want to. You've dragged my old friend Orestes's name in the mud. You've betrayed us all. It would surprise me if you were still alive this time tomorrow."

A metallic click and then dead, empty silence.

The conversation was over, and Manuel Ortega remained standing, holding the receiver, until Danica took it out of his hand.

He frowned and shook his head slightly as if he were trying to concentrate on some serious practical problem.

"They're going to kill me," he said.

"That'll be two of us then," said Fernández, unmoved.

He was standing with one foot in each room, his back to the doorpost.

"No," said Danica Rodríguez with conviction. "They won't kill you. I don't expect they'll even try. They daren't."

The telephone rang again.

"No, the Provincial Resident will not be available until after one o'clock."

She picked up her bag from the floor and rose.

"Come on," she said.

Behind them the telephone rang.

In his bedroom he sat down on the bed and waited. She left him but soon came back and shut the door behind her.

"Undress," she said.

He obeyed. His suit was crumpled and damp, his underclothes soaking. She emptied his pockets and flung the clothes into a heap on the floor.

"Into the shower with you."

He went.

"Lean forward. That's right. Now your front."

Slowly she poured two jars of water over him and he shuddered with cold. Part of his still functioning cell system registered a surprising detail: that she lifted the heavy vessels with such ease and composure.

"You're strong," he said.

"Yes, I'm a strong, healthy girl."

She picked up a clean towel and began to dry him. Her movements were purposeful, swift, and precise.

"You're fine today too," she said. "One doesn't think that about many the day after."

She extracted a little glass vial from her bag, put a tablet in his hand, and said: "Swallow that now and drink a little water."

In the bedroom she took off the bedspread and blankets and turned back the sheet.

"Get in."

He did as he was told, and she spread the sheet over him. He lay on his side, facing the wall, and said: "There's something wrong with me. I'm sorry."

"Yes. You're very tired and a little frightened. You're beginning to feel worn out and you're not used to it. And you've not had more than two hours' sleep. Just think that you've actually achieved something today and be content with that."

"You're looking after me."

"I'm not much good at looking after other people, nor myself, but sometimes one has to. Be quiet now and sleep, I'll be here and Fernández is sitting in the room out there and Gómez is in the corridor. Nothing will happen anyway."

"The revolver," he said.

She got it and put it on the bedside table. The Astra. He stretched out his hand for it and put it under his pillow.

She lit a cigarette, walked over to the window, and stood peering through the slats as she smoked. Now and again she bit at the cuticle around her nails. Without turning around she said: "If you like, I'll get undressed and get in with you. Bruises and all."

When he did not reply she went over to the bed and saw that he was asleep. She walked up and down the room for a while. Then she put her cigarette out in the ashtray and left the room.

"Yes," she said to herself, "someone's going to kill him."

She heard the telephone ring as soon as she reached the corridor.

Outside in the square policemen in white uniforms drove away a crowd of shouting people who had gathered in front of the steps of the Governor's Palace.

16

✳●✳●✳✳

When he woke up, the sheet was stuck firmly to his body. It was Danica who woke him and it was she too who once again poured water over him in the shower. Then she left, and for a few minutes he felt rested and relatively calm. But he picked up the white terylene suit to look at it, he remembered Dalgren's voice and then, as he dressed, it stayed with him all the time, dry and rasping and implacable.

You have betrayed us all. It would surprise me to find you alive this time tomorrow.

He remembered too the member of the Citizens' Guard who had taken aim at him on the corner of Calle del General Huerta and what he had thought of at that moment.

But all the same he believed in his innermost self that he realized that it could not be serious. And he had not been alone either.

When he opened the door to the outer room, López got up from his chair and went into the corridor. López moved silently and cautiously as if walking on his toes. Sometimes he looked like a servile head waiter who always wanted to be available but did not want to irritate his guests by his presence.

The suit was light and comfortable. It fitted him fairly well and when he buttoned up the jacket he found it was full enough not to bulge over the revolver.

When Manuel Ortega had established this fact, he took off the jacket again, unbuttoned his collar and went into the bathroom to shave. He had not done it in the morning, and he was also taking every opportunity to postpone contact with the corridor and the white door into his office.

A quarter of an hour later and it was inevitable.

He adjusted the revolver in the holster, opened the door and saw López sitting in the revolving chair. He took two steps across the corridor, laid his left hand on the knob, and thrust his right one inside his jacket.

López had still not begun to get up. Manuel smiled at his inertia, pushed open the door, and stepped over the threshold.

The room was empty and white and hot, and through the closed door to his secretary's room he could hear Danica. She was talking on the telephone and her voice was stubborn and aggressive and only barely polite.

He went across to the window and looked out. Below by the entrance stood two policemen in white. Five more were sitting smoking on the steps. In the middle of the square stood a little group of people, mostly women and youngsters. They looked as if they were waiting for something to happen.

Danica Rodríguez came into the room.

"How do you feel?"

"Better, thanks."

"Is the suit all right?"

"Yes, thanks. Have you been having some trouble?"

"A lot of idiots have phoned and there's been some commotion outside."

"Threats?"

She nodded.

"Letters too. Seven or eight."

"What do they say?"

"Much the same as Dalgren said on the phone."

"Has Captain Behounek been in touch?"

She shook her head.

"But there is something positive as well. Sixto has sent a letter. A messenger brought it half an hour after the first broadcast. . . . They're putting out the communiqué about the conference every hour," she added.

"Give me the letter and call Captain Behounek. Give me the threatening letters too."

The call came through before he had time to open the gray envelope with the red stamp of the Liberation Front on it.

"Yes. Behounek."

"Ortega. I was expecting to hear from you."

"Well now, weren't there enough people phoning you anyway? I've already got a list of twelve people who have threatened to take your life, ranging from a very high-up potentate with whom you yourself have had the pleasure of speaking, to a taxi driver and the notorious female from the perfume shop. What do you think I ought to do with them?"

"Are there really taxis here?"

"Yes, a few, but I can't think who might make use of them. There's hardly anyone left in the center of the town. Sixty per cent of the apartments are empty. Partly because many people have gone and partly because the buildings are faulty. The ventilation is supposed to be all shot to hell."

Manuel Ortega felt that some of the tension had gone. The everyday tone of the conversation did him good.

"Seriously, I hadn't forgotten all about you. A moment ago I sent a couple of patrols to keep things nice and tidy outside your place. Thought that seemed more sensible than calling up and talking a lot of nonsense."

"People don't seem to like me so much any more."

"Don't say that. My men in the eastern sector report that you've got supporters who write "Viva Ortega" in red paint on the walls. That's not bad. You certainly can't count on equal enthusiasm from all quarters."

"The most important thing at the moment is the conference."

"Quite right."

"Do you think that this can jeopardize it?"

"Hardly. On the contrary, I should think. But . . ."

He stopped.

"But what?"

When Behounek spoke again his tone of voice had changed. Manuel had heard him speak like this once before, in the car on the way to the white villa with blue shutters.

"Ortega, you must listen very carefully to what I'm going to say. You've taken a terrible risk. Personally I think you're wrong, but we'll leave that for the moment. I don't think you've jeopardized the conference, but you jeopardized something else which you at least ought to consider worth something. Namely, yourself. Your position is dangerous. It'll be even more dangerous tomorrow. But it's possible the pressure will slacken within a few days. There are two solutions, but I'm afraid you won't accept either of them. The first is that you get out now, immediately. I can give you an escort to the border and we can requisition a helicopter. The other is that you demand police protection. In which case I'll take you into protective arrest."

"You must see that the one is as unthinkable as the other. The whole assignment would be jeopardized . . ."

"I know. I suggested them only so that you would understand that these possibilities are at hand and that they offer the only chance of saving your life. But then you're choosing to stay and that means you're living in a town where there are twenty thousand people prepared to kill you, as one would kill a prairie wolf or a rat. *And it's impossible to protect you, Ortega.* I'm telling you this as a professional man. I've got seven hundred men in the province and not even with all of them collected here would I dare to guarantee your life. A political murder is the most inexorable thing there is—because the murderer doesn't expect to save himself. He expects only to kill and to die. Even if you had a fortress and an army at your disposal, you still wouldn't be safe."

He fell silent, but Manuel could still hear him breathing.

"Do you know if your secretary makes a habit of listening in to your calls?"

"Yes, she does."

"Excellent. Get your shorthand notebook out then, my girl."

He said this without a trace of humor or irony. Then he paused again.

"Don't forget a single syllable of what I'm going to say. Never leave the building. Don't go into other parts of the building either. Never let your bodyguard out of sight under any circumstances whatsoever. Never open any communications or parcels yourself. Never stand by the windows. Always have your bodyguard investigate your bedroom before you go into it yourself. Don't ever receive visitors except those you really know. Never go about unarmed, not even when you go to the bathroom. Don't put your gun under the mattress or the pillow. Put it on a chair on the right side of the bed at waist height. Make sure the gun is always loaded and the safety catch off. Check that the gun is always in a place where you can get at it in a fraction of a second. Never eat food other than that which I send in to you. Don't take sleeping tablets or any other drug which reduces the speed of your reactions."

He fell silent and seemed to be thinking. Then he said: "Ortega, I'm not telling you this in order to frighten you. You really must remember all this, and you must also keep a cool head. Under no circumstances must you lose control. Your position is to look at the positive side of it, from several points of view. I'll see to the outer guard and I'll keep four patrols—that is, sixteen men—day and night in or in the vicinity of the palace. They should already be there by this time. One man will always be at the door leading to your corridor. That's the only entrance and his instructions are absolutely rigid. That can be good to know, especially at night."

Manuel did not reply, and after a few seconds Behounek shot his last bolt.

"I am very concerned for your life . . . but this time they really mean it. And I understand them."

Manuel Ortega sat at his desk. The telephone receiver trembled in his hand. Several seconds went by before he could break the paralysis and replace the receiver.

Danica looked at him seriously from the doorway. He drew in a deep breath, shrugged his shoulders, and turned to the immobile López.

"Are you aware that the situation has become more serious?"

"Yes."

Manuel discovered that he was still holding Sixto's letter in his hand. He opened it and read: "Prospects improved. Ellerman will be at Hotel Universal at about four today. Arrange police protection for him. Sixto. Acting Chief Politburo. Liberation Front. P.S., You can trust Ellerman. Show this message to your secretary."

The message was hand-written and the writing was large and firm and legible.

He went to Danica and gave her the letter. She nodded but otherwise made no comment.

"This could mean considerable progress," said Manuel Ortega.

"Yes, it's a step forward. Your conference will come off."

"Our conference, I'd say. Old Sixto has evidently made contact with the party leaders."

"I doubt it."

"Why should he have changed his attitude then?"

"Don't you really see why?"

"Yes," he said. "Yes, of course."

"Viva Ortega," she said, smiling a very small smile.

"But what I definitely don't understand is my own inability to understand such a simple connection."

"It's hot and you're still tired and a little frightened," she said.

"Is there any special hidden meaning in his P.S., do you think?"

"There's always a special meaning in everything Sixto does, says, or writes. In this case he means that I shall say: Yes, you really can rely on Ellerman."

"Do you know him?"

"Yes."

"And Sixto you evidently know very well. How did you get to know him?"

"Don't ask me now. I don't want to answer and I don't want to lie to you."

Against his will he was angry, and she noticed it at once.

"I'm hopeless," she said resignedly. "Everything goes wrong. With people I really like I'm always babbling. I talk too much. Now I've got this all unrecognizably tangled up. You already know too much."

"You like me then?"

"Yes. Truly, I think."

"O.K. We'll talk about it another time. We'll get Ellerman here as soon as he shows up at the hotel, shall we?"

"Yes. Don't forget to phone Behounek and warn him."

"Right. You're not a bad secretary either."

He walked over toward the window.

"Manuel! Not the window! Remember the instructions."

"Of course," he said in confusion, and turned toward his own room.

"Manuel," she said again. "You've got to be careful now. Very careful. For several reasons."

At that moment he was thinking about something completely different. They were to talk about Sixto another time. Would there be another time?

When he thought like that the sweat broke out all over his body, and now it was different, cold and sticky, and he shivered as if he had been walking in the rain down Karla-vägen in Stockholm. But perhaps it really was so, perhaps there would be no other time. Perhaps he had only a few hours left to recover all he had neglected to do during the long stretch of careless uneventful years. His wife, his children, his brothers and sisters, his career. And everything else: all the unplayed games of tennis, the boat he never bought, the unread books, the women he had wanted and probably could have had but never did. Manuel, all the soft parts of the body, all the warmth, all the unheard music, all the neglected communion services, all the unspoken truths. No, it must not be like that. He sat down and called Behounek.

"Yes, we'll handle him like a soft-boiled egg. Who did you say—Ellerman?"

"Wolfgang Ellerman. Do you know who he is?"

"For once—no. But call in an hour and we'll see."

"Despite everything, you are a human being! Good-by."

"One more thing, Ortega. Don't forget Captain Behounek's twelve points. For you they are considerably more practical than General Larrinaga's seventeen."

Manuel relapsed into inactivity and immediately fear began to grind within him. Like a churning ache, round and round and round.

There was only one way out: work and more work. And to take the bull by the horns. He stretched out his hand to call up Dalgren, but the telephone beat him to it.

"Yes. Ortega."

"Oh yes, you filthy, lousy pervert of swine. Do you know what we usually do to Indian-lovers here? First, we cut their cocks off and then . . ."

The caller was a woman. He broke off the call and said to Danica: "Must you put that kind of lunatic through? Get through to Dalgren instead."

"Oh yes, you're still alive then?" said Dalgren coldly. "That almost surprises me."

"I'm calling to talk about the peace conference, not to discuss personal antagonisms."

"This, young man, is not a question of personal differences of opinion. You're a traitor and to get rid of you is—how shall I put it now?—a matter of national interest. Moreover, I'm none too anxious to talk to you at all. As the conference is going to take place all the same without your personal assistance, I prefer to leave the business to one of your colleagues."

"Of course, that's fine. One moment and you can talk to Señora Rodríguez. I wish you a pleasant evening."

He succeeded in saying the last words in a lighthearted tone of raillery despite the fact that he was furious, and despite the fact that the churning in his diaphragm was becoming more painful every second.

Three minutes later Danica was standing by his desk.

"They agree about Mercadal as a meeting place," she said, "and they demand that the following shall be there: Dr. Irigo, El Campesino, Carmen Sánchez, and alternatively José Redondo or . . ."

"Or?"

". . . Sixto Boreas. That's wrong. His name isn't that at all."

"What is his name then?"

"Also they're willing to send the delegates whom the Liberation Front nominated, that is, Count Carlos Ponti, Don Emilio Dalgren, Don José Suárez, and Colonel Joaquín Orbal. They make one reservation in that Colonel Orbal is away at the moment and they've been unable to contact him."

"Did you hear what I said? What's Sixto's name?"

"Manuel, don't force me to lie."

"Were you married to him?"

For some reason he said this very violently.

"To Sixto? Married? Good God, no!"

Manuel suddenly remembered that they were not alone.

He glanced quickly at López, but he was sitting as still as usual and his face was completely expressionless.

The day was extremely hot. A white day which became whiter and whiter, hotter and hotter, which hour after hour was stretched out like a steel spring, more and more and more, toward a sudden explosion, as unforeseen as a catastrophe.

As if at a great distance, Manuel Ortega heard his secretary occasionally answering the telephone.

He moved like a sleepwalker into the bedroom and returned, frightened out of his life, with López behind him, his hand on the walnut butt and his heart thumping.

At six o'clock Ellerman came; small, thick-set, curved nose, white linen hat and narrow-striped light-colored suit. He seemed efficient and energetic, sharp, practical, and discerning. Altogether it took half an hour.

"The fundamental difficulty is naturally the time factor," said Ellerman. "One or more of our delegates are not in the country. They must be reached, and certain preparations are necessary too. Let me see, today is Friday the fifteenth of June."

He counted on his fingers.

"Saturday, Sunday, Monday—Wednesday then, at the very earliest Tuesday. The very, very earliest. Preferably Wednesday."

"We'll try for Tuesday."

"But that's really terribly short notice, almost absurdly so. All the preparation on the administrative level, the internal discussions. But we'll try . . ."

"Let's say we'll open the conference on the evening of Tuesday the nineteenth at, say, seven o'clock. Then we can carry on for as many days as we like. I'm sorry I have to force you, Señor Ellerman, but the situation is extremely tense. At the breaking point."

Breaking point, thought Manuel Ortega.

"Yes. I must make a few contacts. You'll have definite confirmation early tomorrow morning at eight o'clock. And the other details are fixed. Written guarantees from the government in my hand on Sunday. At the latest Monday morning. A six-mile demilitarized zone. Complete truce from midnight tonight on, no arrests, no armed action, nothing. It is unfortunately easier for the right-wing extremists to reach their . . . militia, than for us to reach our fighting forces. At the end of the conference, forty-eight hours' grace. And then our delegates: El Campesino and José Redondo—well, why partisan officers at a conference table? But we'll get hold of them, and Carmen Sánchez too, of course. The main problem is Dr. Irigo. But we'll fix that. Otherwise we'll have to postpone the whole thing a day. But you arrange all the practical details here; quarters, printing, broadcasts, and that sort of thing. All right? Excellent. Good-by."

Ellerman rose and picked up his briefcase. He stood looking out of the window.

"Awful lot of policemen," he said. "Very unpleasant. And a lot of demonstrators. Are the right-wing extremists going to kill you too?"

"Yes," said Manuel Ortega.

"Violence," said Ellerman. "I loathe violence of all kinds. And this struggle has to be carried on in this way."

He fell silent and poked at his nose with his little finger.

"Oh well, various people on our side take a different view of violence. There are different sets of values. If only the legal situation weren't so depressingly obscure. You know, the Communist Party isn't banned in the Federal Republic, but it was disbanded by the previous government, which was rather military. So the Party is, so to speak, neither permitted nor forbidden. And the Liberation Front is not officially a Communist organization. This is a matter which must be settled by the highest courts. The government can't decide just like that that the Liberation Front is a Communist movement—and the President knows it. Such a procedure has no legal relevance at all. When Radamek took over, he submitted both matters to the federal courts with the recommendation that the Liberation Front should be declared to be Communist but that the Communist Party should at the same time be made legal. Since then the federal courts have made no move and the matter still stands way down on their list of cases. Here they've got around the whole business by declaring a state of emergency and applying martial law. The only thing I know about martial law after seven years' work is that the generals do exactly as they please. In other words, it's not easy to be afflicted with a socialist view of life in this country."

He stood silently for a moment, rubbing his nose. Danica, behind him, leaned against the doorpost, smiling.

"You know, our party has always been suppressed and has never been particularly strong in any of the other federal states. So the best forces were concentrated here in the south where there was a possibility of making some progress. Now many of them are dead—fine, strong people, real idealists. Only the top layer of the elite is left. The rest are stuck forever in this poor, frightful country. This miserable little feudal province with its millionaires and its military dictatorship. For a hundred years different politicians and different parties have scratched the feudal bosses' backs to obtain backing for their election campaigns. For a hundred years career-mad generals have used this impoverished waste of stone as a springboard to the road to the presidency. And here the people have just starved and suffered and worked themselves to death. How otherwise could anyone earn millions from this desert of stones? And . . ."

"Wolfgang," said Danica Rodríguez.

He started and turned around.

"Aah—I beg your pardon. Talking too much again. Getting pathetic and long-winded, forgetting myself. Lucky I'm not going to be sitting at the conference table—what a lot of prattle—what a bad habit—well, good evening—and eight o'clock tomorrow morning . . ."

He backed out of the room with his briefcase in one hand and his hat in the other.

"He was a criminal lawyer to start with," said Danica, "but he talked every minor case to death. It would take three days to settle an ordinary fight, and then of course he had his political handicap. Now he devotes himself to land cases oddly enough, and to the Party . . . He can be extremely efficient if he puts his mind to it."

"I liked him."

From outside came shouts, the roar of voices, and whistles. Somewhere a windowpane was shattered, briskly tinkling. She looked out.

"Small fry," she said. "Mostly women and children. The police are driving them off. They're carrying placards and streamers."

"What does it say on the placards?"

"Death to the traitor. What did you expect?"

Manuel Ortega lay on his back in the dark with his eyes open and his right hand on the butt of his revolver. He heard Fernández moving about in the room outside. It was half past three and he had been lying like that for four hours.

He had an exhausting day's work behind him, a long and successful day. The conference was as good as settled. People he had never seen wrote "Viva Ortega" on the walls. The truce had come into force. For everyone, but not for him.

He was afraid of the dark but dared not put on the light for fear of what he might suddenly see. He was on the alert for every noise. Had Fernández gone? No, another rustling; he was still there. But could he rely on Fernández? Or López? Or on Gómez? On Behounek? On Danica. On anyone? The answer: No.

"Everything's wrong, Manuel," he whispered. "Everything's been wrong from the very beginning. You're an official and not a hero, however much you'd like to be one. You're no Behounek. Nor a Sixto. Now you must show them that this being normal can mean strength, not necessarily weakness. But you must inure yourself to it. You're being ground between two millstone ideologies and you're surrounded by experts in the art of killing. But are they also expert at dying? Does Behounek lie awake in his official bed too? Or Sixto in his cellar room? Or López at the hotel?"

After Sixto, he thought about the brown-haired Ramón and about the bruise and he was jealous. It came like a balm, but soon left him.

No one was right. Neither Dalgren nor Ellerman. Nor Behounek either. Certainly not Behounek. Nor Orestes de Larrinaga. Nor Ellerman. Not Ellerman.

Point 11. Because of the people's low level of education, it is too early . . . But hadn't every person a right to his own country irrespective of level of education? Should a small number of intruders be allowed to deprive everyone else of all their rights? On the other hand, could people born in this country be called intruders? They had, after all, grown up here, built towns and roads, created sources of energy and earning capacity . . .

This simplified reasoning was no help to him.

He was afraid.

Why could he not be like Behounek?

Or Sixto?

Why could he not hate with the ideological, orthodox person's conscious and powerful hatred?

Manuel, where have your compromises landed you now? What is the formula for a compromise between fire and water? Steam. Yes, of course.

Suddenly he sat straight up in the dark. Cramped, sweaty grip on the revolver butt. Aimed in the dark.

He had heard steps and someone moving by the door.

Then rustling, chewing, and throat clearing, Fernández. He fell back against the damp pillow.

Then the voices came out of the darkness.

"You're a traitor and to get rid of you is a matter of national interest."

"You filthy, lousy pervert of a swine. Do you know what we do to Indian-lovers . . ."

"And it's impossible to protect you, Ortega. I'm telling you this as a professional man."

"They're crazy; they'll try to kill you, if only for the pleasure of it . . . "

"Manuel . . . be careful . . . they mean it."

"Anyone who betrays us, does so only once . . ."

"It would surprise me if you were still alive this time tomorrow."

"True, we didn't kill the previous Resident, but that wouldn't stop us . . ."

Voices, voices, voices.

At twenty to six his eyelids closed. His right hand slipped down toward the edge of the bed and the Astra slid out of his grip. It fell against the chair and then to the floor with a clatter.

A second later the door was open and Fernández had thrown himself into the room, hunched-up and wild-eyed, but several minutes had gone by before he realized what had happened.

He put the revolver back on the chair, stood in the half light, and looked down at the man on the bed. He shook his head.

"Poor devil," he said.

Manuel Ortega heard nothing and did not move. But he was not really sleeping; he had fainted and was unconscious.

17

∗●∗●∗∗

Two steps across the corridor, left hand on the doorknob, right on the revolver, ice in his heart. Fernández on the chair, cramp in his midriff.

Pale, with dark circles under his eyes, Manuel Ortega went into his office.

He avoided the window, and went on into the next room. Danica, in a red dress, thinner and better cut, lower at the neck.

Thank God. He nearly said it aloud. A normal thought for the first time in hours.

She noticed and looked up at him. She smiled, thoughtfully. He remembered his face in the mirror and knew why.

He stood behind her and had forgotten that he might suddenly die without having had time to find out what she had been about to say.

"I didn't have a good night either," she said. "I shouldn't have bothered about that idiot López, but should have stayed here."

López had implied that she might be in the way.

"Well, no one can stop me from staying tonight. I've even brought some things with me," she said, kicking her bag.

"Were you alone last night?"

"Yes," she said seriously. "When it begins to get like this, then I'm either with the person with whom it begins to get like this, or else alone."

"Nice dress," he said lamely.

"Mmm, but I don't like it. I have to wear a bra with it."

"Does it still hurt?"

"Mmm. But not so much now. And the biggest bruise in the history of erotica."

The telephone rang.

"No," he said. "I'll take it."

He felt quite strong now and wanted to test his strength. The voice was low, almost whispering, and it was impossible to make out whether it belonged to a man or a woman.

"Swine, it'll happen soon now, within twenty-four hours, you don't know when, how, or where, only that it'll happen soon and it might be anywhere or any time, because I know, but I'm not saying any more except that within twenty-four . . ."

He slammed down the receiver. It had not gone well. The test had failed.

"Call Captain Behounek," he snapped, and then he went out of the room.

The churning had begun again.

"What are you doing about these damned telephone calls anyway?" he said when Behounek was on the line.

"Well, what the hell can I do? I've a list of twenty-six here on my desk. Of course I can put a man to writing reports and then they'll get fined a piddling sum in about four or five months' time."

"At least call them up and tell them off."

"I've done that in a couple of cases, in fact. But it's stupid. There was one call which the boys listening in thought sounded especially dangerous. Do you know who it was? An eight-year-old child, son of a director of a bank. And do you know what the bank director said? Just this: The boy has got guts, anyhow."

"But you arrested that woman a week ago, the first evening I was here."

"The situation wasn't the same then, and besides, that wasn't true."

"Look, Captain Behounek."

"Wanted to make a good impression, you know. But I did call her up and tell her off. For that matter, what happened to those statistics I sent you?"

"My man is working on them."

"Stop him at once. Hell, I should have told you several days ago but I forgot all about it."

"What's wrong?"

"Everything's wrong. There isn't a correct figure in the whole damned lot. I've got our own statistics here, worked on and finished. You can look at them when you like."

"What do you mean? Are you quite mad?"

"Not at all. I told you, it was the first time. I didn't know you and didn't know what was going to happen."

"You really are astounding."

"Yes, I know. According to those statistics you got, we have fewer outbreaks of violence than anywhere else in the country. They were compiled on the orders of the Ministry when the question of international inspection came up, United Nations control and God knows what else. They were not even done here for that matter, but at the army statistical department. They'll do for all countries and all climates. You only have to fill in the date and the time. Typical fixing."

Suddenly the conversation changed character.

"Captain Behounek, you feel hatred, don't you?"

"Yes. I feel hatred."

"Why?"

"You came with me to the Pérez house. If you'd seen the same thing fifty times before and sometimes much, much worse, then you'd feel hatred too."

"That's no answer, only an evasion. Your own subordinates commit crimes which are just as bad."

"You don't understand. All this stems from one and the same evil root."

"In Spain I heard tell of a doctrine which runs like this: Sometimes ignorance is so great that the teacher has to kill his pupils, for their own sake. Do you think like that?"

"I'm a policeman and hence more of a doctor than a teacher. If you insist on metaphors then all I can say is this: It's an ancient surgical rule that one cuts away flesh and tissue that have begun to decay before one extracts the bullet from the wound. Similarly, one must disinfect secondary infections before one can attack or even get at the seat of infection."

"But . . ."

"Never mind about all that now. Follow my twelve points instead. How's the conference situation?"

"You'll know in half an hour."

"Good. The water mains were in order a quarter of an hour ago, by the way. We can start having showers again."

The conversation was at an end. It could well have gone on longer. Danica and Behounek were now the only people who could distract him. The churning was starting up again. He stared at the maddeningly sauntering Fernández and said, shrilly and wildly: "Can't you sit still, man?"

"This," said Fernández, "is not a good day."

The churning ground and ground in his diaphragm and in the lower part of his chest.

Danica came in. Everything about the conference seemed to be falling into place. Preparations were being made. All clear from Ellerman. All clear from Irigo. All clear from Dalgren. All clear from Colonel Orbal. The apparatus was functioning. Army service personnel had begun to arrange things at Mercadal.

All was well.

Except one small detail. Manuel Ortega, who wanted only to live, but knew that they would kill him.

His thoughts were in a tangle. Repetition, time and time again, of phrases such as: How shall I survive this day even if nothing happens? It's still only eleven o'clock. All those hours. So long. So many.

The weather was the same. The heat was terrific, the air white and molten. The fan whirred ineffectively, only driving yet more heat down from the ceiling. He drank pints of lemonade. He spoke to Ellerman three times. Once to Dalgren's secretary. Once to Behounek.

Twenty minutes to twelve. He was tired and frightened and soaked with sweat. The skin below his armpits and behind his knees had begun to sting. He thought about having a shower but decided it would be best to wait until López came. He did not want them to be changing guard while he was standing naked and defenseless in the shower.

Gómez was standing in for Fernández and was loitering by the window with his short machine gun resting in the crook of his elbow. Now he's looking across the great white square, thought Manuel. As he himself could not go over to the window, suddenly the dismal view of the palm trees and the empty blocks of apartments presented a burning temptation. But he thought too that as soon as he showed himself someone would pull the trigger of a rifle far away, perhaps from one of the roofs. He had heard that a skilled marksman could hit a target at nine hundred yards. If he had a good telescopic sight. He had also heard that one had time to hear the crack before the bullet landed, and even sooner one should be able to see the flash from the barrel. Perhaps one could even take all this in in the right order; the flash, the crack, the window shattering, and then—the bullet.

He also wondered what it felt like to be shot. He had read somewhere that it was like being felled by a club or hit hard in the solarplexus.

The churning ground on and on. Suddenly he was aware that what was being ground away in there was his strength of will and power of resistance, that all established values were being turned into pulp, that slowly but surely he was being filled with grist, was acquiring new and worthless entrails, gelatinous and useless.

Manuel Ortega was blindly, mindlessly, afraid.

He tried to say something but was not certain whether it would not emerge as a weak whisper. He cleared his throat slightly and said: "Gómez, what does it look like out there?"

His voice was calm and steady.

"Empty," said the man at the window. "Three policemen and a cat."

The door opened and López came in. The man with the machine gun nodded and left.

The sweat was running into Manuel Ortega's eyes. He went to the woman and said: "The water is running. What about a shower?"

"Someone had better stay here, though. We can take one in turns. You go first."

"I want to see the bruise," he said childishly.

"Tonight, my friend. You can see it tonight."

O.K., he thought, I'll go first. Hope it doesn't show too much what's wrong with me. The churning ground on. His right leg seemed paralyzed. His heart had begun to trouble him.

López searched the rooms.

In the shower he thought how foolish it was to be afraid. There were police at the entrance and in the vestibule, and there was a policeman at the entrance to the corridor itself. Danica was in the room beyond his. It would be very difficult to get around one of these people without being observed. To pass two of them should be impossible.

He stood under the shower for a quarter of an hour. When he went into the bedroom and saw the bed he suddenly thought that fear would make him impotent that night.

Then he thought that this was definitely wrong, for if one believed that one was not going to be able to, then one would not be able to.

He thought about this as he dressed.

He took a long time over it and his face and neck were already sweaty before he was ready.

In addition to the churning and the strange things his heart was doing, there was something wrong with his testicles, and his right leg felt dead and useless. There was a thumping in his head. He went back to the shower.

Manuel Ortega ran cold water over his wrists, rinsed his face, and sponged the back of his neck with a wet towel. There was something wrong with his heart, as if it had been pumped up until it filled the whole of the left side of his chest.

Then he drew a deep breath, went through the outer room, and, helplessly abandoned to his fear, thought: This is the ninth day and they really have a reason.

He opened the door and saw López sitting on the swivel chair. Manuel smiled at his inertia, then opened the door and stepped over the threshold.

A man was standing in the middle of the room.

For a fraction of a second Manuel Ortega's brain captured perhaps a hundred sounds and visual impressions and arranged them into a proper pattern. Not a man, but a child, perhaps seventeen years old, with a pale exalted face and frightened eyes, well-brushed black hair with a straight white side-part, and the gun held at face level. The gun stared at him with its black eye of death. Time stood still and perhaps in this last thousandth of a second he would have time to see the bullet's shiny nose push its way out of the barrel. He did not know. But he knew, as he had always known, that his sense of security was false, a mere fiction, that the Astra was stuck under his left arm and would never leave its place, that he had known this every time he had opened this door before. He had known that López would never even have time to get up from the chair. He had known all the time that they would kill him, that Uribarri was right that time so terribly long ago, that they were all mad, even the children, for this was a child.

Manuel Ortega had time to think and register all this during that last thousandth of a second. At the same time he thought of names and women, and small children and churches.

Then everything was drowned in the pulsating roar from Frankenheimer's Colt as the man in the linen suit out on the ledge pumped five shots through the closed window into the back of the child. An upright body with an outstretched arm jerked involuntarily three yards forward and hit the wall by the door, first with the gun and then with its face and chest and stomach and thighs, pulpy and dead, with a smack. It stayed there for a brief few seconds as if stuck against the wall, before sliding down to the floor.

Manuel tottered feebly toward the doorway as López grabbed him by the collar and hurled him backward out into the corridor, and neither of them saw how Frankenheimer calmly knocked out the remains of the windowpane with the butt of his gun and climbed into the room. His hearing was the only sense that seemed to be functioning. Manuel Ortega sat down on a chair by the wall and listened to López and Frankenheimer.

López: "How did he get in?"

Frankenheimer: "It looks as if he got in last night and was here all day."

López: "Where?"

Frankenheimer: "In the other room. Behind that folding screen. In that little niche where there are a few coats hanging up. He stood there waiting, a bit cramped of course, but he was quite small. Yes, and Gómez should have covered that niche."

López: "Gómez is an ass. I've always said so."

Frankenheimer: "Well. Depends how you look at it. He has his ideas sometimes. But the kid must have stood in the niche and waited for you to go out. Then he stood here waiting. That's logical, isn't it?"

López: "Where were you then?"

Frankenheimer: "Around. As always when something's up."

López: "Is the girl dead?"

Frankenheimer: "We haven't checked on that, have we? But she's lying on the floor. I saw that anyway."

López: "She's alive, but doesn't look too good. A lot of blood."

Frankenheimer: "He hit her with the butt of his gun. He wouldn't dare shoot. We'll carry her in and then we've got them both in one place."

López: "Has anyone phoned for an ambulance?"

Frankenheimer: "The police. They're fixing that. I think I can hear the sirens now. Or . . . no?"

López: "Yes, I can hear. You fired a lot of shots."

Frankenheimer: "Well. There wasn't much time and I had to catch the kid off balance. I didn't think you were as quick as you usually are. You'd never have got him."

López: "One gets older."

Frankenheimer: "Yes, yes. But my shots landed where they should've. I didn't dare risk breaking the window first. One really shouldn't shoot through glass. Distortion and all that can deceive the eyes a bit."

López: "True, but it worked well this time."

Frankenheimer: "Yes, I think so."

López: "How long d'you think this job's going to last, by the way?"

Frankenheimer: "Don't know. Hell, I'm beginning to get homesick. The old lady and the kids and all that."

López: "The girl doesn't look so good. Pale."

Frankenheimer: "She'll probably die."

Manuel Ortega sat on the chair with his hands clasped and his elbows on his knees. He could see López and Frankenheimer and the two bodies on the floor, but in a strange light, unreal and as clear as glass, and he thought: I'm alive. Thank God. Thank Frankenheimer. Here lie two dead people but I'm alive.

The sirens had fallen silent outside; steps in the corridor.

Behounek came into the room. Lieutenant Brown was with him and a doctor and a photographer.

"How are things, Ortega?"

"I'm alive."

His voice was firm and clear.

"I can see that, but you're as white as—yes, as a corpse."

"Shock," said the doctor. "I'll give him an injection."

Behounek had walked over to the wall.

"What in God's name did you shoot him with? An elephant gun."

"Ordinary .45," said Frankenheimer. "Five shots."

"Must have all hit him in the same spot."

"One's a little high," said Frankenheimer. "The one in the neck. The last one, I guess."

He was standing by the desk, busy with his revolver; he had emptied the chamber and was reloading.

"The woman is alive," said the doctor. "Get the stretcher quickly. Get a move on over there."

"Will she make it?"

"Should think so. She's lost a good deal of blood. Fracture of the skull, perhaps. Hard to say as yet."

"It looks as if he clouted her with the gun butt," said Frankenheimer.

"And you were standing out on the ledge?" said Behounek. "Do you always stand there?"

"Well, in spells, shall we say. It's like this. There's a pillar just to the left of the window. You get there through an opening in the linen closet on the second staircase. Good place, if I may say so myself, real good place. Yes. We put up two small mirrors there. One can't exactly see them from the inside."

Behounek no longer seemed to be listening.

"Brown," he said, "turn that poor devil over."

"I'm alive," said Manuel Ortega, loudly and distinctly.

"Oh, Jesus Christ," said the Chief of Police, making a sign of the cross.

"I still don't understand how he got in," said López.

"No," said Behounek, "you don't."

"With López, it's always the same—he has to reconstruct everything," said Frankenheimer.

"Oh yes. This I can explain to you. This boy knows the building better than anyone else. Knew it, I mean. He had almost certainly crept up through every ventilation shaft and every fire escape in the place. And he also had access to all the keys."

"Well, he must have come in some peculiar way," said Frankenheimer.

"It's possible. He's played here since he was four years old."

Manuel rose from the chair and went over to the Chief of Police. He walked steadily and calmly and his eyes were shining.

Behounek looked at him.

"Shock," said the doctor. "I'll give him an injection in a minute. Then we'll put him to bed."

Manuel took hold of Behounek's arm and looked down at the youngster on the floor. Again he saw the pale narrow face and the hair which was still smooth and black and well brushed. But the face was no longer tense and exalted; the features seemed to have relaxed and now they were simply childish. One of Frankenheimer's bullets had passed clean through the neck; the wound showed above the white collar, but there was not much blood around it. In the buttonhole of the elegant jacket sat a little yellow rosette with a cockade and the initials of the Citizens' Guard.

"Who is he?" said Manuel Ortega, and he heard his own voice echo in the crystal-clear white air.

"His name is Pedro," said Behounek. "Pedro Orbal, Colonel Orbal's son. He's sixteen years old and should be at school at this time of day."

Frankenheimer had put away his revolver. He buttoned up his sagging linen jacket, walked over to the wall, and picked up the black gun that had been left lying on the floor. He looked at it and mumbled absent-mindedly: "Nine-millimeter Browning. Ordinary army issue. Not fired."

"Oh yes," said López.

"This is going to be nice," said Behounek. "Very nice."

18

✳●✳●✳✳

———————————

The room was quite strange to him. So were the bed, the nightshirt, and the whirring noise. It was not a big room but it was clean and neat, with white walls and a light globe in the ceiling. There was no carpet on the floor and only a little furniture: a chest of drawers, a chair, and a small desk. The shutters were closed and in the grayish half light he saw that the noise came from a ventilation cylinder with a built-in fan. It was on the wall, level with the end of the bed, and despite the heat, the air seemed clean and fresh. He was not even sweating.

When he turned on his side he found his watch, cigarettes, and glasses lying on the bedside table. The Astra was there too and when he saw it he felt a jab in his chest and began to remember.

Half a minute later he was soaked with sweat and his hand shook as he reached out for his watch.

It was half past eight and it must have been morning. Everything seemed very still and he could not make out any noise from outside.

"Fernández!" he called.

Nothing happened and he called again twice, his voice hoarse and raucous.

Then he thought he ought to get up. He threw off the sheet and swung his legs over the edge of the bed. He sat with his feet on the warm floor and tried to think. It did not work very well.

His throat was dry and he drank a glass of lukewarm water which had been standing on the bedside table. He looked at the Astra and the cigarettes and the glasses and could grasp nothing at all.

Manuel Ortega sat there and was afraid of a white enamel iron bedstead in a strange room. He was unshaven and wore a cotton nightshirt which came down to his knees. His eyes flickered uncertainly.

The door opened and Captain Behounek came in. He looked as if he had just got up and smelled of shaving lotion and toothpaste. He put his cap down on the desk, flung open the shutters, and turned the fan down.

"Good morning," he said cheerfully.

"Where's Fernández?"

"I sent him home yesterday, him and Frankenheimer and the other two. You don't need them any longer. And yesterday was convenient too, as there was a convoy going north."

He sat down in the only chair in the room and looked cheerfully at the man in the nightshirt.

"I must say you don't look so good, but things'll soon be better. No, don't say anything. I'll explain first, otherwise it'll all be so long-winded. It's Sunday today and it's a quarter to nine in the morning. Yesterday was Saturday and you slept all day. You were awake for a while but I'm sure you don't remember it. We gave you an injection and you went to sleep again. You're in the officers' quarters at the police station, in other words with me. I have the room next door and Lieutenant Brown had this room until the day before yesterday. I've arranged for you to have an office in our administrative block and I've had all your papers and belongings moved here. I won't take the responsibility of having you over there any longer. And we've also got quite a bit to talk about. You had a severe shock at the shooting on Friday and you seem to have been overtaxing yourself before that too. Our doctor says that you should feel a lot better today. He also says I shouldn't mention the shooting when I talk to you, but I won't bother about that. We must be able to talk to each other. Your secretary . . ."

"Danica?"

"Yes, her. I don't know whether you remember that she was knocked unconscious at the time?"

Manuel Ortega nodded. He remembered. He remembered every detail he had seen in the clear white light and he also remembered that he had seen her lying on the floor and that all the time he had thought she was dead or dying and that he had not even minded.

"Well, she's not in much danger. Concussion and a hole in her head. She's in the military hospital and I gather she can leave the day after tomorrow or thereabouts. She sent a letter to you, by the way. And there's another letter for you too which came on the mail helicopter from the capital yesterday morning. And an official cable. They're all here on the desk."

Manuel frowned.

"And the conference?"

"Going according to plan. I've been in contact with both Ellerman and Dalgren and the person in charge at Mercadal."

He looked at his watch.

"May I suggest that you get up and get ready now? The shower and lavatory are on the other side of the corridor. I'll come and get you in half an hour. Then we'll have a talk which unfortunately may well be less pleasant."

"Is there anyone on guard outside?"

"No. No need. You're quite safe here. And your position isn't so tricky any longer either. People think differently about you now. And the shooting has made the right-wing activists halt in their tracks. In fact it's quite calm everywhere. The truce is being honored."

When Behounek had gone. Manuel Ortega opened the door a little and peered out. The corridor was empty but nevertheless he wound a towel around the Astra and took it with him when he went to shower and shave.

Manuel had time to go through his letters before the Chief of Police came back.

The cable was from the capital and ran: CONGRATULA-TIONS STOP A VERY CLEVER AND DARING MOVE STOP BE CAUTIOUS NEXT FEW DAYS STOP IF NECESSARY SEEK PRO-TECTION FROM BEHOUNEK. ZAFORTEZA.

He read through the cable several times and shook his head in bewilderment. Then he looked at the time of dispatch. Friday, twelve o'clock, before the shooting. He put the cable in his pocket.

Then an airmail letter with Swedish stamps on it. His wife had typed four pages about absolutely nothing. It had been raining and the children were well. He skipped most of it. The letter came from a distant and incomprehensible world to which he could scarcely believe he had ever belonged. He shrugged his shoulders and threw the letter into the waste basket under the desk.

The other letter was in a white envelope marked with the official stamp of the military hospital. Along one of the sides was a gray label which read: CENSURA MILITAR.

Danica wrote:

"My friend. Thank heavens you are all right. I don't re-member a thing myself. Have a slight headache and a huge bandage and they tell me I may write a little. I like you. Can't you come here and ask me how I am? Love. Danica."

After "they tell me" there was the beginning of a sentence which had been crossed out. "Manuel, I think I'm beginning to be . . ."

He was still sitting with the letter in his hand when the Chief of Police came to get him. Manuel showed him Danica's letter and took the cable out of his pocket.

"Of course you can go and see the girl," said Behounek. "I'll send a patrol with you."

"Do you understand this then?"

Behounek looked briefly at the cable.

"Yes, indeed I do," he said, and he laughed.

Then he said indifferently: "Just a compliment. They evidently appreciate your work. Come on down to my room now."

Manuel felt as if everything were happening on the other side of a glass wall. A veil seemed to hang between himself and reality. Everything he saw and heard was in some way smothered, and not even here in the corridor at police headquarters and a few feet from the Chief of Police could he rid himself of his timidity and fear.

In the vestibule Lieutenant Brown came forward with some papers. Behounek stopped and said: "Go on in and sit down for the time being, Ortega. I'll be with you in a moment."

Manuel opened the door and started back as if he had been struck. There was someone already in there. Not until he saw that the person seemed not to have even noticed him could he bring himself to step inside, his heart thumping.

The man was perhaps fifty-five, and was wearing polished black shoes and a dark, well-pressed suit. He was rather small, had gray hair and a gray mustache, and his thin face was sunburned and furrowed. He was leaning forward with his hands on the window sill and seemed troubled by the sun streaming through the windowpane. Outside there was a concrete yard and a couple of policemen loading ammunition boxes onto a jeep with a canvas top.

The man by the window was not looking out, however. Probably he could see nothing at all. He was weeping, silently but unrestrainedly. His shoulders were shaking and the tears poured down his cheeks.

Manuel took an uncertain step toward the window but then stopped. The man took no notice of him and seemed unaware of the fact that there was anyone else in the room. Manuel went over to the map and looked at the colored pins for a while. He searched for Mercadal; there were eight white pins there.

Behounek came in and carefully shut the door behind him. The man by the window did not move. The Chief of Police cleared his throat and said: "Well, I don't believe you two gentlemen have met before, have you?"

The man turned around. He was still weeping and his friendly brown eyes were glistening and inflamed.

"May I introduce Don Manuel Ortega, the Provincial Resident, and Colonel Joaquín Orbal, Deputy Military Governor and Chief of Staff of the Fifth Military Command."

Manuel had already taken two steps forward and stretched out his hand. Now he stopped hesitantly. Colonel Orbal took a black silk handkerchief out of his breast pocket and wiped his eyes and cheeks. Then he shook hands with Manuel, briefly and firmly.

"Let's not make this meeting any more painful than it already is," he said. "The fact that I cannot hide my feelings and grief must not influence you. But Pedro was my only child . . ."

He took out his handkerchief again and discreetly blew his nose.

"To you, Señor Resident, I must apologize on my son's behalf. A terrible mistake has been made and the consequences are no less fearful. However, my son was not alone in his misjudgment of your intentions. Many were guilty of the same failure and the overwhelming majority have not yet grasped the motives behind your action."

"Just as well," put in Behounek mildly.

"Well, anyhow, I must beg forgiveness and Pedro has already forfeited his life . . ."

Manuel Ortega had at last succeeded in formulating something to say.

"I hope that you don't for one moment doubt that I am wholly without conscious blame for what happened."

"Gentlemen," said Behounek. "There's been a catastrophe. No one can be blamed for what has happened. No one could have prevented or influenced the actual course of events. I think that any further discussion of the matter will only cause unnecessary pain."

He clasped his hands behind his back and swayed backward and forward on his heels and toes. Then he said: "We can look on this meeting as a pure formality and as an official contact in connection with the coming negotiations. The conference is to be led by you, sir, as Resident, while you, Colonel Orbal, will be the chairman of the Citizens' Guard delegation. To introduce more detailed considerations at this time would be inopportune."

Colonel Orbal nodded absent-mindedly and returned to his place by the window. Without turning around he said: "How many people have been killed here in the last two years?"

"About five thousand."

"And all this comes from the same evil seed, from the same little clique of incorrigible fanatics. We must smash them. We must smash the rats."

"Yes," said Behounek. "We're going to smash them."

Colonel Orbal turned with a jerk and stared at Manuel Ortega.

"I was just standing there and thinking about a strange little detail," he said. "If you were dead, then my son would be alive. I was standing there wishing you were dead. So far as I know, I have never before wished for the death of anyone, apart from enemies of my country in my capacity as a soldier."

He shrugged his shoulders.

"Well," he said, "truth is strange. Life for a life. Now I'll go back home. My wife is suffering terribly from the grief which has overtaken us. You can contact me there then. Good morning, sirs."

Manuel Ortega thought: Colonel Orbal. Leader of the

extreme right wing. Organizer of terror. The protector of the blasting details. A gray old man who wept.

"Oh well," said Behounek, "that went off more painlessly than I had dared hope."

Manuel looked at him. The veil was still there, making everything incomprehensible and unattainable. Behounek took out a cigar, bit off the end, and said: "I'm going on a trip around town now. D'you want to come too?"

Manuel shook his head.

"No. I'd rather stay here."

"You can feel quite safe with me. At least, as safe as I feel myself. I'm going to see Dalgren."

"Dalgren has as little interest in meeting me as I have in meeting him."

"You're wrong. His attitude had changed radically. When he saw the stand that the Ministry of the Interior has taken, he, like the rest of the inner circle, realized that publishing Larrinaga's idiotic proclamation was a trick to win the confidence of the Communists and to persuade them to agree to the conference."

"But it's not like that," said Manuel. "I've never thought of it in that way at all."

"I know that," said Behounek drily. "But so far I'm about the only one who does."

He went to the door and put on his cap.

"You won't come?"

"No."

"You daren't?"

"No."

"I understand."

He stopped, as if he had just thought of something else, and said: "But I know what you can do instead. Go up to the hospital and see your little friend with the beautiful feet."

Manuel shook his head.

"Silly," said Behounek: "You'll have three policemen and a

covered jeep with you. It's four minutes away and the town is virtually empty. I'll go and order a car. It'll be outside in five minutes."

He left.

As the white jeep passed the sentries, Manuel Ortega was seized with panic. He broke out in a cold sweat and hunched down, trying to press himself as far into the corner as possible. The policeman looked at him in astonishment. He could feel the Astra against his ribs, but it made no difference. It had already failed him once and could no longer give him an illusion of safety.

Danica Rodríguez was lying in the officers' department, in a small air-conditioned room with white walls. Two of the policemen went with him to the door, but stayed outside, as did the nun who had shown them the way and unlocked the door.

The woman in the bed looked pale and thin and her lips were dry and split. She no longer had a bandage around her head, but they had shaved off some of the hair from her scalp and put on a dressing. Her eyes were large and dark gray and serious.

Manuel sat down on the edge of the bed. After a moment's hesitation, he kissed her on the forehead and said: "Hello. How are you?"

"Better. Headache's gone. And you?"

"Not bad."

"You don't look too good. How's everything going?"

"Very well. The conference starts tomorrow."

"Manuel, lean over a little nearer."

He obeyed.

"Listen," she said. "I didn't ask you to come just to have a chat and be told everything's all right."

He did not know what to say. Moreover, he felt nothing special for her, at least not at that moment. She went on: "First of all, I'll tell you about what I didn't want to talk about before. I'm a member of Irigo's Communist Party and I work to a certain extent with the Liberation Front. That's why I wanted this job, and I managed to wangle it in the end. I would have got it before, in Larrinaga's time, except that he insisted on having a male secretary, an adjutant. And what's more, Sixto is my brother. I'm telling you this because I want you to know, now that you are alone."

"I see."

"No, you don't see. When I woke up yesterday I had a feeling that something didn't quite add up in practically everything we've done."

She fell silent.

"Is that all?"

She looked at him with huge clear eyes and said so quietly that he had to strain to catch the words: "Manuel, could the conference be a trap?"

"How could it be?"

"I don't know. But somehow or other everything went so smoothly. The right-wing extremists never wanted to negotiate before, and now they've agreed to everything. Could it be a way of getting hold of these people whom they've never been able to catch before, who have eluded Dalgren and Orbal and Behounek and the police and the army for years?"

"Neither the government nor the President would dare or even be able to commit such a breach of faith. They've even issued written guarantees."

"I know. But still . . . Are you absolutely certain all the same that something isn't awry? You must find out. Now. Today."

"Yes," he said. "I'll look into it. But I'm almost certain your misgivings are unfounded, that you're wrong."

"But you promise?"

"Yes."

Now that he was near her he began to feel differently. He was conscious of her physical presence under the white blanket. At the same time he felt safer and less afraid. He even managed to smile.

"How's the bruise?" he said.

"Still there. If it weren't so awkward I'd show you. They've given me such a peculiar nightdress."

"Well, see you the day after tomorrow."

"Day after tomorrow?"

"Yes, you'll be out then."

"No one has said anything to me about it. The patient is never told anything. It's like being in prison here. They even lock the door."

"Typical army."

"What bad luck we have when we're about to sleep with each other."

"Be all right the day after tomorrow."

"Yes, I've had enough of this nonsense now."

Suddenly he said: "Danica."

"Yes."

"I like you so much."

She stretched up her hand and, putting her strong thin fingers on the back of his neck, she pulled him down against her shoulder, and whispered in his ear: "Manuel, I told you from the start that I'm not worth having. Everything I try just goes to pieces."

She let him go.

"Wait, I want to show you something."

He sat up.

"Some mail came yesterday," she said. "I had a letter which had been forwarded from Copenhagen. From my husband— yes, we never got a proper divorce. I liked him so much, but it went wrong. You see, I destroy those I like and I don't know how or why. We met five years ago in the capital. The Party was allowed then and we got out a newspaper together. He wrote well and everyone said he was a born journalist and propagandist. We had such a good time together, but then it began to go wrong. Piece after piece began to fall off—we tried to glue them on again but it just went on breaking up. And it was nearly always my fault, I think. Last time we met was in Copenhagen eighteen months ago. It was . . . well, it didn't work. Then he left. This letter is the first word I've had from him since then. Take it and read it. I want you to read it."

He looked at the envelope. It was typed, with a Czechoslovakian stamp on it, and it had been mailed in Prague.

"I like him more than anyone else in the world," she said. "I want to be good and not hurt him. Read it."

Manuel opened the letter. It was quite short and looked as if it had been written by a child. The handwriting was large and round and uncertain. He read:

"Dear Dana. I have wanted to write for a long time but I find it difficult and could not do it but the doctor says that it is good for me if I do and now I am trying to. When I left you I went to France and then on to Spain and it went well and then I went to Bulgaria and across the border to Greece. That did not go well because they took us there. They beat me a lot every day for three weeks, I think it was, and then I was not very well. Then they let me out and I got across the border to Sofia and then came here. It is good here but I don't seem to be able to do anything. Nothing comes to anything and the doctor says I must go out and he has bought me a brown suit and a hat too but I don't seem to be able to. Dana dear this is not at all what I meant to say but I have been writing it for several days and it doesn't get any better and the doctor says send it. Hope you are well. Your Felipe."

At the bottom of the letter someone had added a note in English in red ink and very small handwriting:

"Dear Mrs. Rodríguez. From several points of view it would be a good thing if you could reply to this letter. Yours faithfully, Jaroslav Jiracek, M.D., Bulovka Hospital, Prague."

Manuel Ortega put the letter back on the table by her bed. "Are you going to go there?"

"Give me a cigarette, will you please. I suppose you're not allowed to smoke here but to hell with that."

She took a few nervous puffs and then said: "I don't know. No, yes, no. I can't do anything for him anyway. I know what it'll be like."

He had no reply to that, so he sat silent for a while.

Suddenly she said: "Manuel, what is it that we are doing? What is it that everyone in the world is doing?"

At that moment the nun came in. Her long black habit trailed on the floor.

"I'm sorry," she said, "but you may not stay any longer now."

Danica put her hand on the nape of his neck again and he went to her, lying with his nose against her throat.

"You won't forget."

"No."

"If anything's wrong, you must warn them."

"Yes. See you tomorrow. Darling."

"Yes. See you tomorrow."

In the small white air-conditioned room the veil had vanished, but as soon as he was sitting in the car it reappeared. He sweated and pressed back into the corner.

"Oh, my God, as long as I can get away from here," whispered Manuel Ortega.

19

✳●✳●✳✳

It was half past nine when Behounek opened the door and said: "Come on—let's go to the club and eat."

Manuel Ortega had not seen him since long before the siesta. He himself had sat in his room, made a few calls, and seen everything slide into place, smoothly and with precision. The preparations in Mercadal were complete. Irigo was to come in a chartered helicopter the following morning. Everything was perfect.

The day had been hot and suffocating but no worse than usual.

He had also thought quite a bit about Danica Rodríguez and her questions, and he had formulated some of his own. These questions were troubling, but on the other hand he had watertight evidence to show that Danica must be wrong. In his safe lay the government's promises and guarantees, signed by Radamek and his Prime Minister, documents which could not be false.

He had been afraid all day, not terrified or agitated, but more the victim of a passive fear, a helpless, creeping unpleasantness which made him feel weak and ineffectual.

Manuel went with Behounek to the club. They ate an expensive and very bad meal and talked about inessentials. At eleven o'clock they drove back to headquarters. In the big hall, Manuel Ortega said: "Captain Behounek, may I ask you one thing?"

"Of course."

"Is the conference a trap?"

"Come on into my room."

The Chief of Police closed the shutters and switched on his desk lamp. They sat opposite one another.

"Yes," said Behounek.

"I asked: Is the conference a trap?"

"And I answered: Yes. Or more precisely: It is a wolf pit set for the country's most dangerous enemies."

"What'll happen?"

"They'll be arrested."

"By you?"

"Yes. Or, if you prefer, by the Federal Police."

"I'll stop you doing it."

"No, Ortega, you won't stop me."

"You forget that I still have some authority. I can ask for military assistance."

"Where from?"

"You're overlooking the fact that there are two thousand regular infantrymen in the immediate vicinity of the town. You're also overlooking the fact that I can still reach both the Minister of the Interior and the President by cable. That is, assuming that you do not intend to use force against me."

"Ortega, let's get this clear once and for all. It's high time. First: There are no troops here. Just a force of about sixty or seventy men for guard duties. I really thought you knew that. The night before you came the Third Infantry Regiment was moved north. Together with all other regular forces of the Fifth Military Command they've been on the alert for eight days along the northern border of the province. For eight days those troops have been in control of all roads and communications. That's why poor Ruiz couldn't let you have more than three vehicles, why he had to order out even the cooks and tailors and orderlies to the pumping station and the reservoirs. He had no regiment at all. That's why I was afraid too—yes, really frightened—during the rioting a week ago. As far as the other thing goes, you needn't cable the

Minister of the Interior. You can call him up, right now, and get through to him in twenty minutes."

"Aren't the lines still cut?"

"The lines never were cut. But the army installed a control post at the border and let through only certain calls."

Manuel Ortega stared at the man in the white uniform.

"But you can't call up the President," said Behounek.

"Why not?"

"Because at the present moment there is no President. Radamek left the country today, this morning."

"But the government?"

"The government will be dissolved at about six o'clock tomorrow evening."

"And you think that this gives you a free hand to break all the promises that the outgoing government has given? No, Captain Behounek . . ."

"One moment, Ortega. I am a federal official, as you are, and I act according to orders."

"What orders? From whom?"

Behounek rose, unlocked the safe in the wall, and took out several papers.

"Here," he said, "you will see the orders for the arrest of the six Communist delegates. Signed by the Prime Minister. This was flown here yesterday."

"Jacinto Zaforteza is not the Prime Minister."

"But he will be at seven o'clock tomorrow evening, when this order is to be carried out."

"And who will be President?"

"Who do you think?"

Manuel Ortega burst out laughing, a half-surprised re- signed laughter. He leaned his elbow on the edge of the desk and rested his forehead against the palm of his hand.

"Yes, of course," he said. "So simple. General Gami."

"According to rumors I've heard, nine of the commanders in the field out of thirteen support General Gami's candidacy."

"You call it candidacy too. A candidate who has thirty thousand regular troops on the alert, ready to march against the capital and take over all the important positions?"

"Well, call it what you like. That, however, is the situation."

"Will Orbal be Minister of Defense?"

"Hardly. But a general and Commander-in-Chief of the Fifth Military Command."

"And you yourself?"

There was a long pause before Behounek replied. First he looked at the wall map, then at Manuel Ortega. Finally he said: "I shall get my reward tomorrow evening."

"When you arrest these poor people?"

"Yes. Then I hope to be allowed to leave this province, forever."

"And I am to be sacrificed?"

"Not at all. You have, as far as I can make out, done your duty very well. You've even performed a miracle, though it was unintentional. The appointment itself probably won't exist much longer, but in the administration there's rarely a shortage of appointments for faithful workers."

"Then it's my honor that's to be sacrificed? Don't you consider . . . ?"

"What don't I consider?"

"That I'm committing a terrible betrayal against these poor people?"

"That's the second time you've used that phrase, Ortega, and the first time was once too many. These poor people bear the blame for the sacrifice of five thousand lives during the last two years. Their struggle was senseless from the very beginning, bound to fail. It resulted in chaos, confusion, and degradation in which people were turned into mad dogs. Like those three mineworkers in Pérez's villa. Like Colonel Orbal's sixteen-year-old son. Like . . ."

"Like yourself, Captain Behounek . . ."

"Yes, like myself. That's absolutely true."

He fell silent and drummed his fingers on the top of the desk.

"Do you think I'd overlook such an important detail as myself and my own actions?"

"You yourself are evidence of your own rightness, then?"

"Yes, unfortunately."

"And if I reach over the desk and pick up the telephone and tell Ellerman and warn him, what'll you do then?"

"You won't warn Ellerman. And that's why you'll never know what would have happened if you had."

Manuel was still sitting with his head in his hands. He felt an emptiness rising within him and thought about the churning ache.

He changed his position and put his clenched fists under his chin and looked at Behounek. The Chief of Police was sitting quite still with his arms on the desk and his hands loosely clasped.

Manuel leaned forward and pulled the telephone toward him. He lifted the receiver.

"Hotel Universal, please. . . . I want to speak to Señor Wolfgang Ellerman, please."

There was a long wait before Ellerman replied. He had evidently been asleep, for his voice sounded harsh and confused.

"Yes, Ellerman speaking."

"Ortega. Sorry to disturb you, but it's a matter of the utmost importance."

"Yes?"

A moment later.

"Yes? Are you there?"

"Can you give me the exact time of Dr. Irigo's arrival tomorrow?"

"Between half past nine and half past ten. I can't be more precise than that, I'm afraid."

"That'll do. Thank you. Good night."

Manuel put down the receiver and pushed the telephone away. He put both elbows on the table, clasped his hands, and pressed his knuckles against the base of his nose. He listened to his heart.

Behounek had not moved once the whole time. Neither had he said anything and it was impossible to determine whether he was looking at anything at all. Now he said: "I loathe playing with hidden cards. Therefore, before we continue this conversation, I must let you have a look at one more document."

He extracted one of the papers.

"These instructions are for you," he said. "It was intended that I should give them to you tomorrow, an hour before the beginning of the operation. Here you are."

Manuel took the document and turned it and twisted it before breaking the seal.

The government's memorandum was in the form of a personal letter; it was prefaced with a few conventional phrases but came swiftly to the point.

". . . owing to the President's sudden departure for reasons of health and the consequent necessity to re-form the government, the situation is now considerably altered. General Gami's first measure as President is to eliminate the threat from both internal and external enemies of the nation. In these endeavors he has the government's full support. To this purpose the Federal Court has today made two announcements. First: The Federal Court confirms (rejecting President Radamek's proposal) the legislature's bill declaring the already disbanded Communist and left-wing socialist parties in the country illegal. This means that all members of Communist or crypto-Communist organizations, from 12.00 p.m. today on, can be regarded as reasonably suspected of crimes against the laws of the state and should be considered a threat to the security of the nation. Second: The Federal Court confirms that the ideological orientation of the so-called Liberation Front is clearly Communist. (In this respect the Federal Court has aligned itself with both the legislature and ex-President Radamek.) I therefore urge you to treat all relevant matters in accordance with the above judicial decisions.

"To ensure a smooth interim period a military state of emergency in your province is to be reimposed from 1800 hours today on. This will be lifted after a short period of time. The Federal Police have been granted unlimited authority to apply martial law.

"I advise you to cooperate closely with the Chief of the Federal Police, Captain Isidoro Behounek, who has received detailed instructions in this matter.

Zaforteza. Prime Minister"

Manuel Ortega folded the paper and leaned back in his chair.

"This is the end," he said. "And your name's Isidoro, is it? I didn't know that."

"Yes, isn't it awful? Children should have the legal right to rechristen themselves when they've reached a reasonably mature age."

"Call up the Federal Court and tell the commissionaire that a new law on the matter must be confirmed within twenty minutes."

The Chief of Police smiled.

"Listen, Captain Behounek. Here I am, sitting here, and in my hand I have an order which is dated tomorrow and which among other things contains two decisions made by the country's highest judicial authority, which will also be made public tomorrow. The order is written by someone who thinks he will be the head of the government tomorrow and is issued by a general who is thinking of becoming a dictator tomorrow."

"Today, Ortega, all this is happening today. It's already a quarter to one."

"It seems to mean that Gami, whom I have never met but who obviously is just an ordinary power-mad officer, before he has even succeeded in making himself dictator, can direct the highest judicial authorities and the country's legislature."

"You forget Zaforteza. He has been the Minister of Justice in three governments."

"What does he look like, this Gami?"

"Like most generals. Nothing special. Slightly corpulent. Red-nosed. Fat wife. Four children."

"Does this mean that the death sentences are also already prepared?"

"In principle . . . yes. Only three of them are completed however, those on El Campesino, Irigo, and José Redondo. I've got about twenty blanks, though. All signed by Colonel Orbal."

"And who will fill them in?"

"I shall."

Manuel Ortega felt that the cocoon which had separated him from the world now enveloped the man on the other side of the desk too. He said: "If we could get on to a less formal level, I would like to ask you: What pressures do you think could have persuaded Radamek into making this sudden exit?"

"Well, informally speaking, I can say this: Radamek and the whole of the Liberal regime had gotten to the stage where it was a question of blinding the opposition here at home and gagging the talkers abroad. It has been dependent on the support of the army all the time and has certainly never taken one single independent decision. Zaforteza has been the driving force in the cabinet and he is in all respects the general's man. As far as Radamek is concerned, I'm convinced that he did everything for money. He could hardly be described as hard up when he left the country yesterday."

"And yet it was he who created the Peace Force," said Manuel."

"Yes," said Behounek, glancing at the map. "He created the white police, the Federal Police, the Peace Force."

"And when the Peace Force goes to a village everyone runs to the woods and women hide their children under rags and piles of sticks."

"There are no woods here, but you're right in principle."

"How many village populations have you wiped out, as in Santa Rosa?"

"About ten, perhaps. Always for the same reason. They've helped El Campesino's murder gangs hide or flee. Sometimes they themselves have plundered and killed."

"Do you feel very unhappy when you think about it?"

"Sometimes, yes. But not often. You exaggerate in your mind the drama of what happens on such occasions. In fact it's just routine, no grand gestures. Usually at five in the morning. That's a time of day which doesn't invite melodramatic actions. But many have died, that's true. Who is to blame, then?"

"Now we're back there again. And I repeat. The blame is yours."

"Because I obey orders?"

"Yes."

"It's as well, both for you and for me, that you're wrong. The blame lies with men like this Cuban, El Campesino, who have taught impoverished illiterates to kill. With ridiculous theorists like Irigo and Ellerman and with spreaders of hatred like Carmen Sánchez."

"And with madmen like Isidoro Behounek."

"To some extent, yes."

"With madness."

"And, Ortega, with inconsistency, don't forget that."

"As I said."

"One must choose a side."

"Must one?"

"Yes, definitely."

"Have you, Captain Behounek, ever played with the thought of letting mercy go before justice?"

"Many times, but not in cases like these."

"Then it's unrealistic to expect a certain mildness on your part tomorrow? Some kind of barter?"

"Let's sleep on it."

They went to their rooms.

Between three o'clock and three minutes past three in the morning on June 19, Manuel Ortega, formerly an assistant trade attaché in Stockholm, thought:

I must call Ellerman. I must call Ellerman. I must call Ellerman. If I call Ellerman, I am staking my life and in any case destroying forever my career and my livelihood. I would be officially guilty of failing in my duty and would end up in prison. The logical thing would be for them to kill me at once. If I break the promises made to the Liberation Front, then Sixto will kill me. I must flee, immediately. Nevertheless, I must call Ellerman.

Suddenly: Manuel Ortega, you're a federal official. Your duty is to obey orders until those orders are rescinded.

Nevertheless, I must call Ellerman.

Why must you call Ellerman? Because you happened to say you would to a nymphomaniac you want to sleep with? That's irrelevant.

But you must.

You know that you're not going to call Ellerman. The churning has stopped. The grinding is over.

Conversation along a stony mountain road, in the front seat of a white Land-Rover with a canvas top.

Ortega: "Why did you tell me all that yesterday?"

Behounek. "Because I wanted you to know exactly what you were doing. So that you will never at any time be able to say, not even to yourself, that you were acting in good faith or under the influence of surprise. However you act now, you are doing it fully conscious of the fact that you have analyzed the situation, even if during a sleepless night. In the future you can probably deceive others, but I don't want to give you the chance of deceiving yourself."

Ortega: "You took a considerable risk."

Behounek: "I considered it was a small one. You're an official. You fight according to orders with your papers, as I do with my gun."

Ortega: "I've still got a couple of hours."

Behounek: "Time's running out. Besides, you're not capable of making a decision. You're frightened and tired. The easiest decision is always not to make one."

Ortega: "For that matter, was it you who arranged the murder of Larrinaga?"

Behounek: "No, that was an internal army affair."

Ortega: "Who was Pablo Gonzáles?"

Behounek: "You've a good memory—but that wasn't his name."

Ortega: "What was his name?"

Behounek: "Bartolomeo Rozas. A Communist worker we arrested and executed a few days before the murder."

Ortega: "And the real murderer?"

Behounek: "Don't know. One of the young right-wingers they brought here from somewhere. I just supplied the identity papers. They didn't even bother to inform the officer in command of the escort. And the murderer was shot, much to his surprise. He probably expected that they would . . . let mercy go before justice."

Ortega: "Would you under *any* circumstances let mercy go before justice?"

Behounek: "Hardly any."

Ortega: "What about our barter?"

Behounek: "What barter?"

Ortega: "I offer my honor and refrain from warning them. You offer your hatred and refrain from killing them."

Behounek: "That's no honorable barter, because you won't warn them anyway. Besides, I've certain orders to take into consideration, just as you have. We're officials."

Ortega: "I can still call Ellerman. Some of these people can still be saved."

Behounek: "You never consider the question whether they are worth saving. You never think that perhaps we can save ten thousand other people by killing these six. For that matter, shall I arrest your secretary?"

Ortega: "Not if it can be avoided."

Behounek: "Of course it can be avoided. If I want to avoid it. You probably know she's a Communist and even a member of the Party."

Ortega: "Have you known that all along?"

Behounek: "Almost. She's down on our books. A miracle she succeeded in duping the ministry."

Ortega: "It can be avoided then. But are you thinking of avoiding it?"

Behounek: "Let me make a proposal for once. I arrest your secretary and in exchange we refrain from executing Carmen Sánchez. Both will get prison, perhaps five or ten years. You can choose between having Carmen Sánchez dead or Danica Rodríguez free—or both in jail."

Ortega: "Do you mean that seriously?"

Behounek: "Of course not. And I won't suggest exchanging your secretary's life for the six people we're going to execute tonight."

Ortega: "Thank you. Why must it take place tonight?"

Behounek: "In a few days the state of emergency will be

lifted, no one knows when. Then the time for death sentences will have gone."

Ortega: "And Danica Rodríguez?"

Behounek: "Can go of course. For that matter, she's not very dangerous. A little naïve, half-intellectual. And she sleeps around. It may be tempting but it's not a good method. Nearly always ends badly."

Ortega: "Spare me your wisdom."

Behounek: "Certainly."

Ortega: "Strangely enough, right up until this morning I thought it was fear that had broken me. Only now do I realize that it has been you."

Behounek: "It's neither. We are wholly victims of ourselves, our own thoughts and our own actions. I was the first victim of my activities down here."

Ortega: "You're beginning to be banal."

Behounek: "I'm a little tired. You see the houses over there on the other side of the quarry?"

Ortega: "Yes."

Behounek: "That's Mercadal."

Manuel Ortega, you, at the desk on the platform. Behind you your assistant and a secretary you've never seen. And in front of you the faces.

You speak: "The other delegates should be here by now. They've been delayed by their deliberations—internal procedural matters, I imagine."

Human faces. Which have names.

Irigo—white-haired, wrinkled old man's hands, horn-rimmed glasses. He is trembling a little—he is afraid.

El Campesino—partisan expert from Cuba, tall and strong, and brown eyes, restless, watchful—afraid.

Carmen Sánchez—slim with short hair, defiant. Already biting her nails—afraid.

El Rojo Redondo—heavy and large and coarse, hairy

wrists, wiping the sweat from his forehead—already afraid.

Two more men but neither of them Sixto. Not Sixto.

These will die. But you are alive. Thank you, God. (Must go to mass soon. Thank you, Frankenheimer. Thank you, Behounek.)

Treachery and already they know it.

That uproar—those overturned chairs—those cries. Those white uniforms—those odds against—those machine guns— those glittering chains between the handcuffs—those metallic clicks in the locks—that roar of engines—those looks—that distant reality—those faces on the other side of the veil.

Manuel Ortega remained sitting at the chairman's desk while the police took out the prisoners. Captain Behounek had not put in an appearance.

Ten miles from the town they saw the fireworks and the bonfires. Red, green, white, purple, the rockets drew rising curves across the night sky.

In the beam on the spotlight in front of the radiator they could see yellowish-gray gravel and a great many stones and once a little lizard. The heat had become more oppressive and sultry after nightfall. The night lay over the countryside like a sleeping hairy black animal.

"They're already celebrating the victory," said Behounek. "General Gami's appointment has been made official. Colonel Orbal is probably speaking from the window of the Governor's Palace."

"Are the rockets coming from the villa area?"

"No, from all over the town. Fifty thousand rockets and roman candles have been distributed. Suggested by the Citizens' Guard."

"To usher in the new President?"

"Naturally. Then there'll be executions for a week or two. But as soon as they're dealt with, he'll remember his old province and lift the state of emergency. The people will be happy and will be able to walk about in their own streets. He'll become a hero for a few days. General Gami knows how to do it all. He's neither the first nor the last to climb onto these people's necks on the way to power. As I said, it's all routine."

Manuel Ortega lit a cigarette.

"Is the prison van behind or in front of us?"

"In front."

"Have you seen them?"

"No, I'll be seeing them in good time."

They drove in under the first banners, saw the first portraits and the swinging placards. Viva Gami! Viva Orbal! Viva la República!

"Viva Ortega," said the man sitting beside the Chief of Police.

"Yes. One can indeed say that," said Behounek. "There'll be several extra masses. Shall we go to one?"

20

●●**

The cellar was large and cold with a concrete floor and whitewashed walls. Along one of the walls stood a wooden table on trestles and under it was an old ammunition box with rope handles and metal edges. To the right of the table was a gray steel door.

Along the opposite wall stood the six Communist delegates. They were still bound, but the police had now fastened the handcuffs to staples in the wall and they could no longer leave their places. The woman was leaning with her head and shoulders against the wall, but the rest were standing more or less upright, rocking on the soles of their feet.

In the middle of the room Lieutenant Brown was standing with his legs apart and his hand on the butt of his revolver, and along one wall stood three policemen in white uniforms. Their machine guns lay in a row on the wooden table a yard or two away from them.

The steel door opened and the Chief of Police came into the room.

He was bare-headed but otherwise was dressed according to regulations, in boots and newly pressed uniform with his gun in his belt and the strap diagonally across his chest.

"Good day," he said. "My name is Behounek."

He placed himself a few yards from Lieutenant Brown and looked at the prisoners with benevolent interest.

"You are condemned to death," he said. "The execution will take place by firing squad but without military honors. It's due to take place at nine-thirty, that is, in . . ."

He looked at his watch.

". . . exactly twenty-five minutes. The formal sentence will be read out to you immediately before the execution."

He looked at the floor for a moment and rubbed his lower lip with his right forefinger.

"Well," he said. "Which of you is El Campesino?"

The Cuban raised his head and looked at him. The man had watchful brown eyes; he was frightened, but not without a trace of defiance and expectation.

"Set him free," said Behounek.

Then he turned around and went over to the table, pulled out the box, and selected something from it—a lead pipe about a foot long and two inches in diameter. He weighed it in his hand.

The Cuban was free and had taken three steps away from the wall. He was standing with his head bowed, massaging his wrists to get the blood circulating normally again.

Behounek walked across the floor, very calmly, and without taking his eyes off the man for one moment. One step away from him he stopped, bit his lower lip, and rocked his body a little with his heels off the floor. Then he hit the Cuban a tremendous blow on the back of his neck with the lead pipe.

The man fell headlong and for a few seconds lay still on his knees and forearms. It looked as if he were alive, but he was probably already dead; he fell at once onto his side and lay immobile with his eyes open and knees drawn up.

Behounek turned around, took two steps toward the wooden table, and threw the lead pipe back into the box. Then he returned to the wall.

It was absolutely quiet in the room.

Again he rubbed his forefinger along his lower lip and looked at the prisoners in turn. Finally he stopped in front of the woman, who was standing farthest to the left in the row.

"Carmen Sánchez," he said absently. "Beautiful Carmen Sánchez."

The girl had short black hair and was wearing faded jeans, wellington boots, and a dark-blue blouse.

Behounek gripped the front of her blouse and ripped it down so that the buttons spun off. Underneath she was wearing an ordinary bra, clean and white against the dark skin. He stuck his forefinger in the middle and tore it apart. She cried out in pain as the straps cut into her sides and back. The cry was shrill and childish. Then he thrust his hands between her trousers and the brown elastic skin and jerked. He did not succeed at first and a vein in his temple swelled as, with a tremendous effort, he tore her jeans and pants apart.

The only sound to be heard in the room was the noise of rending material and ripping seams.

He took a step back and looked at her. Her breasts did not look especially firm and her nipples were round and small and pale brown. She was not as thin as one would have thought, seeing her dressed. The skin of her stomach was a trifle slack, as if she had once given birth to a child, and the hair below was sparse and reddish brown.

From her body rose a faint smell of sweat and enclosed body warmth.

"Not much," he said.

Then he looked at his watch and said to the policemen: "You've got nineteen minutes. Do what you like with her."

Lieutenant Brown leaned over the man on the floor and said: "I think he's dead, sir."

"Shoot him anyway," Behounek said, and left the room.

Manuel Ortega was sitting in the visitor's chair in the Chief of Police's room. He was pale and sweating and his hands trembled as he struck a match and tried to light one of his dust-dry cigarettes.

Behounek came into the room, unbuttoned his tunic, and flung himself into the swivel chair behind his desk.

He bit his thumbnail thoughtfully and seemed to look beyond the other man to a point far away. Then he said: "Have you ever killed anyone? I mean actually—by force?"

"No."

"Then you've got something to be thankful for."

Manuel stared at him.

"You see, the first time one kills, one burns one's boats in some way. One deprives oneself forever of the right to what one has left behind on the other side. One cannot gather any of it up. It's lost and gone."

"What is lost and gone?"

"It's hard to explain, and besides, it's supposed to be the same for everyone, but I find that hard to believe. If I say that you can never live again as you lived before, that you can't love, can't feel you're yourself and be happy about it, not even sleep with a woman or get dead drunk, then of course you won't believe me. Nevertheless it's true. You can, of course, do all that, live, be happy, sleep with women, whatever you want to do, but you can only do it in a technical sense. Your technique can be improved, but it's all a bluff. You can never deceive yourself, at least not for long. You soon realize that."

"You're really destructive."

Behounek rose from his chair, laughed, and walked around the desk.

"Isn't it absurd?" he said. "Isn't it absolutely ridiculous to think that I was once a happy man? Yes, it's true. I remember it very well. Together with a woman. Sometimes I wake in the night and think I remember what it feels like."

He paused.

"Now it even seems absurd that I still have a wife and children sitting in a house somewhere, having a good time, and even thinking about me occasionally. But it's true. I have a wife and children."

"I, too," said Manuel Ortega.

"You're right of course. I am destructive, in my way. Often I feel as if I had for months and years vegetated in a mad distorted picture of the world, in which all meaning is perverted and where everything is wrong or must soon become so. But which of us do you think is the most destructive, I with my monomania or you with your sick desire to please everyone? Although you know all the time that you're inadequate? There are perhaps a hundred thousand people in this province whom you've led astray with your talk and your actions. You've built a tall lookout tower for them. From up there they could see in perspective an existence and a future which will never materialize. Where is that building today?"

"It's collapsed."

"And who knocked it down?"

"I did."

"Have you thought that if your crack shot on the ledge hadn't been so quick on the draw, you would have been, for ten years or more, a martyr and a hero of this province? Perhaps they'd have put up a statue of you in the middle of the plaza."

The sound of a distant salvo of shots penetrated through the stone walls, and then another. Behounek pricked up his ears and counted on his fingers. Then he mumbled: "El Campesino, Irigo, Carmen Sánchez, El Rojo Redondo. They've lived with me for eight months. So palpably, here in this room. Now they've gone. And I am left."

He began buttoning up his tunic and then he picked up his belt from the desk.

"Well, Ortega, where shall we eat? At the club?"

"I suppose so."